The Secrets in Silence

Nicole TROPE

The Secrets in Silence

ALLEN&UNWIN
SYDNEY · MELBOURNE · AUCKLAND · LONDON

First published in 2014

Copyright © Nicole Trope 2014

Allen & Unwin
83 Alexander Street
Crows Nest NSW 2065 Australia
Phone: (61 2) 8425 0100
Email: info@allenandunwin.com
Web: www.allenandunwin.com

Cataloguing-in-Publication details are available
from the National Library of Australia
www.trove.nla.gov.au

ISBN 978 1 74331 749 5

Set in 12/18 pt Minion Pro by Midland Typesetters, Australia
Printed and bound in Australia by Griffin Press

10 9 8 7 6 5 4 3 2 1

MIX
Paper from
responsible sources
FSC® C009448

The paper in this book is FSC® certified. FSC® promotes environmentally responsible, socially beneficial and economically viable management of the world's forests.

Hey babe, how are you enjoying the view so far?

Autumn

1

'Emergency services.'

'Yes, it's my daughter. I need an ambulance for her. I need an ambulance right now! My daughter is passed out and bleeding. She's bleeding everywhere.'

'Is she breathing? You can say you don't know?'

'Um, she's . . . is she breathing? Yes, she's breathing, but there's blood everywhere—it's all over the bathroom.'

'Do you know where the blood is coming from?'

'I don't—I don't know. It's all over her pants. All over her pants. It's all over the floor. It's everywhere! Jesus, where's it coming from?'

'Sir, you need to calm down so we can help you.'

'My wife is a nurse. She says it's from . . . where did you say? I don't know! I don't understand! Look, you need to send an ambulance now!'

'All right, sir. Take a deep breath. An ambulance is on the way. Can you confirm your address for me, please?'

2

Minnie turned her body one way and then another, angling herself into the tight cubicle.

'There should be a law,' she puffed to herself as she always did. Once she had managed to close the toilet door she stood for a moment and breathed in and out, swallowing the bitter taste of her shame at her unwieldy body. She waited patiently for her racing heart to resume its normal rhythm, dabbing at the sweat on her forehead and upper lip with the ends of her long red scarf. The short walk had brought on a hot flush, making her long for a bath of ice to sink into. She stood quietly until she felt her body calm itself.

'Right, let's get this show on the road,' she muttered. She lifted her large bag with slightly trembling arms and hung it on the hook at the back of the door, pleased to find the small metal piece still there. She had no idea why anyone would want to steal the hook off the back of the toilet stall door, but it wasn't the strangest thing she'd ever heard of being stolen.

Last year someone had stolen a plant right out of her front garden. It was an orchid and just beginning to bloom. The thief must have come equipped with a bucket and spade to dig up the garden in the middle of the night. Minnie had been too shocked by the act to actually be upset at the loss but she had missed the beautiful pinks of the flower.

She had walked all the way across the shopping centre to get to this bathroom. It would have taken most people only a few minutes, but for Minnie it had been a marathon. She knew the inside of her thighs would be red-raw. She preferred this bathroom because it was usually empty. The shops on either side had closed down and it was far away from the hub of the super-markets and fresh-food stores.

Minnie preferred the privacy of the empty bathroom when she absolutely could not hang on until she got home. If she went into the big bathroom near the busy part of the centre she had to endure the looks of disgust from other women waiting. Teenage girls giggled. Young children stared open-mouthed. Although the sight of a large person was not exactly unusual, children were still shocked by her size. The bathroom in the busy part of the centre was large and airy, however, the cubicles were still small, and she would have had an audience as she manoeuvred herself into one. It was better to be alone when such a thing was necessary. At home the bathroom was bigger and she could almost pretend that she was a normal size. It was the one part of the house she and her mother had changed.

Minnie lifted up the folds of her rose-patterned dress and stepped backwards towards the toilet. Her hands were tugging at her underwear when she heard a sound like a hiss of air.

'Good Lord, Mum, what on earth could that be?' she whispered.

The sound could have come from her own body for all she knew. The bigger she grew the more precarious her control of herself seemed to become.

But she would have to check. Sitting on a toilet that you couldn't see was difficult enough without wondering what may or may not be lurking in the bowl. Who knew what might crawl up through the horrors of the sewerage system? In America people found alligators in their toilets.

She pulled her underwear up again and smoothed down the material of her voluminous dress and then shuffled around one step at a time so she could peer into the toilet.

Afterwards she would thank God for her strong bladder and her still-beating heart because who'd imagine you could find such a thing in a shopping-centre toilet?

She didn't scream because Minnie was not a screamer, and panicking took too much energy, so after just a moment's stunned observation she reached down and plucked the blood-covered infant out of the toilet.

'Look at this, Mum, just look at this.' She grabbed the baby under the arms and said, 'Lord, give me the strength to deal with this.'

The baby's feet had been down by the S bend and its head had been resting just below the rim.

As Minnie picked it up it gave a tiny high-pitched wail. The bathroom was cold but the baby was warm and slimy. It could not have been long since it was safe inside a womb.

'What an undignified start to your life, little one,' Minnie murmured.

She wondered where the mother might be. Had Minnie seen her? She could remember passing a few people on the way to the bathroom but it was her habit to stare straight ahead or at her lumbering feet and avoid meeting anyone's gaze. Eye contact made some people think it gave them the right to smirk or make comments. She could recall blood red painted toenails in high black stilettoes, black boots and her own red-veined feet, but she had not seen any faces.

The baby was still attached to the placenta by the cord, Minnie noticed.

'The cord needs to be cut, Mum, I know that much. It was on telly the other night, remember?'

Gently she placed the baby back into the toilet bowl then rummaged in her gold-and-green-flecked bag for a clip and her nail scissors.

'A lady is always prepared,' her mother would have said.

'Never imagined I would have to prepare for something like this, Mum,' muttered Minnie.

She knew what to do from the birth documentaries. She never tired of watching them. It was the same as those girls who starved themselves while watching cooking shows—an exquisite torture.

The scissors in the documentaries always looked huge but she would have to make do. The cutting never looked like it bothered the baby. She hoped that was true. She closed her eyes and thought for a moment about how the cord had been held by the capable doctor. In the documentaries they usually let the father do it. How hard could it be?

Minnie placed the clip where she thought it should go and then waited a minute before sawing through the tough sinew with her nail scissors. It was a revolting feeling but she didn't think about that. She needed to free the poor creature from its tether.

Once the baby was free of the cord Minnie lifted it out of the toilet again and listened for any sounds to indicate someone else had entered the bathroom.

There was only faraway outside noises from the shopping centre.

The birth documentaries always showed the ecstasy on the mother's face once the pain of birth was over and the infant was safely on the breast. Minnie liked the part where the mother and baby saw each other for the first time. It always seemed as though they recognised each other. She looked at the baby in her arms. Its eyes were closed but as she watched it opened them just a little and gave her a grey lizard look.

Minnie felt a bit like crying herself, like the women in the documentaries, but that would achieve nothing.

'What are we going to do about this then, Mum?'

The quiet of the bathroom was broken only by her own heavy breathing and the light wheezy breaths of the baby.

They were alone.

Then the baby began to cry properly and Minnie felt her mind cloud for a moment before her hands took over. Cradling the baby in one arm, she grabbed the scarf from around her neck whilst still holding the greasy creature under the arms.

She could barely move in the cubicle.

She pushed the infant to one side and held it under her arm, supporting its head as she had seen the doctors on television do. It was slippery and writhing and she was terrified she was going to drop it. She flipped the lid of the toilet down and laid the scarf across it. She placed the now-screaming baby on top of the scarf and wrapped it up tight until it resembled a red cocoon with only the nose and mouth exposed. She tucked the ends of her scarf into the bundle and held it up to view with a critical eye.

'What do you think, Mum?'

The child's cries had begun to ease as soon as Minnie

began wrapping it. Now it was silent. Its eyes were closed as though it had expended all its energy with the small protest it had made.

Minnie held it up and put her ear to its chest. She felt the tiny chest move up and down, and nodded.

She turned back around again and opened the door of the stall.

The bathroom only had three toilets in it and it was still empty. Minnie breathed a sigh of relief and was aware of the urgent pressure on her bladder again.

'Fuck,' she said out loud, almost enjoying the uncharacteristic feel of the word on her tongue.

'Sorry, Lord, but I'm sure you must understand my loss of control,' she said.

She reversed back into the stall and closed the door again, catching sight of her large bag on the hook.

She looked down at the sleeping infant, then opened the bag with one hand and placed it gently inside. The baby huffed a little but made no other sound.

'Good,' said Minnie and then flushed the toilet to wash away the blood and muck from the baby. She had to flush twice, and the wait to allow the cistern to fill felt interminable.

She used the toilet and then flushed again and manoeuvred herself out of the cubicle, holding the bag in her sweaty hands.

She put the straps of the bag over her shoulder, washed her hands and left the bathroom.

Minnie trudged quickly through the shopping centre towards her car. She kept one hand in the bag and on the small chest, making sure that the swaddled child was getting enough air. Her bag contained a loaf of soft chewy bread she had bought just before realising she needed the bathroom and she fancied that it made a comfortable bed.

As she moved through the shopping centre Minnie looked behind herself continually—expecting to be tapped on the shoulder at any moment. Her heart skipped in her chest and she had to keep wiping at the sweat on her face.

She wanted to shout with joy when she saw her car but she just kept moving. She got into her car and removed the baby from the bag, placing it gently on the seat next to her with the bread as a bolster. 'Let's get this show on the road,' she said as she backed slowly out of the parking space. 'Let's get this show on the road.'

Once she was free of the shopping centre carpark she began to giggle and she could not stop until she pulled into her driveway at home.

'No going back now, Mum,' she said.

Inside, Minnie fired up the heater and unwrapped the baby slowly.

'So you're a girl,' she said, and the baby began to wail again.

'Look, Mum—it's a little girl. Imagine that. Who'd want to leave a poor little thing like her, do you suppose?' She shook her head. 'Well, thank the Lord you have good lungs,' said Minnie to the baby. 'I bet you're hungry, little girl. I need to get you some food and some clothes and—oh my, there's a lot to do.'

The baby's cries grew louder and more frantic.

'Now, that's enough of that,' said Minnie. 'You need to hush and I'll take care of everything. You're safe here now with me. You're safe with me and Mum.' She closed her eyes for a moment. 'Lord God, guide me and protect me in this endeavour and keep this little one safe.'

She wrapped the baby up again and lifted it to her chest. It smelled like soil, like the earth and slightly of blood. Minnie bounced it against her large breasts and the baby closed its eyes again.

Newborns could sleep for a long time after birth, according to one of the doctors on television. The TLC channel screened one baby show after another and Minnie would sit on her red velvet couch night after night drinking in the images of babies and their happy families as she pushed indiscriminate amounts of food into her mouth.

'Who'd have thought I would ever get the chance, hey, Mum?'

Minnie knew she needed to get organised.

There was no way she could go back to the shopping centre but there was a 7-Eleven down the road. She could walk there and pick up enough to get by for a couple of days, and order online later.

At no point did she consider calling the police or letting anyone know what she had found.

'The Lord works in mysterious ways,' her mother had always said.

And that was good enough for Minnie.

3

'Mr Sanderson? Mr and Mrs Sanderson?'

'Yeah, that's me. I'm Max Sanderson.'

'Mr Sanderson, I'm Dr Elias—I've been treating your daughter. She is your daughter, is that correct?'

'Yes, I'm Tara's father. And this is Tara's stepmother.'

'Is Tara's mother here?'

'No, she's ah . . .'

'Oh, for God's sake, Max. I'm Alicia Sanderson, Dr Elias. I'm Tara's stepmother and I have been for the last ten years. Her mother is currently at Peace Hills.'

'The psychiatric hospital?'

'Yes. My wife—that is, my ex-wife—suffers from bipolar disorder and schizophrenia.'

Max and Alicia and the doctor were all silent for a moment, swallowing the intimate details that had just been shared. Max shook his head, clearing it of thoughts of his ex-wife. 'What's wrong with Tara? Is she okay? Why was there so much blood? Where was it even coming from?'

'Perhaps you could come with me; there's a small lounge just down the hall.'

Dr Elias was tall and thin and he loped off down the hallway without waiting for a reply.

Alicia grabbed Max's hand and they followed the doctor into a small room with a tan leather couch, a water dispenser and a lush green pot plant. Max wondered if the plant was real and had to restrain himself from reaching out to touch the thick waxy leaves.

They sat gingerly on the couch. Alicia knew exactly what they used rooms like this for, and even though she knew that Max was terrified and that she should feel nothing but anxiety, she felt more weary than anything else. She dropped Max's hand and crossed her arms over her chest.

Tara had slammed out of the house that morning after claiming to be unwell and whilst Alicia had felt she should have gone after her she was just grateful to be free of the girl's sour presence for a while.

'Mr Sanderson, as you know Tara was brought into the hospital by ambulance a short time ago. She was taken into the emergency room immediately and I was called in to help with the situation. I'm the obstetrics resident on call today.'

'But that's for . . . for pregnant women. Isn't that for pregnant women, Alicia?'

'It is, Mr Sanderson. We examined Tara thoroughly and we have stopped the bleeding.'

'That's good, right, Ali? That's good, isn't it?'

Alicia nodded. She wanted to shout at Max to shut up. She knew what was coming.

'Mr Sanderson, the extensive bleeding was an indication that some time in the past twelve hours your daughter has given birth. The bleeding was the result of a secondary postpartum haemorrhage. This can be caused by an infection or, as in your daughter's case, it can be caused by a piece of placenta that was left over in the uterus.'

'What do you mean she's given birth? That's not possible— it's completely impossible. You must have made some sort of mistake. The bleeding must be from . . . from something else.'

'I'm afraid not, Mr Sanderson. It's clear that Tara has recently given birth.'

'Will she be all right?'

'Yes, Mrs Sanderson—she will. We caught it in time and although she needed a transfusion she'll be fine.'

'But I don't understand—how could she be pregnant? She's only fifteen . . . she's so young. We never knew. Alicia, why didn't we know?'

'Five minutes ago I was only her stepmother,' thought Alicia. 'Now I'm supposed to have the answers.'

She sighed. 'I don't know, Max. You know what she's like . . .'

'Oh, for fuck's sake, Alicia, let's not dump on the kid now,' said Max.

'I'm not dumping on her, Max. I'm just saying that she's very secretive. She spends more time in her room than anywhere else and she's always dressed in all those layers. She could have been hiding anything under there.'

'You're a nurse, Alicia.'

'I work with women after they've had the baby, Max. Please do not make this my sole responsibility.'

'I'm not, Alicia, I'm just saying—'

'Mr and Mrs Sanderson, our current concern is for the baby.'

Max and Alicia both blushed. The doctor's presence had been forgotten.

'The baby?' said Max. How could Tara have a baby? She was just a baby herself.

'Yes, Mr Sanderson—the baby. Your daughter gave birth a short time ago and we have no idea where the infant is. The baby may have been stillborn or it might be alive somewhere. I've called the police and they'll be here shortly.'

'The police? What the fuck for?'

Alicia placed a warning hand on Max's arm.

'I'm sorry, Mr Sanderson, but it's mandatory for us to report cases like this. We have a duty of care to the child.'

'Have you asked Tara where the baby is?'

'She did wake up for a little while but she wouldn't answer any of our questions. She has drifted off again, which is normal. Perhaps if you asked her . . .?'

Alicia rose. 'Can you tell us which room she's in?'

The doctor stood up and opened the door to the corridor. 'Walk straight through those doors and up to level two. She's in room 204. And Mrs Sanderson?'

'Yes?'

'She's given birth on her own. It must have been a very traumatic experience. A psychiatrist will be along to see her soon, and I'll be back after I've seen some other patients. I think we need to take things slowly and—'

Alicia put her hand up. 'I understand what you're saying, Doctor. I'm not going to attack the girl, but we do need to know where the baby is. The sooner we get this sorted out the better. Come on, Max.'

Max walked behind Alicia, letting her lead the way. Even in places she'd never been before Alicia took the lead. In a hospital Alicia was even more comfortable taking charge. He watched his feet move, trying to go back over the last few months. Had Tara seemed to be gaining weight? Alicia was right about the layers but he'd assumed it was the fashion—he'd even worried that she was trying to conceal some huge weight loss; he'd read about teenage girls doing that in some book or other. But then work had been chaos the last few months and he'd . . . well, he'd let Alicia sort it all out at home. How was he supposed to run the marketing department and do everything else as well? His staff was just waiting for the next round of cuts—everyone's job was on the line. The GFC was over one week and not over the next; his whole department teetered permanently on the brink of collapse. There were endless things to worry about.

So maybe he hadn't been home as much as he could have, but Alicia had been there. Why hadn't she noticed? Wasn't that the sort of thing a woman would notice? Sometimes it seemed like Alicia went out of her way to avoid Tara. The girl was difficult, that was true, but she was fifteen—all fifteen-year-old girls were difficult, weren't they? Was she more difficult than most? Were her moods an indication of something else? And now this . . . what the fuck could all this mean?

Why hadn't they noticed?

'Max, are you listening to me?'

'What? Sorry I was just . . .'

'Max, we need to present a united front on this. We have to be firm and get her to tell us what happened. This could be a very real problem for her now that the police are involved.'

'I know that, Alicia. Don't you think I know that?'

'God, I'm tired,' thought Alicia.

•

In room 204 Tara lay in a hospital bed with her eyes closed. Her face faded into the grey-white of the sheets and her blonde hair was matted and greasy. An IV filled with something clear snaked out of her arm. Even her lips were white. Max stared at his little girl and flashed on the time she had leapt from the top of the fourth stair onto the wooden floor below and broken her wrist. She had come to tell him with white lips and glistening eyes. She'd been four at the time. Her mother was having another stay in hospital in an attempt to get the medication right. She never really came home again after that, but at the time he and Tara were still hopeful, still waiting.

Max sat down on a chair next to the bed and stretched his arms behind his head. Each time Sasha went into hospital he had hoped that this time they would get it right. This time something would click and Sasha would respond and she would come home wanting to stay connected to reality, that she'd be like the woman he'd met at university. Eventually he grew to hate himself for being so stupid, for continuing to hope. He hated himself for it but it couldn't be helped.

Tara had screamed bloody murder when he took her to the emergency room for the broken wrist. She knew that when you went to hospital you stayed there for a long time. That you would miss birthday parties and school concerts. Her mother had been gone for six months by then and even though Max still prayed every night that she would return to them he had started seeing other women. Secretively, guiltily, he'd started seeing other women. He was cheating on his wife. He didn't explain it away; he just accepted himself for the shitty husband he was. He

craved the physical presence of a woman. For years his relationship with Sasha had been more like the relationship he had with
Tara than that of husband and wife. He cooked and cleaned and
told her to take her medication and called her during the day to
make sure she was coping. The more paternal his role became
the less possible it was to see himself as her husband. He was
crap at one-night stands and always felt ashamed when he paid
the babysitter but fuck, he was a man as well, wasn't he?

When the doctors finally shook their heads at him and told
him to give Sasha another year or two or three he'd started
seeing Alicia. She was a one-night stand that turned into something else. He'd been upfront about it. She knew he was married,
knew where Sasha was and she was okay with it. He had never
lied to Alicia.

The first time he went out with Alicia he told Tara he was going
to work. She had just turned five; she still believed anything he
said. 'How many lifetimes ago was that?' thought Max, staring at
his ghostly pale daughter.

The night he went out with Alicia she chose the restaurant
and then she suggested what he should have. She spoke to the
waiter and ordered the drinks and when his meal came and he
mentioned that the steak was overdone Alicia sorted that out as
well. Max hadn't had to open his mouth or lift a finger. He had
felt himself relax, truly relax, for the first time in years. Alicia
told him to come up for coffee and then she helped him take
off his shirt. He hadn't had real emotionally connected sex with

anyone since before Tara was born. He was so fucking grateful for Alicia. So fucking grateful.

Now, more than ten years later, Tara didn't look much bigger than she had when she was five. Underneath the covers he could see the rise of her stomach where a baby had recently nestled. A baby?

He wanted to stroke her hair and have her sit on his lap. He wanted to tell her that everything would be fine and he couldn't even begin to think of how to ask her what had happened to the baby.

How could she have had a baby? It was a ludicrous thought. Max dropped his head into his hands.

'Hey, Tara,' said Alicia, and Max looked up to see Tara had opened her eyes.

'Hey, little girl,' he said.

Tara simply stared at them.

'You passed out in the bathroom,' said Alicia. 'Your dad had to break the door down.' She didn't mention that the blood had seeped under the door, pooling in the hallway and congealing on the burnished floorboards. She didn't say anything about the boys screaming in horror and she didn't talk about the mess she would have to clean up when she got home. She didn't say that the boys had sobbed in the back seat as she and Max sped over to her mother's place to drop them off. And she didn't tell Tara that Anne had screamed when the boys tracked bloodied footprints onto her cream rug.

For just one moment she wanted to describe it all to her so the girl would know just how much trouble she had caused. Then she felt shame wash over her. 'When did I get to be such a horrible bitch?' she wondered.

Aloud she said, 'They've given you a transfusion because you lost a lot of blood but the doctor says you'll be fine. You'll feel really weak for a few days,' Alicia added, taking comfort in at least having something of value to say.

'Where would Tara have gone to have a baby?' she asked herself. There was a park near the house and a shopping centre within walking distance but those places were always full of people.

Tara turned to look at Max. Her eyes widened. She had the same dark brown eyes as her father. So dark that they sometimes seemed black. Ethan had them too.

'Oh, sweetheart, why didn't you tell us? Why didn't you say something? We would have helped. You could have died.' Max grabbed Tara's hand and was grateful to feel her fingers tighten around his. But she said nothing.

'Tara,' said Alicia gently, 'you need to tell us where the baby is. We need to find the baby and make sure it's okay.'

Tara looked at Alicia, looked through Alicia, and then she turned her head slightly to the side and closed her eyes.

'Tara,' said Alicia.

Max stood up and put his hand on Alicia's arm.

'Leave it now, Ali. She needs to rest. Just leave it. Why don't you go home now? I'm sure your mother is finding the boys a handful. I'll stay here tonight and we'll sort all of this out tomorrow.'

'But the doctor told us we need an answer, Max. There is a baby somewhere that needs medical attention.'

Max placed his hand on the small of Alicia's back, propelling her towards the door while he talked. 'I can't think about that now, Alicia. Tara needs my attention. I'll try and talk to her but you know that even at the best of times she doesn't respond to being badgered. Just go home and I'll deal with this.'

Alicia nodded her head curtly.

Max could see she was hurt, that she felt excluded, but he needed to give Tara some space. Alicia had a way of taking up all the air in the room.

He went back to the chair and sat down again, placing his hand over Tara's small white one. It felt like a completely useless gesture and Max found the texture of her soft pale skin unfamiliar. 'How long has it been since I've touched her?' he thought. It could have been weeks but it could also have been months. When she was little she was always climbing into his lap or holding his hand or touching his face to get his attention. He was always touching her, too. Little children were so open to physical contact. He rested his hand on Ethan's shoulder and stroked Michael's neck while they talked, and he kissed them goodnight and good morning. He was sure he had done the same with Tara but at some point he and Tara had stopped hugging, stopped touching at all.

Max closed his eyes and tried to think about the last time he had given his daughter a quick hug or the last time he had seen Alicia do the same. If they had hugged her more or touched her more, surely they would have picked up on the pregnancy. It wasn't something you could hide in a hug. He opened his eyes again and looked at his daughter. She had, over the years, become more defensive, more prickly. She hadn't wanted to be touched but he should have done it anyway—even if he had just stroked her hair . . .

'God, I'm so sorry, love,' he said to Tara.

She opened her eyes.

'I'm sorry,' he said again.

Tara just stared at him.

'I'm so sorry this happened to you, baby,' he said. 'I'm sorry that we didn't . . . that I didn't see something, notice something. I'm sorry I didn't notice you. Can you say something? Just tell me you're going to be okay?'

Tara continued staring and Max couldn't think of anything else to say. Last week he'd been having a beer with Dave, commiserating over the mess Dave's divorce was making of his life, and he'd felt a small sense of satisfaction that his life had finally settled into the kind of steady rut that some people thought of as boring. Work was crap but work was always crap. It was the same for everyone. Alicia and Tara didn't exactly get on but they were civil to each other and the boys were just a pleasure. He knew he could go out to work every day and come home to a tidy house and a cooked meal and a sense that things were under control. It was so different to the years he had spent with Sasha that sometimes he couldn't quite believe it. Back then he would come home after a day at work and feel stomach-flipping trepidation at what he might find. Some days the house would sparkle and there would be cakes and muffins on the table and a roast in the oven. Tara would be playing with something that had been made during a complicated craft project and Sasha would have a fixed grin on her face. She would be too busy to sit down and eat, too frantic to talk and he would try to see the order and her busyness as a good thing. He would try not to ask about the medication. If he did mention it she would throw up her hands and simply walk out, so he tried to keep quiet and just subtly work out whether or not she had taken her pills.

Some medications didn't work; some worked but she wouldn't take them. And then a few days would pass and he would come home to find her curled up on the couch with Tara spoonfeeding her peanut butter. The house would be a complete mess and he would know that they would have to start again.

He regretted his smugness now, regretted feeling like he had a handle on things. Quite clearly he didn't. Who knew what those years with her mother had done to Tara?

Alicia suggested a psychologist for Tara every now and again but Tara wouldn't even consider it. Psychologists and doctors put you in hospital and you stayed there for longer each time until one day you didn't come home at all. And the older she got the more Tara knew about her mother's disease. She'd searched the web and she knew that it ran in families, knew there was a genetic component.

'It'll start with one visit to a therapist, Dad, and it'll end with me sitting next to Mum in Peace Hills.'

'That's crap, Tara. You've been through a lot. *We've* been through a lot. Just talk to someone. They may have something valuable to say.'

'I'm not sick, Dad—there's nothing wrong with me.'

'Tara, you know that the therapists didn't give your mother bipolar disorder. You know that, love.'

'That's not what Mum used to say. She said she was fine until you started dragging her off to see people. She said there was nothing wrong with her until she started therapy and pill-popping.'

'But, Tara, that's not the truth. You know what it was like when she was home. You can't remember her before she started therapy but I do, and there was something very wrong.'

'Well, I'm not baking five thousand cakes and I'm not lying around in my pyjamas all day. I'm fine.'

'I just want to help you, Tara. I want you to be happy.'

'I know Alicia would like someone else to deal with me . . .'

'Not this again, Tara. Alicia is trying to help.'

'Then tell her to leave me alone.'

He should have insisted Tara talk to someone but she seemed to be doing all right. He had met Alicia and Tara had essentially had a mother for the last ten years. Things got a bit difficult when the boys arrived, but that was normal sibling rivalry, wasn't it?

'Oh, poppet,' he said now to his still daughter. 'What's happened to us?'

Tara closed her eyes again.

Her body felt like there was something heavy lying on top of it. She couldn't imagine finding the energy to move, to lift her arm or to open her mouth. She felt drained and slow. There was pain everywhere and she could feel blood trickling out of her, like a heavy period. She had no idea where the blood could have come from or what she was doing in the bed in the white and grey room. Her hand felt odd, like there was something attached to it, and she wanted to turn over and give it a shake but she couldn't find the energy. She couldn't focus on anything or think straight. It was easier with her eyes closed. Something had happened, something bad but she had no idea what. She heard her father sigh and then the creak of the chair as he leaned back.

'It hurt, Daddy,' she wanted to say. 'It hurt so much.'

4

Minnie lay the swaddled baby on the floor again. The scarf was filthy with blood now but it would have to do. She would have loved to give the poor creature a bath but she had so many things that needed to be done first. The baby's earthy smell filled the room. It was a mingling of blood and soil and was not at all unpleasant. The poor little creature didn't look happy and Minnie's own hunger pangs reminded her that the baby needed feeding. 'The poor thing must be starving, Mum.'

She emptied out her bag and put some folded towels into it. The baby was comfortable enough and she seemed happy to be asleep again when Minnie swung the bag back and forth a little. She stepped outside with the bag and noticed movement in the front garden three houses away. It was always the first place she looked now.

She immediately turned and went back inside.

She had begun to sweat again and she could feel the slight tremble in her hand. They were out in the garden.

The boys, Minnie called them in her head, although the term 'boys' was a little too benign for the three men who had moved in. They were young—very young—but they carried with them years of anger and cynicism. Minnie could feel their hunched-up fury from three houses away.

Their front yard was the only unkempt one on the quiet street. It was routinely filled with beer cans and household rubbish. Now an old sofa had taken up residence in the garden as well. The garbage bins overflowed and the smell mingled with the general air of menace that seemed to emanate from the house.

The street was an old one lined with small, neat fibro houses. One or two of the houses had an extra level tacked onto the top, but for the most part the houses were single levels with two or three bedrooms. The cladded walls were all painted in white or cream, with only the accent colours on the trim changing from house to house. Minnie's house had a blue accent, the one next door had a rust colour and across the road there was a house with the shocking choice of purple. There had been talk in the street when that choice had been made by the two elderly gentlemen who lived in the house. June who lived next door had been upset at the time, but everyone was used to it now.

Minnie had lived in the street all her life and never thought to change anything about her house. It wasn't like she and her mother had ever needed any extra room. They had redone the bathroom, but her mother had deemed that a necessity.

'We have to be able to fit in our own shower, don't we, love?' she had said.

The kitchen still had laminate bench tops and brown veneer cupboards but Minnie looked after it so well the kitchen could have been done five years ago or fifteen years ago. The Lifestyle Channel had lots of programs on how to give your house a 'retro' look.

Everyone in the street was more than a little houseproud. June and Lou gave out rose cuttings in spring and the same pink and white roses bloomed happily up and down the street. The house where the boys now lived used to look exactly the same as all the others, but almost within days of them moving into it the garden was dying. June speculated that they actually urinated in the garden at night. 'Like animals,' she whispered to Minnie as though the occupants of the house could hear through walls. Minnie privately thought that the garden had understood, as all living things would, that it would no longer be cared for and had just given up.

The pink and white roses had been the first to go. Now that it was autumn the grass in the garden was mostly weeds and soil. 'I have to resist the urge to go in at night and fix things up,' said June, who felt physically hurt by the neglected patch.

They had moved in suddenly one Saturday afternoon in the first days of summer. June and Minnie had been enjoying a cup of tea in June's front garden. Minnie didn't often leave the house but her weekly visit with June was something she wouldn't miss. Each Saturday afternoon Minnie hauled herself across the road and perched on a garden chair next to June, who would be waiting with tea and chocolate cake.

For a time that afternoon they had discussed the warm weather and the possibility of a predicted heatwave and then a multicoloured van covered in foul graffiti had roared up the street and stopped. Minnie had felt her face heat up as she sat next to June while words like 'fuck' and 'dickhead' screamed at them from the van's painted side.

They had watched in silence, expecting it to take off towards the nearby highway but instead it had remained parked in front of the vacant house three doors down from Minnie's own.

Susan and Patrick had lived in the house for as long as Minnie could remember, but when they died within months of each other their daughter had not known what to do with the house.

'I have to keep it, Minnie. I can't let go of the last place where they were happy together,' Mary told Minnie when she came to clear it out. 'I'll rent it out for a year or so, give myself some time to decide.'

Minnie had nodded, picturing some delightful young couple who would move in with a child or two and fill the street with a little bit of noise. Minnie was the youngest in the street now. All the children of the long-time residents had moved further away from the city to where the homes were more affordable.

Minnie yearned for the shouts of young children and the chaos of families in the street again. She was happy to watch.

But there had been no young family to take Susan and Patrick's place. Instead, two men had climbed out of the front of the van and then opened up the back doors to let a third man out. They were all dressed in tight jeans that slid off their narrow hips, exposing grey underwear. They began unloading the van, filling the air with 'fuck' and 'wanker' and occasionally spitting on the sidewalk. Minnie had never imagined that three such young men could exist. 'Sent straight from the devil—Jesus, save us,' her mother would have said.

After a while one of the men—the one with spiky blond hair— had walked into the middle of the street and looked directly at Minnie and June, who were sipping their tea in silent horror, and said, 'What the fuck are you two ugly cunts looking at?'

His words were slightly slurred, which Minnie attributed to all the beer that had been drunk as they moved between the house and the van. The garden was already filling up with cans. June had blushed almost scarlet and Minnie had stood up slightly but then sat down again heavily on the chair. She had no idea what to say. The man had laughed and his friends had laughed with him and then they had gone inside and closed the door of the house.

Over the next few weeks June watched the activity in the house and reported everything to Minnie.

'There's another one who looks like a boy who visits all the time. He comes in a school uniform sometimes. I wonder if his parents know what he's doing. I think they'd just want to die if they knew who he was spending time with. He stayed over on Friday night but went back home again on Saturday. He always looks a little shifty to me—like he's afraid of getting caught.'

Minnie watched out for the young one and thought about telling him to stay away from the dreadful three in the house but she never got up the courage. He didn't even look old enough to shave and he didn't seem to swear as much as the others. He was mostly quiet, in fact.

'It's that shopping centre,' said June. 'I told Lou it would bring the worst of the worst into our neighbourhood and then they built that ridiculous skate park with the ramps and God knows what kind of people hang out there.'

'The centre's been there for a long time now, June,' said Minnie, mildly. June didn't like to be contradicted.

'More's the pity, I say,' said June.

No one on the street had any idea what to do about the new residents. They slept all day and played loud raucous music at night, and they could be heard fighting and swearing until dawn.

It had not taken the young men long to turn the house into a small piece of hell.

The police turned up every now and again, but people on the street were increasingly afraid of calling them. After a visit from the men in blue, one of the boys would run up and down the street screaming, 'Which one of you fuckers did it? Get the fuck out here, you bastards. We'll kill every fucking one of youse.' The threats would continue for a while until the alcohol or something else kicked in and then whoever was doing the yelling would retreat back to the house.

And then of course there was the matter of William. June and Lou had adopted William when he was only a kitten. He had grown up with their children and spent the last years of his life asleep across Lou's feet. As a kitten he had wandered around at night, occasionally catching rats and bringing them home for June. 'You filthy thing,' June would say when she found William's latest present, but she always said it with a smile on her face. Minnie or her mother would occasionally find William at the back door of their house and give him some milk before returning him to June and Lou. Others in the neighbourhood did the same. William was certain of a warm welcome wherever he went.

After the boys moved in and started blaring music all night long, Lou had taken it upon himself to have a chat with them.

June had not mentioned her first interaction with them. 'It's his heart, Minnie,' she had whispered. 'He'll go mad if he finds out what they said and I just don't think his heart could take it.' She had tried to dissuade him. 'You forget you're seventy-eight, Lou,' she said. 'You don't have to solve every problem anymore.

And what about what happened with the television? You know they're the ones who took it.'

'The police found no evidence of that, June. Perhaps we've misjudged them. Time to mend a few fences and give a bit of fatherly advice, we all have to live in this street.'

'Why don't we give the police another call?' said Minnie.

'They're only young,' said Lou. 'The trouble with kids today is that no one has shown them the right way to do things.'

Minnie had nodded as Lou talked. She didn't really think he had any idea of how to deal with the young men, but Lou was a retired paramedic and he liked to tell Minnie that he had 'seen a few things that would make your hair stand on end'.

'Just leave it to the police,' June said. 'Why do you always have to be the hero of the street?'

'Now, Junie,' said Lou, 'there's nothing to worry about. They just need to be told to calm down.'

He had marched purposefully over to the house and stood by the gate talking to all four of the boys as they lounged in the garden. The street was hot enough to melt shoes by then and Minnie had stood with June watching Lou gesture and then trying to hear what the one with the spiky hair was saying. The young one looked at his feet a lot and almost immediately after Lou finished talking he walked towards the bus stop, presumably to make his way home.

Lou had returned with his shoulders back and a smile on his face. 'He says they're sorry to have bothered anyone and that they'll try to keep the noise down if we leave off calling the police. I said we would. It's all part of being good neighbours. We need to understand that they like to have a little party every now and again. We were young once, weren't we?'

Minnie had looked over to the house and caught the eye of the tall skinny one with the shaved head. He had given her a creepy smile and then waved.

That night the music couldn't be heard but it was also the night William disappeared.

'He barely moves anymore,' said June the next morning after she had paced the neighbourhood looking for him. 'Where could he have gone?'

By the end of the day most of the neighbours were out looking. Minnie sat on her front step and kept an eye out. Her size made walking further than the end of the street difficult.

Eventually they found him three streets away in someone's garden pond. 'There's no way he could have walked that far,' said Lou. 'Someone must have taken him.'

June didn't cry—she knew he was just a pet—but Lou wiped his eyes and blew his nose loudly. They buried him in the front garden and 'the boys' watched from their yard. They drank and laughed all through William's sad little funeral.

No one suggested that it might have been the boys—no one said anything—but the next night one of them knocked on June and Lou's door and said innocently, 'We found this collar on the street. It doesn't belong to that cat of yours, does it?'

June wanted to go to the police. 'And tell them what?' said Lou. He had taken the collar and put it in a box he kept next to his bed.

That night the music was back up to an ear-splitting volume. Lou didn't say anything about going over to talk to them again.

Minnie wore earplugs when she went to bed and quietly spent thousands of dollars on security. As soon as the sun set she pressed a button and the shutters came down on the windows. She double-locked her security gate and then triple-locked the back door. The only way into the house was through the roof, so Minnie complained to an exterminator about rats and he set traps all through the roof cavity. No one was getting in without Minnie hearing it. Every now and again she worried about a fire. There were news stories of families who couldn't make it out of their houses in time because of all the locks and bolts. 'I trust in the Lord to keep me safe,' she would intone when those thoughts entered her head.

She had also called Mary, but Mary was going through a divorce and seemed distant and angry. 'They pay on time every month, Minnie,' she said. 'I'm sorry that you don't like them but I really can't deal with that right now.'

'Where do they get the money from, do you think?' Minnie asked Lou.

'Oh, I'd say they're all on the dole. It's easy enough to leave school and get the government to take care of you.'

'The devil makes work for idle hands,' Minnie's mother would have said. She had silently knitted hundreds of blankets for 'Godless savages', sitting next to Minnie making sure that she studied for her bookkeeping course without interruption. Minnie studied the numbers and listened to the click of her mother's plastic knitting needles. She had wanted to give up when the stares of other students at the college became too much to deal with or when an exam was looming but her mother's moving hands allowed no argument. 'I'll leave you with a trade if nothing else,' her mother had said and now Minnie was, of course, grateful.

Minnie's mother had never accepted a handout and Minnie wouldn't either.

'That's our taxes paying for that horrible lot,' said June. 'Our taxes.'

The boys kept paying the rent and music wasn't illegal. They hadn't actually done anything except be unpleasant. Nothing that could be proved anyway. Not yet. So there was nothing they could do. General drunken threats sounded silly when Minnie whispered them down the phone to the kind policewoman.

'So they threatened to kill you?' she asked.

'Well, not me,' Minnie said.

'So who did they threaten to kill?'

'Well, no one in person. I mean it was just a general threat. Just a sort of shouted threat to everyone in the neighbourhood.'

'You know, ma'am, if you are feeling threatened you can take out an apprehended violence order.'

'Wouldn't I have to go to court for that? Wouldn't they have to be told?'

'Yes and of course yes.'

'Oh,' said Minnie as she pictured herself walking into court to be stared at and then spending the rest of her life terrified that one or all of 'the boys' would exact revenge. 'No, thank you,' she said. 'I'm sure it's not really that much of a problem.'

Standing inside with the baby in her bag, Minnie contemplated her options. She was afraid of the boys but she had never been as afraid of them as she felt now. Never as afraid of them as she was when she had someone other than herself to protect.

There was no way she was going to expose the baby to their cruelty. Mostly they just shoved Minnie aside and called her a 'fat cunt'. Minnie didn't worry about the insults, but if they shoved her and she dropped her bag the baby would get hurt. If the baby cried then they would want to know what she was doing in the bag. They could do nothing. They could be too drunk or stoned or lazy. But they could also decide that today was the day they needed to amuse themselves with her. Minnie couldn't run and she couldn't really defend herself. Having the baby only made her more helpless.

'What should I do now, Mum?' she said.

She walked back and forth across the living room once or twice.

Eventually she picked up the still-sleeping baby and tried using one of her long thin scarves to wrap the child close to her body. It didn't fit so she used two scarves tied together and then she donned her mother's old overcoat. She looked a bit fatter but the baby was completely protected. She moved a piece of her dress aside so that she could feel the baby's breath directly on her skin and know that it was safe.

'Right, little one,' said Minnie, 'let's get this show on the road.' The phrase had been handed down from her mother and Minnie remembered that even as a small child she had been constantly encouraged to 'get this show on the road' for anything that required movement. It was her mother's way of encouraging them both off the couch and out into the world or it was used as a way to make it through tasks that sometimes seemed insurmountable. 'What a show this is,' thought Minnie as she pulled open the front door.

Outside it was cold and dusk was drawing near so Minnie set off at a brisk pace for the 7-Eleven. She kept her head down and by the time the boys registered her, she was gone.

'Jesus, look at her go,' one of them shouted at her back, but that was all.

Minnie accepted the insult gratefully. She ignored the chafing of her thighs and the pain in her muscles and she kept moving as fast as she could.

'Not far now,' she kept saying to herself. Her lungs burned and the sweat dripped everywhere but she could not stop moving. There was no time to rest.

Not far now.

5

The store was filled with schoolchildren filling up Slurpee cups and throwing things at each other and for once Minnie was glad of the bustle. Usually the stares and sly giggling made moving up and down the narrow aisles torture, but today she pushed past people without thinking twice.

She lifted her hand as she came in and saw Lela nod as she rang up newspapers and chocolates for a frazzled-looking woman with five children.

'Just stop it, for God's sake, just stop it,' the woman was saying to the smallest child, who kept pulling at her pants leg.

Minnie wondered if the woman knew how lucky she was but she supposed not. Five children was, to Minnie, an abundance of fortune but the woman was probably just worn down and weary. Growing up, Minnie had always imagined the friendly bustle that went on in houses filled with children and she had vowed to be the mother in such a house one day. By the time she realised that even commonplace dreams were not for everyone it was too late to attempt to do things alone. And now whenever she felt a hot flush signalling the arrival of menopause she would be consumed by a feeling of loneliness and despair so strong that she had to sit down until it passed.

Yesterday she would have stood gazing at the woman and then piled her basket high with treats to soothe her soul, but today . . . today was different.

She went to the back section, where she knew she would find everything she needed. It was going to cost a fortune, but that was the least of her concerns. She grabbed nappies, two bottles and a tin of formula, some dummies, soap and a small pack of vests that had obviously been sitting on the shelf for years. There was nothing else for babies except a display of small rattles with lion faces and shaking paws. Minnie took one of those as well, even though she knew it was ridiculous.

She went to the counter and placed everything in front of Lela, who just raised her eyebrows. Minnie had not bought anything to eat. It was the first time she would ever leave the store without at least half a dozen chocolate bars.

Lela had thick eyebrows and dark expressive eyes and she smoothed her headscarf down, which Minnie knew meant she was working out just which question to ask first.

Behind Minnie, two teenage boys holding giant Slurpee cups began shoving each other and one bumped into Minnie, pushing her forward.

Minnie's hands went automatically to her front to protect her secret parcel. She felt a momentary jolt of rage. She wanted to turn around and swing a fist at the boys.

'If youse boys don't bloody calm down you can shove off outa here,' said Lela in a loud voice.

Lela's ocker accent never failed to make Minnie smile. She was a delicate-looking woman who had been sent from Pakistan to marry the son of an old friend of her father. In quieter moments at the shop Lela lamented her husband's stupidity, but always with a wry laugh that told Minnie there was some love there.

Lela was the one who'd pushed her husband to open the 7-Eleven and twenty years later she basically ran the show. Her children were grown but she still didn't look much older than the young woman she had been when the store and petrol station first opened.

'My cousin is coming to stay,' said Minnie before Lela could say anything else.

'Cousin?'

'Yes, she's a second cousin on my mother's side and she has a baby and, well, she's only really young so she's really not coping, you know? So I told her she could come and stay.' The words came out in a rush. Minnie had prepared them all the way to the store and was pleased she had thought to change niece to cousin

43

at the last minute. Lela knew she was an only child. Lela knew most things about her. Lela knew about her failed hopes, Lela knew about her mother and how hard it was for Minnie to get through the day sometimes. Minnie tried to buy her petrol at night mostly, when families were busy with dinner or curled up together watching television. Minnie knew the time of day when she could almost certainly find Lela alone and she would fill up her car and then buy enough to fill up her stomach. She usually got through one or two chocolate bars as she and Lela chatted. Sometimes Lela suggested that Minnie eat less chocolate but she only ever made the suggestion gently.

'How long is she going to stay for?'

'Oh, who knows?' said Minnie, who knew exactly when the cousin was going to disappear and leave her with a child to raise by herself. 'Imagine her just leaving like that,' she would say to Lela. And she knew that Lela would nod her head at the stupidity of youth and they would both agree that the baby was better off with Minnie. But that scenario was for later. Now Minnie had to get past Lela's questioning gaze.

'Babies are a lot of work, Minnie,' said Lela.

'Oh, I know,' said Minnie, 'but you'll help me—help us—won't you?'

'Of course. In fact, I have some stuff you can have if you don't mind hand-me-downs. I was saving them for my grandchildren but Ahmed has no interest in ever finding a wife and Malika just screws up her nose when I ask her what she wants me to keep for her future children.'

'Well, I guess she'll buy everything new.'

'Oh, yes—Miss Important Lawyer with her doctor husband wouldn't dream of using secondhand clothes.'

Lela never missed a chance to boast about her children and Minnie smiled and nodded, feeling a small surge of joy at the thought that one day she might be able to do the same thing.

'I'd love to have anything you can give me, Lela. I want to give the poor little thing everything I can.'

'You're a good cousin,' said Lela as she began ringing up Minnie's purchases. The baby began to wriggle and squeak and Minnie coughed loudly and then kept coughing while she paid Lela to cover the little noises the baby was making.

'You right?' said Lela.

'Just something in my throat—but look, there's a big queue. I'll come by next week and show you the baby.'

'Yeah, see you then,' said Lela, already looking to the next customer. The teenage boys had stood patiently whilst she served Minnie.

Minnie felt relief wash over her as she exited the store. The cold air was fresh on her face. She opened her coat a little to get some air to the baby, who immediately started crying. Minnie hurried along with her head down. She just needed to get home.

•

Minnie unwrapped the screaming baby and laid her in front of the fire. The baby needed to eat but the bottle needed to be cleaned first and she was sure that she needed to use boiled water to make the formula.

There was something black and disgusting on the red scarf the baby had been wrapped in and Minnie didn't want to think about what it could possibly be. The baby was filthy but was obviously inconsolable with hunger.

'Look at the poor thing, Mum. I can't wait to clean her up.'

She would have to order some sort of book about caring for babies and she would need to get the baby to a doctor. Babies needed to see the doctor, didn't they? She felt a momentary sadness that she had reached the age of forty-seven without knowing anything about children except what she saw on television.

She tore open the package with the nappies in it and fumbled about for a bit until she got the nappy on the baby and then she left her screaming while she went off to make a bottle of formula. The formula tin came with instructions, thank Jesus.

Ten minutes later the sound of the baby crying was beginning to drill straight through Minnie's head. 'It's driving me completely crazy, Mum.' Her stomach cramped with hunger because she had neglected to eat afternoon tea, but she had more important things to do.

She tested the bottle on the inside of her arm and, finding it still too hot (though she had no real idea how hot a bottle should be), she ran it under some cold water. She thought that babies would probably like something to be lukewarm.

In the living room she scooped up the screaming baby and held the bottle to her lips, but she continued to cry. Minnie could feel herself beginning to sweat again. The room was very warm and the baby was wriggling and screaming. Minnie uttered up a small prayer to God then squeezed the nipple of the bottle. A few drops fell onto the baby's tongue. Instantly she stopped crying, clamped her lips around the bottle and began to suck.

'Well thank you, God, for your mercy,' said Minnie.

The baby sucked for a while and then it stopped and wriggled around. It let go of the teat and scrunched up its face.

Minnie lifted her up and put her against her shoulder. Maybe she'd had enough. The baby burped and then Minnie felt her little body relax. Minnie resumed feeding her. They went on in this way until the bottle was almost finished and the baby clamped her lips together.

'Right then,' said Minnie.

She took the baby into her bedroom and put her down on the bed. The whole house was warm now but Minnie didn't want to leave the child in just a nappy for too long. She looked so tiny in the middle of the king-size bed that Minnie had to smile. She opened one of the dresser drawers, pulled everything out then padded it with towels. She grabbed a clean scarf from the floor, silently thanking her mother for the staple Christmas present, and wrapped the baby up again. She laid the sleeping child inside the drawer.

She watched the baby girl for a moment, listening to the silence.

It had been an extraordinary few hours.

She felt like she could sleep for a week.

Her bed beckoned but there was just so much to do. The house was a complete mess and even her bedroom—her sanctuary, with its large bed and mahogany desk and chest of drawers— looked a sight.

'No going back now, Mum,' she said.

She was starving but she was getting used to the empty feeling—except it wasn't really an empty feeling; it was more like a hungry body asking for food. It had been a long time since Minnie had tried to distinguish between the two.

Minnie went to the kitchen, where she gulped down a glass of water, and then returned to her bedroom and sat down at her desk. She opened the computer. *What does a newborn baby need?* she typed.

Twenty-eight million results came up.

Minnie started reading and after half an hour she retrieved her purse from her bag, took out her credit card, and started spending.

6

'Where's the baby?' said the doctor.

'Where is the baby?' said the policewoman.

'Where is the baby?' said the psychiatrist.

'Where is the baby?' said Alicia.

'Where's the baby?' said her dad.

'I'm lost,' Tara wanted to say. 'I'm lost. Isn't anyone going to find me?'

The words were trapped inside. Sometimes she opened her mouth to let them out but they wouldn't budge.

Outside the hospital window the rain settled in for the day and inside people came and went and asked the question. They had searched everywhere for the baby. They had gone to the park and the shopping centre and walked the streets around her house knocking on doors, but no one knew anything about a baby.

Tara knew the least of anyone.

'You need to say something—eventually you're going to have to talk,' said Dr Elias softly.

Tara looked at him and shook her head. She couldn't talk. She touched her throat to let him know.

He brought in another doctor to examine her.

'I don't think it's that she can't actually talk. I think it's selective,' the second doctor said.

Sometimes Tara put her hand on her stomach and felt the soft wrinkled flesh and she wanted to throw up because it felt so gross. She didn't know what had happened. They kept asking the question but she didn't understand why they were asking.

The time before the hospital was simply black. There were no images she could grasp, nothing to give her a clue. There was just black.

Her father slept in a chair that night. If she had been able to speak Tara would have said, 'Go home, Dad. I'll be fine.' But she kept her mouth closed and when she felt herself dragged up from sleep with a racing heart she opened her eyes and felt the comfort of his presence, as she had on nights when she had climbed into bed beside him dragging her blankie and doll. His black-grey beard aged him and his bloodshot eyes made him look angry.

Early the next morning he chewed on a piece of toast from Tara's uneaten breakfast and barked at people in his office on his mobile phone. He had risen through the ranks of his firm to be head of marketing but he didn't seem to be that happy about it. 'It's a load of crap', Tara had heard him say. 'Endless reports and meetings so I can tell some client that people really are interested in a new kind of butter. It's all buzzwords and bullshit.'

'Go back to accounting,' Alicia said.

'I hated that even more,' her father would reply.

Tara understood that they had the conversation about his work just to have it and not because her father would ever change anything. He had too many responsibilities, too many people to take care of. Tara wondered how much her stay in the hospital was costing.

She still viewed her father's work the same way Ethan and Michael did. They all understood that daddy went to work early and came home late and had a lot of people working for him but beyond that they didn't think about it. Tara had never been able to dredge up the interest to ask him what his work actually meant. But it kept the money coming in.

Her father stayed with her until Alicia arrived bringing a bag filled with sushi and muffins and cake, like food would solve the problem.

'Go home and get some rest, Max. I'll stay until it's time to pick up the boys from school. I've told the clinic I won't be able to do my shift for a week or two.'

'Call me before you leave,' Tara's father said, and then he leaned down and rested his lips on Tara's forehead for a moment.

At the door to Tara's hospital room he took a deep breath and hunched his shoulders against the world outside and left.

Alicia watched him go and Tara saw her shake her head at how strange and defeated he looked.

Tara saw him on the news an hour later covering his face and pushing against the cameras stationed outside the hospital. She couldn't quite see the desperate man shouting 'No comment' as her father.

Alicia turned the channel to an awful soap opera.

'How did they find out so quickly,' Alicia murmured to Tara. In the absence of an answer she laid all the food out on a hospital tray in front of Tara. Tara didn't want to eat but she could sense Alicia's agitation building and so she sat up and obligingly pushed some sushi into her mouth. It was her favourite kind and she knew that Alicia would have had to go to the sushi restaurant one suburb over to get it.

'Thank you,' Tara wanted to say and 'I'm sorry I've caused so much trouble,' because she understood as she had understood for many years now that she was a great source of 'trouble' to Alicia.

Later that day when Dr Elias returned to check on Tara, Alicia pounced on him as he walked through the door.

'How on earth have the press found out about this,' she said without even greeting the doctor.

Dr Elias shrugged his shoulders. 'Slow news day, I suppose, and of course the police have been looking for the baby. They would have spoken to a lot of people.'

'Did someone from the hospital tell them?' said Alicia, and Dr Elias shrugged again. Tara wanted to throw her glass of water at him. 'It's unacceptable,' said Alicia. 'This is a private family matter. You have a duty to protect your patients.'

'I understand that you're upset,' said Dr Elias, 'but if having the information out there leads to us finding the baby surely that's a good thing?'

Tara watched Alicia deflate. She sank into the chair next to the bed.

'I feel like the whole country is talking about us,' she said.

'Where's the baby?' said the woman with the perfect hair on the television.

Inside her head Tara could feel the question growing, could feel it taking over until it became part of her breathing.

As the hours passed she felt the truth nudging at her. If she closed her eyes she was beginning to see snatches of images. Things that flickered quickly and then faded to the black that stopped her from knowing what had happened.

She remembered the pain and she remembered running and she remembered large red-veined feet stuffed into blue canvas shoes. But everything else was black.

She could not remember the baby.

They brought the psychiatrist back to try again and he stared at Tara and Tara stared at him. She watched his eyebrows move up and down when he started to talk. He went on and on about the need for her to acknowledge what had happened and the need to find the infant so it could be saved.

'Help us find the baby, Tara, so we can save it—so we can save you,' he said.

'You need to communicate with us if you can,' he said.

He took Tara's hand in his and forced a pencil into it. His hands were soft and dry and they turned Tara's stomach.

'If you could write something down to help us that would be good,' he said.

Tara held the pencil. She rolled it between her fingers and rested it on the paper but she could not get her hand to move. She felt heavy and boneless. The pencil rolled off the bed and clinked onto the floor.

The psychiatrist sighed. 'You need to find a way to communicate, Tara,' he said, and then he kept talking until eventually Tara got tired of watching his eyebrows and she closed her eyes and floated into a light doze.

She listened to the soft slap of shoes on the floor of her room as the psychiatrist gave up and left and then she heard the heavy tread of her father return to take over from Alicia.

'Go away,' she wanted to say to all of them. 'Go away and let me think.' She knew that if they stopped talking at her she would be able to piece the puzzle together. Why did she remember a pair of blue shoes? Where had she been going? Why was there so much pain? She touched her jelly stomach under the blanket and wondered how she could have fitted a baby in there. The thought was absurd enough to make her laugh but the laugh died in her silent throat.

In a whisper, Alicia told her father what the doctors had said. 'They think it could be a sign of . . . of.'

'She's not her mother—she's not,' said Tara's father.

'We know it's a genetic condition,' said Alicia. 'We have to face the possibility, Max. She may have the same condition as her mother. It's not normal behaviour to hide a pregnancy and abandon a newborn somewhere. It's not normal to choose silence. We don't need the doctors to tell us that.'

'No!' shouted her father and Tara's eyes flew open because they had to know she was awake now. 'No medication. She needs time. I'll give her time. We'll take her home—she'll talk to us at home, I'm sure of it. But no pills. I won't go down that road yet . . . not yet. I can't just yet.'

Tara watched Alicia fold her arms and then she had to move aside for the police, who were back with more questions.

'Where do they get all these words from?' thought Tara.

'This is very serious,' said the policeman with blue eyes. 'We are going to have to charge her with abandoning a baby at the very least and there may be a murder charge to follow if we find the baby and it has not survived.'

'Maybe it was dead when it was born,' said Tara's father.

'They can tell these things, Max,' said Alicia.

'How can they tell them? How do they know? How do they know?'

'Max, please. We all want what's best for Tara and the baby. You aren't helping things by being like this.'

'I'm not "being" like anything, Alicia. I want to know how they can tell these things.'

'They check for signs that the baby breathed air—something it wouldn't have done if it had been stillborn.'

'Oh,' said Max and then he was silent.

The policeman nodded. He looked younger than her father. Silence made her invisible. Everyone talked around her and through her and she wanted to open her mouth and shout, 'I'm here! See me? I'm here,' but her mouth stayed closed and the conversation went on around her.

'I need to get the boys from my mother,' said Alicia but as she turned to go Daniel Walters arrived. Tara watched her father and Alicia sag a little, as though they could relax now that the cavalry had arrived. Daniel Walters kissed Alicia on the cheek and shook her father's hand but he didn't say anything to Tara.

'Thank God,' said her father.

'Now, I don't want you to worry about a thing. They haven't charged her with anything yet and I'm not going to let them push her too much. Tara is our main concern,' and here he finally looked at Tara.

'You remember Daniel Walters,' said Alicia to Tara. Tara nodded. Daniel brought papers over to the house and drank bourbon with her father.

When the police and Dr Elias returned for one more attempt to get her to talk that day they found Daniel waiting for them.

'Tara is still recovering from an incredible trauma and if you persist in this line of questioning it is quite possible that you will cause the girl to have some sort of breakdown,' he snapped the moment the policeman began his questions.

'Mr Walters, we are concerned about the baby. If she has left it somewhere there may be a chance that it's still alive,' said Dr Elias, who had been nice to Tara at first but now seemed mean.

Alicia gave the doctor a look. Alicia was a nurse and Tara understood that the look said, 'No, there is no chance.'

Alicia had to go and get her own children from her mother's house. Tara knew Ethan and Michael hated going to visit Grandmother Anne. She hated mess and constantly told them to 'keep the noise down'. They were only seven and five and Tara felt sorry that they were stuck with Anne because of something she had done. She wondered if Alicia had told them anything about their big sister.

'I'll call when I'm home,' she said to Tara's father but he was in the middle of a whispered conversation with Daniel. Alicia closed the door behind her.

The police and Dr Elias stood on one side of the room and her father and Daniel stood on the other.

Tara watched them all. The room was too small to hold all the people who were concerned for the baby. Tara felt sad for the baby that might be dead but she had no idea what to do about it. It couldn't possibly have anything to do with her.

'I'm taking her home,' said Tara's father.

'It's only been twenty-four hours,' said the doctor. 'She needs more time to recover.'

'Alicia's a nurse, she can take care of her,' said Tara's father.

Tara knew Alicia had no desire to take care of her.

'You'll need to surrender your passports and there will have to be visits with a therapist,' said the policeman.

'Fine.'

'Fine.'

Everyone was angry and defensive. Everyone talked to Tara with their voices on quiet and their thoughts on secret but Tara knew it was all her fault and still the words wouldn't come and the blackness persisted.

7

Tara's room had silvery-pink butterflies on the wall and there were one thousand songs on her iPod.

Her room looked strange to her now. She was a stranger in it. It didn't seem logical that she had walked out of it two days ago and thrown her whole world into chaos.

She had a closet full of clothes that hadn't fitted her for some time. She pulled out her short skirts and tight jeans and couldn't imagine that she had ever worn such things. She had grown bigger and bigger before the blackness.

She had grown bigger because of the baby; because she'd been pregnant.

She had grown bigger and bigger and there was a reason for the bigness, for all the space she was taking up even when she had wanted to be small and invisible. She had been pregnant.

Preg nant

Pregn ant.

Pregnan t.

You could say some words inside your head over and over again until they lost all meaning. In her bedroom she thought back to the time before the blackness had descended.

There had been fear and humiliation. There had been the horrible feeling of something strange moving inside her body. That was pregnant. That was pregnancy. She had been pregnant.

She had dreamed it might burst through her stomach and try to eat her.

She had ignored it at first. Her period was not something she paid attention to. It appeared suddenly every month, leaving her with stained pants and a craving for chocolate. When she realised what was happening she looked up some stuff on the internet. It confirmed what she already knew. All those stupid lectures in personal health and development class had been right. It was possible that it just took once or twice. And not even a good once or twice. Just a rushed, hurried pushing and then it was easier not to look at him. It played out better in her fantasies. They should tell you that in the classes.

The swelling was disgusting. It was disgusting and she had covered it up. Even when she was so hot she thought she would melt she had to keep it covered. Layers and layers of clothes went on top of the parasite inside her. Some days she had to sneak food from the kitchen. It was eating her up from the inside just like she had dreamed. She covered it up and she pretended it wasn't there and she got through the bigness. She waited for it to be over.

She had no plan for what to do when the pains started. She didn't know when the pregnancy was supposed to end but she had some vague dates off the internet. You could calculate your due date. Due date for what? The end of your life.

There were hundreds of websites filled with round smiling women and single-toothed babies. The posts were all joyful and filled with glee. 'I'm nothing like these women,' Tara thought. 'I can't be having a baby.'

She knew what was supposed to happen but she didn't want to know.

In the months leading up to the blackness she remembered wanting to go to sleep and wake up when everything was over. She thought about telling her father; the words almost tripped out when she was with her friends. She wanted to tell, desperately wanted to talk to someone, but it seemed that everyone was in on the conspiracy. Everyone pretended it wasn't happening so she could pretend the same thing.

'You're a smart girl, Tara,' her father had said when he held her hand as she lay in the hospital bed. 'How could you have thought that you could ignore this?'

'I didn't think,' she wanted to say, but of course she couldn't even get her mouth to move. 'I didn't think.'

Two days ago, when the pain started to bite, she went to tell Alicia that she needed help but Alicia had been folding washing and talking to her mother on the phone.

'What is it?' she had snapped at Tara.

Tara just shook her head and walked to the front door.

'Too sick to go to school but not too sick to go out to the shopping centre, I suppose,' said Alicia.

Tara had felt another pain bite into her stomach and she had squeezed the door handle and waited for it to pass, then she walked out the door.

'I don't know, Mum,' she heard Alicia say. 'She hangs out at that ridiculous skate park next to the shopping centre. I'm sure she's off to meet that boy. I have no idea how to deal with her anymore.'

'Then don't fucking deal with me,' Tara thought, and now when she went over what had happened that day, it was the last thing she could remember. Maybe it was the last thing she wanted to remember. There were other things that crept up on her. Blue shoes, excruciating pain, fear.

'I have no idea how to deal with her anymore,' Alicia had said.

Did Alicia have any idea of how to deal with her now? How to deal with this? Did anyone have any idea at all?

'Why can't I remember the baby?' she wondered. 'Did I leave it somewhere? Can you forget a baby like you forgot your sports bag?'

Her body felt weak and tired and she lay on her bed and slept for hours. She wished that she had kept a diary or a journal or something that could have told her who she had been before all this happened, but she had never been someone who wanted to record every day. There were a lot of days that she just wanted to forget.

That afternoon Tara's father retuned to work so he could 'put out all the Goddamn fires'. He kissed Tara's forehead and left her to her heavy dreams in which her father kept trying to climb up the side of a building engulfed by flames. Tara shouted down to him from the top window but the heat was too great and he could not find a way to rescue his daughter.

Alicia brought food and water up to Tara, checked her temperature and handed out pain medication but she was silent on the topic of 'the baby' and Tara was grateful for the reprieve. She knew it would not last long.

On the news that night the lead story was different. There was a celebrity getting a divorce. There was always a celebrity getting a divorce.

•

'Try, sweetheart,' said her father when he came home. He brought a tray up to her room and sat on her pink beanbag looking uncomfortable in his suit. 'Try to say something. If you can tell us anything it will help. If you can tell us where the baby is we can sort this all out.'

He handed her a silver pen and the special little notebook he carried around with him so he could write down all the things he had to remember. Tara opened the book and flipped over pages and pages of small numbered points. Her father had a lot of things to remember.

She held the heavy silver pen in her hand and rested it against a new page, wondering if she should number her recollections. If the memory of the baby could fit into the little notebook surely it couldn't be so bad.

Her father squirmed on the beanbag and waited.

The pen touched the paper and made a circle. It went round and round, pressing deeper and deeper into the page. The circle filled itself in with black lines. The page tore.

Her father sighed and got up to go downstairs and eat dinner with his uncomplicated, unfucked-up family. Tara was used to his disappointment.

'If you could just try to be a real part of this family it would make things easier for everyone,' he had said many months ago after she'd had another fight with Alicia.

'It was my family first,' she wanted to say, but no one ever said everything they wanted to say except her mother—and look where that had got her.

Tara turned on her computer and her story was all over the internet.

Look at me—I'm someone.

No one was supposed to know who she was because Daniel Walters was making sure that her identity was a secret. She was a minor. Minor as in small and not important. But her father had been all over the news. People weren't stupid. The world couldn't hide its secrets anymore.

Her friends had left messages on Facebook but Tara couldn't bring herself to read them yet. Instead she read the articles that had bloomed overnight like spring flowers. Articles that were filled with words like 'allegedly' and 'police' and 'homicide'. And she read the comments. Hundreds and hundreds of comments. Didn't people have anything else to do?

Oh, that poor little thing, left alone in the cold. The mother should be jailed for life.

That is why teenagers should not have sex. They don't under-stand about consequences.

How could the family not have known she was pregnant? What kind of people are they?

That poor, poor little baby. What a horrible way to die.

I think we should give this family peace. The girl is obviously sick or mental or something.

Children should not have children. Where was her mother?

What kind of a person does this? She should be shot.

On and on they went as the world pulled her apart and left her to put herself back together again.

8

Minnie startled into wakefulness to the roar of a motorbike. She pushed herself off the bed, noting her own sour smell and wrinkled clothes, and peered into the drawer.

The baby slept—filthy in her new multicoloured cocoon but peaceful.

It was ten o'clock.

Minnie had woken to the baby's cries every two hours. She wouldn't eat or sleep and when Minnie finally got her to close her eyes again it was only minutes until she opened them. Eventually, at three o'clock in the morning, the baby had filled her nappy with black stuff that would have made Minnie panic if she hadn't known from her research online that it was called meconium. She seemed to settle after that and sucked her bottle for only a few minutes before drifting into sleep. Minnie missed dinner and a shower and simply collapsed onto her bed.

'Right, little one,' she said to the sleeping baby. 'You keep doing that and I'll get things under control. Some of your stuff should arrive today.'

Minnie showered and cleaned up and ate an apple before the baby woke up. And then the day belonged to the infant.

Minnie finally managed to bathe her before her lunchtime bottle—or at least what she thought of as lunch, because she could see that now the days and nights were divided up by hours rather than meals and the clock. Feed every four hours all the websites said, but there were some that said to let the baby lead the way if it was breastfed. Minnie felt an ache in her breast when she read this. What did it feel like when your baby drank from your breast? she wondered. 'No use asking for the moon,' her mother always said.

Bathing the baby was a tricky process that involved filling up the laundry tub and testing the water again and again. The special bath thermometer hadn't arrived yet so Minnie dipped her elbow and hand and wrist into the water, trying to judge if the bath was just right for the baby.

The baby started to cry the moment Minnie began unwrapping her and got more and more frantic as Minnie tried to work out how to lower her into the water without dropping her. But when her little body hit the water she was instantly calm. She seemed to know and understand the weightless feeling of being in the water.

'Does she miss being inside her mother, Mum?' said Minnie, and she pushed down a small stab of regret that the baby had never been inside her.

Silence descended and Minnie felt her own body relax. She moved the baby back and forth, studying the perfect little body, marvelling at the tiny fingernails. 'Hush, little baby, don't say a word,' sang Minnie and the baby opened her eyes, which looked darker today, and looked directly at Minnie. Minnie held her breath, terrified to move in case she startled the baby. 'Hello, little one,' she said in a quiet singsong voice. 'I'm Minnie.' And then, because she couldn't help herself, 'I'm your mum.'

The baby stared and stared. Minnie felt locked into her gaze, held in this perfect moment. 'This must be what it feels like to truly be in love,' thought Minnie. 'This must be what everyone talks about. All those mothers on the television who cry when they see their babies and then give up their whole lives for them—this is why.'

She and the baby looked at each other, suspended by the water and the silence.

She could feel the water cooling down. The front of her dress was soaked.

'Time to get you cleaned up,' she said. She leaned over and placed her whole arm in the water to support the baby so she could use the other hand to pour some soap into the water.

She made slow, connected movements across the baby's body, revelling in the feel of her soft skin. When she poured some of the soap over the baby's head and massaged away the last remanent of her birth, the baby closed her eyes and heaved a great sigh. 'You like that, don't you?' said Minnie.

When she was completely clean, Minnie took her out of the water and placed her on a large towel she had laid out on the counter next to the tub. The baby made her disappointment at the end of her bath known, but her cries petered out once Minnie had her dressed in a nappy and little vest and wrapped in yet another clean scarf.

'We'll soon have special blankets for you, little one, but this will have to do for now.'

She fed the baby and settled her back to sleep easily and then the doorbell rang.

The deliveryman had a name tag that identified him as Matt and thin arms with bulging veins. He studied Minnie carefully, perhaps trying to assess exactly where she fitted in the life of the baby he was delivering so many things for. Before Minnie could speak he made up his mind as to who she was. 'When's the baby due?' he said with a smile. It was obviously part of his job description to make friendly small talk with expectant mothers.

Minnie looked down at her bloated stomach and sighed. 'Next week,' she said with what she hoped was a smile that told a tale of excitement and joy over the coming baby.

'Right,' said Matt, who had no idea how long women could have babies for but this fat one sure looked old.

He went back to the van to collect the rest of the stuff. There was thousands of dollars' worth of stuff. His boss had been delighted. Most women shopped around and bought a little bit here and there and only ordered the really big stuff from one store, but this woman had bought everything, right down to a month's supply of nappies.

'That's the last of it, love,' he said, even though the word felt strange in his mouth. The woman looked old enough to be his mother.

Minnie tipped him ten dollars, grateful for the absence of the boys. She had no idea what she would do with the boxes once she had unpacked them. She would have to keep them inside until she could take them apart. Lou and June had placed the box for a flat-screen television on the pavement only to have the fancy new television disappear in the night.

The police could find no evidence that the boys had taken the television but Lou had stood in the garden and gone on and on about not buying a new one. Minnie knew that a replacement had been brought in at night and the boxes quickly disposed of; Lou just wanted to make sure the thing stayed in his house.

The police had interviewed 'the boys' about the missing television, just like they had interviewed them about the missing lawnmower that had disappeared from the house at the end of the street and the iPhone that disappeared from the house where Lilly lived—only two doors down from Minnie.

They always had an iron clad excuse and the street had never really been crime free. No one could prove anything.

If Minnie bought something new or expensive she broke down the box and then cut it into small pieces so it could have been anything and nothing.

Minnie looked at the sleek pram sitting in her living room and thought how pleasant it would be to stroll up and down the street on a sunny day with the baby wrapped up warm and tight. She could finally join June on her daily walk. June was always trying to encourage her to get out of the house and into the fresh air. Minnie could never see the point. Now she felt a stab of excitement at being able to show the baby to June. June and her mother had been friends for years and Minnie had overhead many whispered conversations about 'poor Minnie'.

When she was in her twenties Minnie had hated June just a little for her constant sympathy. In her thirties she had nodded as June dispensed reams of advice—gleaned from where Minnie had no idea. In her forties Minnie had taken to avoiding June whenever she could, but then her mother had fallen ill and June swung into action, providing empathy and support.

Now Minnie looked forward to having tea with June once a week. She was just about the only person Minnie ever had a real conversation with, other than Lela. June tried half-heartedly to get Minnie to diet or exercise every now and again, and Lela occasionally showed her a new meal replacement or diet pill, but mostly the two women in Minnie's life saw beyond her size.

'You cannot weigh two hundred and fifty kilos and survive, Minnie,' Dr Benson had said once when he saw her at the supermarket.

Minnie was mortified at his unprofessional outburst and hated him for it, though she recognised he was just desperate for her to help herself. He had looked down into her overflowing trolley and actually gasped at the frozen meals and chocolate bars.

Minnie had wanted to shout at him. She had wanted to yell and scream and spit right there in the supermarket, especially when Dr Benson's pretty wife sidled up to him with three bunches of asparagus in her hands.

'Easy for you to say,' she had muttered and pushed past them both.

She wanted to take the baby to Dr Benson to show him that she was capable of more than just eating, but Dr Benson would ask questions and try to find the cousin who had supposedly left the baby. She would need to find a new doctor for the baby and tell another lie about just moving into the area or something like that.

'I hope I can keep all the lies straight in my head, Mum,' said Minnie as she surveyed the things that had arrived for the baby. 'I know it's wrong, Mum, but you only have to look at her to know she needs us. Poor mite.'

Things for the baby took up the whole living room. The neat little room no longer looked like it belonged to her. Minnie could feel that her world had shifted. In her head she saw two giant wheels with interlocked cogs and she watched as one moved against the other. They were both rusty because nothing much had changed for Minnie for years and years. Even after her mother died she simply added the overwhelming grief to her day, but she could feel the wheels move now, could feel the enormous change that had taken place.

There was a pram in grey with patches of pink and a highchair with pink-checked padding. There were babygros and socks and jumpers and tops, all in shades of pink and lilac. There were towels and face cloths and packets of nappies for newborns. There were vests and toys and a cot that needed to be assembled and lined with the pink floral bedding and soft pink blankets. The numbers had ticked up on the screen as she had ordered and Minnie had imagined someone rubbing their hands with glee over the amount. They had promised next-day delivery and here it was. It had taken the man three trips to get it all inside and now suddenly the house that was the perfect size for Minnie and her mother was small for a baby and all the things it needed.

'Imagine needing all this stuff for one little baby, Mum. Where shall we put it all?' said Minnie, but she knew the answer.

•

As the baby slept Minnie munched a piece of toast and talked herself round.

The room had been empty for two years already. Minnie was surprised to realise that so much time had passed. The first days and weeks and months felt like they would last forever. But then the outside world muscled in through the television and her clients grew tired of waiting for her to return calls and she had to focus on something else and now two years had passed.

Minnie had never imagined she would need to move things around, never imagined that she would have to open the cupboards and pull out the clothes to make room for someone else. There was never going to be someone else in her life. Minnie had made peace with that long before her mother got sick.

She had nursed Charlotte until the end, holding her hand as she took her last breaths and her heart stopped. Minnie had understood on some level that her mother would eventually die but the reality was a different story altogether.

It seemed to Minnie to be completely impossible that her mother had actually left the world. For the first few days after the funeral she had simply assumed her mother was resting or out shopping or visiting a friend.

One night her mother chased her through her dreams, shouting 'I just want to say goodbye,' but Minnie would not stop to listen.

The next day Minnie had climbed out of bed and prepared herself a huge breakfast of eggs and bacon and pancakes and syrup with squares of chocolate floating in butter. She sat in front of the television and ate and ate and ate until the ad break. An old man lectured her on getting funeral insurance and it hit Minnie with all the force of a boulder that her mother was gone. Really, truly gone.

The loss left such a great hole that one night Minnie nearly choked to death trying to fill it. The large piece of chocolate had dislodged itself just in time and Minnie had sat on the couch shaking with disbelief for a few minutes before she went back to eating.

Minnie thought about suicide but couldn't fit into the bathtub to slit her wrists and she had no idea how many pills she would need to put her large body to sleep.

'Too fat to kill myself, Mum,' she said one night, and then she had to laugh because Dr Benson was worried about her dying.

People at church were kind but she went less and less after Charlotte died. When they were together Minnie had been able to withstand the stares of the other parishioners. Alone she was just a large island surrounded by a sea of whispers and sympathy. She had to stop herself from being angry with God. Charlotte would not tolerate anger towards the Lord. 'He never gives us more than we can handle, love. Trust him on that.' But she did feel jealous that God would have the advantage of Charlotte's company while she was left alone on earth with nothing more than television and cake.

To Minnie, she and Charlotte weren't just mother and daughter; they were allies against the evils of the world and in particular the evils of men. They had been ever since that one and only time when Minnie was four years old and her father had come in to kiss her goodnight and started stroking and touching and eventually sticking his fingers where they shouldn't go. Minnie's breath had left her and she felt her eyes widen and burn with fear. The fingers hurt but her father kept muttering about how good it was and pushing and pushing. Minnie thought she was going to throw up when her mother's voice came from the doorway. 'Just what the fuck do you think you're doing?' Her father had leapt off the bed and turned with his pink sausage shrivelling in the hand that had not been poking about in Minnie.

Charlotte threw him out that night, kicking and swearing and threatening to call the police.

'As if I had any choice.' Her father had gestured at her mother. 'Who'd want to climb on top of that? Who'd want to touch that?'

Charlotte had opened her mouth wide and laughed in her husband's face. She stood up straight and tall and Minnie was suddenly aware of how very small a man her father was.

'So that's how you avoid the poking fingers,' thought Minnie. 'You have to be big.'

'Bye, Minnie,' said her father and Minnie hid her head in the body of her fluffy rabbit and crouched in a corner.

'She has nothing to say to you, you horrible little pervert,' said Charlotte.

'You always were a ballbreaker, Charlotte,' he replied.

'You never really had much to break,' said Charlotte, and then she slammed the door and turned to face her daughter, who was a small ball of misery and guilt.

'Never mind, love,' she said. 'It wasn't your fault.'

She dressed Minnie up in her gown and slippers and they went off to the store for ice cream. They sat together on the couch with the flickering television until Minnie fell asleep and the whole incident seemed very far away. Minnie knew she was safe and would always be safe with her mother, and it seemed to Minnie that they had never really moved off the couch.

Sometimes Minnie stood and stared at the wedding photo of her parents which maintained pride of place on the mantel as if to legitimise Minnie and give her credence in the world. In the photograph her mother was plump and pink, bursting out of the white satin wedding dress. Her father, whose name was George, looked pleased and proud with his hair neatly flattened against his head. At five years old Charlotte was just her mother and she could only see the woman who loved her but at ten she would gaze at the picture and note the difference between Charlotte then and Charlotte now. She would not have left room in the picture for George.

'I just wanted to get married I suppose,' Charlotte had said in one of the rare conversations about George that happened after Minnie grew up and reached an appropriate age for such discussions.

As she grew older Minnie understood from books and television that a father was an important part of a family. As a teenager she supposed she should miss his presence but he had been a peripheral figure in her young life. He existed on the edges while Charlotte raised her only child.

'I wanted a child more than anything,' Charlotte confessed one night.

'So you married him just to have me?' Minnie asked, and she had been warmed by Charlotte's nod.

The loss of George had not been felt too greatly by either Minnie or Charlotte.

Her mother had gone to work and she had gone to school but they would always come together at the end of the day and sit in quiet contentment, eating and watching television.

Television and comfort food made up for all the trials and tribulations both women encountered out in the world. Charlotte went to night school and studied bookkeeping and went to work in a large firm, where she was given a small office in the basement that she had to squeeze in and out of every day.

Her first instinct was to confront anyone who stared or laughed at her, but she knew enough to keep quiet because she needed the money. She never missed a day of work and she never spoke to anyone either except if it related to work. Charlotte would hear the other unmarried women in the office chattering about their Friday nights out and supress her longing to be invited along. 'I have Minnie,' she told herself, and Minnie unwittingly became her best friend and reason for living.

Minnie had friends when she was in preschool, despite being terribly shy, but as she grew older and larger she found herself alone more often. When she did bring a friend home the little girl would soon grow bored with the ritualised eating that characterised Minnie and Charlotte's afternoon tea and would never want to come and play again.

In high school Minnie hung out in the library waiting for the bell to ring so she could go back to class and sit quietly in the back row.

Minnie needs to contribute to class discussions was always written on her report cards but when she did raise her hand the teachers seemed not to see her. She was as invisible as a large person could be. At fourteen Minnie longed for a friend, but she could not quite see how such a thing could happen. 'How do I start a conversation?' she wondered.

For a while there had been boys—more boys than she would have imagined possible. They were hypnotised by her gigantic breasts and didn't seem to care about the size of her waist. Charlotte preached abstinence and self-control but Minnie knew that she needed to take the chance while she could. One boy named Joel had come to tea and told Charlotte his parents were religious and so Charlotte had allowed Minnie to go for walks and to the movies with him. Joel had greasy hair and smelled strangely of lemons but his sweaty hands made Minnie's heart flutter.

They had sex at the back of the park and Minnie found it painful and ugly but she loved his attention. After they had been together for a few months he broke up with her in the middle of the schoolyard, declaring her to be 'too fat to find it'.

Minnie had felt removed from the scene and watched from above as those standing around giggled and other boys high fived Joel. She could see the smirks on the faces of those who had engineered her humiliation.

At home her mother shoved Joel into the same category as Minnie's father and they went for five courses of Chinese food. Thinking of Joel always made Minnie hunger for spring rolls and plum sauce.

After that there were no more boys. At first Minnie was afraid of wanting to feel again and then she was so big that she blended into the walls at school and at TAFE. But through it all she still had her mother. At the end of each day there was something on TV and a takeaway menu. It was enough. It had to be.

On Sundays they went to church together and Reverend Sam made God sound like the perfect man. He was all loving, all forgiving and all knowing; what else could you want in a man? He came to you gently and only wanted the best for you. He was perfect. Minnie and her mother both kept their crushes on Reverend Sam a secret.

And then Charlotte was sick.

Minnie watched the deterioration of her mother in baffled silence. Once the doctor had declared there was no hope all Minnie could do was cook, but Charlotte had finally had enough food. She wasted away while Minnie sat glumly on the couch finishing off two portions and seeking solace in the American sitcoms. It seemed to Minnie that if she could just keep her mother's space open in the cycle of cooking and eating and mindless sitcom consumption then her mother would surely have to return to her rightful place on the sofa. June came over every day and tended to Charlotte as a sister would. When Minnie thought about those few months now they were glossed over with the faces on television. In her mind the deathbed scenes in movies all featured Charlotte.

Minnie had started crying for Charlotte a week before she drew her last breath and kept crying for weeks afterwards. She was aware on some level that she was crying for more than just her mother. She cried for the hopelessness that was her life. She cried a little for her absent father as well, though she could barely remember the man.

The tears never stopped the food going into her mouth. She cried while she cooked and cleaned and ate and worked, and just when she had begun to suspect that her face would be permanently wet the tears had slowed, until she only needed to shed tears for her mother once a week.

Now Minnie stood outside her mother's room and said a prayer and then she waited for God to answer her, but God was obviously busy right then.

She tiptoed into her mother's room. 'What do you think, Mum? Do you mind if I put the baby in here?'

The room was cold and silent. The door had been closed for two years, except for the once-a-week dusting it received. The pink furry blanket her mother had clung to as she writhed and sweated through the agonies of her end was clean and stretched tight across the bed.

Minnie sat on the bed preparing for the tears that would surely come, but she felt strangely unable to cry.

Through the silence in the bedroom she fancied she could hear the strains of her mother's favourite hymn, 'Be Still My Soul'.

She hummed along: *When disappointment, grief and fear are gone, Sorrow forgot, love's purest joys restored.*

God might have been busy, but Charlotte was watching.

'You're right, Mum. It'll be nice for you to have some company.'

She stood up and got to work.

Winter

9

Tara climbed out of bed and got dressed. She needed to get out.

The winter sunshine streamed into her room, beckoning her from her lethargy. She had been a runner before something stopped her . . . something. She shook her head and looked out at the garden. She wanted to feel the pavement under her feet. She wanted to feel the tightness in her chest that gave way to a heart-pounding peace when she hit her stride. She couldn't run now, though—not yet. She hadn't exercised for too long. She would have to start again.

The white blobby thing that was her belly had held her back from that for the longest time but now it was gone. She wouldn't be able to run yet, but she could walk.

Her father had encouraged her to run. He liked her to stay fit, as if by being physically strong she could stave off the genetic time bomb that ticked in her brain.

'Boom,' she thought but did not say, even though she opened her mouth.

She was as mystified as everyone else over the loss of her voice. She wanted to talk, she wanted to give them the answers—even though she had no idea what they were—but her voice remained lodged deep inside her.

Every few days her father would hand her a pen and some paper and wait for her to write something.

'Just write anything, Tara—anything at all. I don't care. Write down a joke, write a word, just write.'

Sometimes he got angry and swore and then Alicia would lead him away and calm him down. Tara held the pen but it felt bizarre in her hand. The very act of holding it made her hand sweat and her heart race. One day she wouldn't even hold the pen. Her father was really pissed off that day.

'Type something,' said Alicia when they were home alone together.

She handed Tara her laptop and folded her arms.

Tara placed her hands on the keys but her fingers wouldn't move.

She couldn't tell them what they wanted to hear. They didn't want her to write or type 'Hi' or 'I'm fine' or 'I'm sad', regardless of what they said. She knew they only wanted an answer—the answer. She didn't have it although there were moments when it felt possible that if she began writing the truth would come spilling out onto the page, drowning her in the dreadful thing she had done. She couldn't explain to them how afraid she was of that happening. When she was alone in her bedroom at night she scrolled through the messages on her Facebook page and she held her hands poised over the keyboard, just waiting for them to work, just waiting for her fingers to drop onto the keys and let the world know she was still here . . . but she couldn't type a word.

Tara could feel intense frustration radiating off Alicia and her father. She spent most of her time hiding from them in her room.

It was so easy just to lie on the bed listening to music until all that filled her head were the words of songs. Words that belonged to someone else were easy.

She listened to songs about love and heartbreak and she didn't think about the answers that they were all waiting for.

But today Tara needed to get out.

'Where are you going?' said Alicia when she found Tara at the front door with her keys in her hand.

Tara looked at her feet. Alicia had a hard time believing the words were stuck. Tara could see her purse her lips and shake her head a little when her questions were met with silence. Tara knew that Alicia thought she was playing some sort of game. Alicia hated the amount of attention her silence commanded. Tara didn't blame her. She hated it herself.

Before all of this had happened there had been whole days when Tara got by with just a shrug or a grunt. Once, just for fun, she had spent the whole day in silence, just to see if either Alicia or her father noticed. Only her little brothers cared and even they gave up quickly when she didn't respond. They knew enough to leave her alone if she didn't specifically say she wanted to play. At the end of the day Tara had felt triumphant at her ability to avoid conversation with Max and Alicia, but in bed that night she had been overwhelmed by a sadness that she remembered from bad days with her mother. Was she so easy to overlook in the chaos of family life?

From her friends Tara knew that there were times when everyone felt invisible. No one's parents understood them.

'My mother is so busy worrying about who my father may or may not be fucking that she just looks bored when I try to talk to her,' Jody said.

'God, I wish,' said Emma. 'My mother sees me and starts a lecture.'

'I think Alicia hates me,' Tara had said one day. She had just thrown the words into the conversation and waited to see what her friends would say.

'She's always nice to us,' said Jody.

'God, Jody, you're so stupid,' said Emma, and then one of the cute year twelve boys walked past and there were other things to discuss.

The police were angry with her silence, the doctors were frustrated and Alicia and her father were distressed but still the words would not come.

She was seeing a therapist chosen by the courts. Everyone hoped Dr Adams would coax the words from her mouth. It was difficult to charge someone with something if they couldn't answer any questions or speak at all. Daniel Walters told them he would keep charges from being laid.

'He's good—I'll give him that,' said Alicia to Tara's father when she saw the bill.

'He buries everyone in paperwork,' said Max. Tara pictured the police and the doctors standing in a room surrounded by piles and piles of paper. 'Will he bury me in paper too?' Tara wondered.

Ethan and Michael didn't mind that she had nothing to say. She could still play Monopoly and watch Nickelodeon with them.

'Sometimes I don't . . . sometimes I don't wanna talk either,' said Ethan when Alicia lamented Tara's silence.

'Yeah, me too,' said Michael, and they would both wind their arms protectively around their half-sister.

Tara would try not to smile when Ethan and Michael defended her but she couldn't help feeling a rush of warmth at their uncomplicated, undemanding love.

Now Tara waited patiently for Alicia to stop her from walking out the door but Alicia said nothing. Tara could see her holding back not just the words that would prevent her from leaving the house right then but the endless words and questions about what she had done. And Tara understood that two people could use silence if they needed to. Max was at work and the boys were in school. Tara was not supposed to be alone ever. It was the only reason she was allowed to stay home.

Finally Alicia seemed to come to some conclusion and said, 'Please don't go further than the end of the street, Tara. If you disappear they will have us arrested.'

Tara nodded her head even though she knew it wasn't true.

'Your dad will be back in an hour so I can go and do my shift down at the clinic,' said Alicia, and Tara nodded again.

Alicia stepped towards her and Tara felt the flash of a thought. Did Alicia want to hug her? She stepped back, away from any possible touch from her stepmother, and Alicia noticed the flinch and stepped back as well.

Tara closed the door quietly behind her and raised her face to the sun.

10

Alicia went to put another load of washing in the machine.

She had toyed with the idea of asking Tara to help but knew there was really no point. The girl's silent presence made her jumpy. It was easier just to do the work herself.

She shouldn't have let her go out. It could lead to all sorts of trouble but it wasn't something she was going to think about. She took a deep breath and pushed the buttons on the machine.

'Time for a coffee, I think,' she said aloud to the empty house.

In the kitchen she sipped her coffee and pictured Tara walking down the road to the park or the shopping centre. She was wearing the leather jacket Alicia hated, but she knew if she ever mentioned it that Tara would live in the thing. There was a time, before the boys were born, when she and Tara had enjoyed shopping together. Tara would trail patiently behind her, and try on everything Alicia suggested without complaining.

'I did my best, didn't I?' she said. But there was no one around to reply, no reassurance was forthcoming, and Alicia was afraid to ask the question of anyone but herself.

When Ethan was born, eight-year-old Tara had hovered protectively by his cot, daring anyone to upset her new baby brother. Alicia let her help, let her be involved, because the psychologist said it was the best way. Tara was an excellent big sister. When Michael came along Alicia had seen that Tara's interest in babies had waned but she still wanted to be part of things. And then life got busy and Alicia had to work and raise three children and Max left early and came home late and somewhere along the way her relationship with Tara got kinked. If Alicia thought back over the years she couldn't quite pick when it had happened. It seemed that one year Tara was this joyful, helpful little girl and then the next she was angry and moody and not exactly a pleasure to be around. It was nature's way and Alicia knew that. Teenagers were supposed to be awful so that their parents could accept the fact that they would eventually leave. So parents could celebrate it even. But what if you could not remember the child as a newborn clinging to your breast for their survival? What if you could not see the face of a two-year-old in the angry scowl of your teenager?

Occasionally Alicia would wonder what was going to happen

when Ethan and Michael barrelled into the teenage years but she couldn't imagine ever not loving them, not wanting to protect them.

'I'm a bad person,' she thought on the worst days. 'I'm a wicked, evil stepmother.'

'Is it possible to really, truly love a child that isn't your own?' Alicia had asked her friend Meg when she and Max were still just at the beginning.

'Of course it is,' said Meg. 'People adopt kids and foster kids and love them as much as if they had given birth to them.'

'I'm a bad person,' Alicia thought whenever an argument with Tara left her seething with dislike for the girl.

But then she would try for days and weeks to be patient and understanding and Tara would screech and shout and whine and complain and Alicia would be worn down again into antipathy for the girl.

And there were other concerns with Tara as well. Her mother sat in Peace Hills and stared at a world only she could see. The older Tara got the more Alicia found herself watching the girl, searching for signs that she would be like her mother. She understood Tara's growing resentment but she had to make sure her own children were safe.

Now she watched the boys talk to her silent stepdaughter and felt a twinge of jealousy at how much they loved her.

'I think it's great, Ali,' said Max. 'One day we'll be gone and then at least they'll have each other.'

Alicia knew what she was supposed to think and feel. Over the last few years it had come as a great shock to her that she was not the benevolent force for good in the world that she had always pictured herself to be. Even as a child her mother had always said, 'Alicia's going to be a nurse; she is such a sweet caring girl.' Alicia had accepted this as the truth. She was sweet and kind and caring and she would be so for the rest of her life. She loved nursing, loved being the one person who could help someone feel better, loved that she was an emotional help as well as a physical help, and now that she looked after mothers and babies she loved the way they came to her in a fog of exhaustion and despair and left feeling as though they could make it through another week. Alicia could connect with anyone—she understood that the most unlikable people were the ones most in need of your patience and love—but with Tara she failed utterly. Tara gnawed at something inside her and no matter how much she told herself the girl was suffering from the demons left to her by her mother, she still could not summon the endless reserves of compassion and patience that she knew she needed in order to keep the peace with her stepdaughter. Alicia had always been a giver; Tara grabbed at everything with both hands. Alicia had loved her once—not a complete unconscious love like the one she felt for Ethan and Michael, but she had loved her. Now as she thought about her stepdaughter, whose face was set and voice was silent, she hated her a little.

God, that was such an awful word, so filled with anger. Did

she actually hate Tara? She hoped not. It was devastating to think that she might feel that way towards her desperate step-daughter. Just the thought of it made her uncomfortable. She was not supposed to be capable of such a destructive emotion.

Tara's face was thin to the point of gauntness and her dark eyes seemed haunted but Alicia was struggling to dredge up even a small amount of sympathy for her. She had got herself pregnant and then abandoned the baby. Alicia felt sympathy only for the poor creature that had probably died a cold and lonely death. The fact that she felt little for the child she had been raising for the past ten years was profoundly upsetting. It led to questions not only about her marriage but about her own place in the universe as well.

She could count up all the slights if she chose to. Had the slights come before she suggested Tara see a counsellor or after-wards? Alicia couldn't remember. She liked to list all the ways Tara had tried to hurt her. It meant that their estrangement couldn't be all her fault . . . could it? There was the time when Tara had a part in the school play and brought home an invi-tation addressed only to Max. Or when Tara got her first period and didn't tell Alicia until months later, choosing to talk to the school nurse instead. Or the time when Tara stated loudly at the parent/teacher interview, 'My father is working and my mother couldn't come so my stepmother Alicia is here.'

The list grew longer as the years passed. Once Alicia had lost her temper during an argument over curfew and screamed,

'It's not my fault your mother can't take care of you.' She had immediately regretted the words and tried to apologise but Tara had walked away, telling the story to Max that night in a whispered conversation.

There was so much anger brewing in the child that sometimes Alicia feared for all of them. And now she had gone and done this terrible thing. This terrible, terrible thing. When she looked at Tara now she knew the girl was missing something. Inside her was a darkness that Alicia had no idea how to deal with. She tried not to think of the poor infant. She wondered briefly how long it would have taken the baby to die, how much it had suffered, and felt her skin grow cold. Once you were a mother the only needs that mattered were those of the baby. Why hadn't Tara felt that? What was wrong with the girl that made her able to walk away from an infant that had kicked and turned and lived inside her?

She took care of babies for a living, for God's sake. How could she have any compassion for someone who had abandoned an infant to suffer and die? At night she prayed that the baby had been stillborn. It would explain why Tara couldn't speak. It would allow Alicia to find the crack that showed a little light. If Tara had simply left her own child to die it would mean there was something very wrong with her. How could she have helped to raise such a person?

But then she would think about how Tara was with the boys. Children understood when someone had no desire to connect with them. Tara had taken care of the boys all their lives. If she babysat them Alicia would find them warm and clean and happy when she came home. She played with them and talked to them and hugged and touched them. She was an excellent big sister. Whenever Alicia despaired at her behaviour she would remember what Tara was like with the boys and know that there was more to her than her teenage mood swings.

So then why had this happened? Why had she kept this enormous secret from her and Max and then allowed her baby to die?

The thoughts chased themselves around her head at night, keeping her from sleep and making her stiff and angry with the boys during the day. And then Alicia was afraid that it was just the beginning of what would happen. Sometimes she scared herself with a future vision of herself and Max living the rest of their lives caring for two people who could not care for themselves. Two people who should never have had anything to do with her at all.

She hadn't been looking for a man with a child and a wife who spent most of her time in a psychiatric facility, but Max had dirty blond hair and dark eyes and when he smiled he couldn't hide the despair that followed him around like a lost puppy. She had made the same mistake that countless women did—she had fallen for a man because she wanted to save him. Even now she still wanted to shield him from the hurt his own child was causing him. She had not expected that he would divorce his wife and propose marriage, but once she accepted she was determined to be the best possible mother for Tara.

The first year of their married life Alicia had been conscious of both Tara and Max watching her all the time, waiting for her behaviour to change, waiting for her to turn into Sasha. Sasha who was so beautiful and so broken. Alicia worked hard to remain even tempered, to always have things under control and to always be the voice of reason. Tara came to her more and more, and when the boys came along Alicia thought she could pat herself on the back. Job well done. But then Tara started keeping things from her and wanting to visit her mother and talking back. Maybe she should have handled it better?

If she and Max had taken a more casual approach perhaps Tara would not have found that strange boy Liam to hang out with. Alicia sighed, 'maybe this and maybe that and if I had and If I could', but who really knew what the right way to do things was. Certainly she could point to herself and acknowledge that she and Max had done it the wrong way but now it was too late and nothing would be achieved.

11

Tara wandered down the road, listening to her feet hit the pavement. She breathed in and out slowly, smelling the smoke from a real wood-burning fire somewhere in the neighbourhood. The chill in the air was sharp and fresh. She was wearing her skinny jeans again. She hadn't been able to fit into them for a long time. It was six weeks since she'd been in the hospital and she felt exactly like her old self except . . . except for the fact that she couldn't find her voice. Her voice was missing.

She walked to the end of the street and waited by the park. Her friends at school would be heading into class after the recess bell.

She wondered if she was still a topic of conversation or if they didn't really think about her anymore.

When Lulu had left the school they had all made her a card and held a party and then they cried on her last day. But then a few weeks passed and Lulu was in Queensland with her mother and her mother's new husband and she didn't know what had happened at school that day and she didn't know that Teresa and Mario were going out and that Mario had hooked up with some strange girl when he got drunk at a party and the whole story was too complicated and took too long to explain. Eventually even when Lulu was online she wouldn't be included in their conversations because she talked about people they didn't know and things they hadn't experienced.

Tara grew cold at the thought of returning to school. She knew she would have been the subject of gossip everywhere from the toilets to the teachers' lounge, but by now the whole school would have moved on to some other story. When she returned they would accept her silence for a short time but after that they would grow bored with her. There was always the chance that she wouldn't be allowed to return, of course. The police wanted to charge her with something called manslaughter but her father wasn't going to let that happen. No one could find the baby they all kept talking about, so how did anyone know it was dead? Still, that hadn't mattered with that woman on the news—the water polo player. They sent her to jail forever because she said she gave the baby away but couldn't prove it. Tara was a minor and 'mentally unstable', according to Daniel Walters. Her dad didn't like her to listen to him talking to the lawyer but Alicia said she needed to be kept informed. Tara only tuned into the conversations every now and again anyway. Mostly she thought about Liam and how much she wanted to see him. She walked over to the park equipment and sat down on one of the swings, pushing herself gently back and forth, scuffing her shoes in the dirt. She had to admit to herself that the real reason she had wanted to leave the house was to see Liam. She had thought about him every day of the last six weeks. She was happy to wait for him for the rest of the day but Alicia would be angry if she stayed out for so long. 'Half an hour,' she thought. 'I'll give him half an hour and then I'll go.'

The park had always been their place to meet. Every night at five she had gone out for her run and ended up at the park. Liam had always been waiting. Some days they would find a private space at the back and some days they would just talk. Tara preferred it when they talked. Mostly she would talk and Liam would listen and play with her hand.

She always went for her real run after she had seen Liam. She felt lighter and faster after she had seen him—but that was before it all went wrong. She knew why it had fucked up. She understood. Liam had been very angry with her and then she had been even angrier with him and then it was over.

Tara felt the phone in her pocket. She could have texted him, but then he could have contacted her, too. Her story had been all over the news even though they weren't allowed to mention her name. He had met her father—only once, but they had met. Her father hadn't liked Liam but Tara hadn't expected him to. Tara ran her fingers over the screen but didn't unlock the phone. He must want to see her, to speak to her. He must want to because she couldn't believe that she could need to see him so desperately and that he would feel nothing. Sometimes when they had been together it felt like they were the same person. She would watch his chest rise and fall and realise that their breathing was in sync. It had been love, it was love, it was . . . it was just . . . something. But he would come.

He could be at school. Maybe he had caught the study bug that all the HSC students did and started working as he raced towards the end of the year. She hoped it was the case but you never knew with Liam. His friends were a problem. They weren't at school anymore and Liam hated the fact that he was still stuck in the same routine. At least he had hated that once. Who knew what he thought now? They hadn't seen each other for so long that it was possible he had changed completely. He could have left school or found another girlfriend or . . . but she wouldn't think about that. She would come to the park every day and, until there was a reason not to, she would believe that one day he would be there waiting for her.

She smiled into the sun and thought about how he would sit next to her on the bench and take her hand. Liam liked silence.

He preferred not to talk.

Maybe he knew where her voice was.

12

Minnie waited weeks to name the baby. She was too tired to do more than feed, change and bath her. The baby was unrelenting need. Feed me, burp me, hold me, rock me.

She grew a little each day. Sometimes she would wake up from a nap and Minnie could actually see that she had grown in her sleep. At night, after taking her milk and having a bath, the baby would nestle against Minnie and burrow into her. Minnie would sit in the rocking chair that had once belonged to her grandmother and sing hymns until the baby was heavy with sleep. Minnie would feel her heart slow and her soul rejoice at the wonder of the small creature in her arms. She had to hold herself back from squeezing the child too tightly. The baby's eyes grew darker and darker and settled on a brown that looked almost black in some lights. Her eyelashes were long and thick. Mostly she looked at Minnie. Minnie talked to her constantly or she sang to her or she prayed for her. The baby never tired of looking at Minnie and Minnie was always happy to meet her eyes.

Minnie worked in snatches so she could sleep and keep up with the housework. Some days she managed to have breakfast and lunch and some days she just got by on apples. Her clothes suddenly felt oversized and she had to go through her closet and find some loose pants that she had long since grown out of.

She seldom left the house. Instead she tended the baby and rehearsed the story she would tell the neighbourhood and Lela.

June had been delighted to hear about the baby that would be joining Minnie.

'You'll have to invite us over as soon as your cousin moves in,' she had said. 'Lou and I would love to help. How old is the baby? What's her name?'

Minnie had left the baby sleeping in the house when she went across the road to tell June the news about her cousin. The whole time she stood and talked to June she had been praying that the baby would not wake up; June liked to chat.

Then she had called June a few days later and told her that the cousin had arrived but both she and the baby were suffering from colds. Higher and higher went the tower of lies.

'You can certainly come over and see them, though,' Minnie had said, knowing that June was terribly afraid of getting sick; even an ordinary cold could turn into pneumonia, after all.

A week later Minnie told her she had caught the cold as well, and then the new little family needed time to recover. June left chicken soup on the doorstep. Minnie consumed it gratefully over a couple of nights.

But now, after all these weeks, it was time to move forward with the plan. It was time for a new story.

Minnie recited the story to herself to practise.

'My cousin brought her over and she stayed for a couple of days but then she told me she had plans to go out one night and would I mind watching the baby. I said, "Of course not. Go out and have a good time." You know how difficult it can be for a new mother; I wanted her to have a few hours to herself. But she didn't come back. I'm sure she'll return and I just don't want to get the police or social services involved until I know she's gone for sure.'

Minnie could imagine June nodding her head and tut-tutting along with her about young people making foolish choices. Hopefully they would all just accept the baby belonged to Minnie now.

Because of course Minnie knew the baby belonged to some-one else.

'It was all over the news, Mum—they're looking for a lost baby,' said Minnie, but she didn't call the police.

'They must be frantic, Mum,' said Minnie, but she still didn't call the police.

'The mother is just a girl. She's only fifteen. She didn't want the baby, Mum. She left her in the loo. That's not the kind of mother our girl needs,' said Minnie.

'They searched the centre, Mum, so the girl must live nearby. They say they've looked and looked but found no evidence. Imagine that, Mum—no evidence of a baby at all.'

'You'd make a wonderful mother,' Charlotte had always said.

Who knew what kind of life a teenage girl could give a tiny baby? Children needed to be raised by stable adults.

They hadn't shown pictures of the girl—only her father. The man looked worn down. He had held his hands up in front of his face and barked 'No comment' at the cameras. He didn't look like he would make a good grandfather for the baby.

They hadn't charged the girl with anything, not yet. Apparently she was in a 'fragile mental state'. Did the girl miss the baby? Was that the reason for her mental state?

Some websites said that the girl was not talking and others said that she couldn't remember what had happened to the baby. People left comments on the websites. Dreadful, angry comments. Once Minnie might have felt compelled to leave a comment or two herself. It wasn't fair that some people were never allowed the joy of a child and others squandered the blessing with neglect or abuse.

Minnie prayed on the question of whether to go to the police or not. She asked God to give her a sign—any sign so that she would know exactly what she should do but God had other things to do.

'The police will just take her away, Mum, and we'll never see her again. Even if they don't put me in jail we'll never see her again.'

It would be the right thing to go to the police. Minnie knew that. She knew that all she would have to do was bundle up the baby and walk into any police station and explain. It wouldn't take them long to work out if the baby Minnie was taking care of belonged to the girl. DNA testing made everything clear.

'It could be a different baby, Mum,' she said, but she knew it wasn't.

At night when the baby slept she wrestled with herself, trying to find reasons why she should be allowed to keep the baby. She would wake up some mornings determined to do the right thing. She would dress herself and the baby and get ready to leave the house to go to the police station, but each time something would stop her. The baby would need a nappy change or she would get fussy or she would start crying for no particular reason.

'She doesn't want to leave us, Mum,' Minnie would say, and she would sit down on the couch and wait for the time to pass until she needed to feed the baby again.

They probably wouldn't charge the girl with anything anyway. She was a minor. Teenagers got away with all sorts of things these days. Just look at the boys who lived three doors down.

Once the police had cruised down the street and taken one of them away but he was back the next day, smirking and swearing about 'fucken idiot coppers'. Minnie thought it was Leo, who was tall and skinny and filled with bits of silver, but it could have been the one called Callum, who looked a little older than the rest. The only one she could identify properly was Brent. He was hard to forget. His spiky hair and flat stare unnerved everyone. He knew people were scared of him. People had probably been scared of him his whole life.

The boys weren't scared of anything. Minnie wondered if the girl who had left her baby was scared.

'What shall I do, Mum?' she said as she rocked the baby to sleep, but her mother had nothing to add and the prayers went unanswered. Finally Minnie got up one morning and resolved that today would be the day that she marched into the police station and told the truth. She got as far as reversing the car down the driveway with the baby buckled into her special seat and then she stopped.

In the winter sun her body felt chilled right through to the bone.

The police would charge her with kidnapping or something equally awful and, even worse than that, there would be cameras and her large body would be splashed across newspapers and television and the internet. She could see quite clearly that at that very moment she was poised right on the edge of a precipice. If she moved forward all that was waiting for her was the fall but if she stepped back, if she left well enough alone, there was a whole world of experience to come. A world that she had always prayed for, always dreamed of and always felt she deserved.

Her hands gripped the steering wheel and her breath came in short pants. She would not give up the child. The decision had been made.

'She's better off with us, Mum,' said Minnie. 'We'll take good care of her. I'll go to church and get Reverend Sam to baptise her.'

•

The baby slept and fed and slept again, and then one day she smiled at Minnie and Minnie knew that even though it was a sin—a terrible, dreadful, go-straight-to-hell sin—she would never go to the police with the truth.

Minnie stopped thinking about the teenage girl and her angry father. 'What shall we call her, Mum?'

The baby sighed and opened a little hand that had freed itself from her soft wrap.

'Something simple, I think. Something everyone can spell. Something that can be an adult or a child.'

The Duchess of Cambridge was on the television planting a tree. Everyone called her Catherine now, but before she married a prince she was just plain Kate.

Minnie liked the name Kate.

It was unpretentious. It meant you could be a painter or a princess. You could be anything with a name like Kate, really. If the baby grew up beautiful she could be a model like Kate Moss or if she grew up looking more like Minnie she could simply be Kate who did the accounts from home.

Minnie didn't want to saddle her child with a name like her own. Knowing instinctively that she would only ever have one child, Charlotte had named her daughter after a goddess. Minerva was the goddess of poetry, medicine, wisdom, commerce, weaving, crafts and magic. It was too much for a little girl to live up to—especially a chubby little girl whose main occupation in life was eating.

Kate could be lived up to or it could be just your name. Minerva became Minnie as soon as she could. Teachers in school always tittered a little when reading out her full name. The humiliation of being so un-goddess-like haunted Minnie. Kate would not know that experience.

'Her name's Kate,' she told Lela when she finally left the house for the first time. She had practised putting the pram up and down at home so that she would seem confident and in control.

'And you say your cousin hasn't been back for weeks?' said Lela.

'No, I haven't seen her and she never had a mobile phone as far as I can tell. Her parents both passed away years ago—you know, from . . . um . . . drugs. That's why I said I would help her. I figured we're both on our own, you know.'

'You really should call the police, Minnie. You don't want to be saddled with this child for the rest of your life.'

'Oh, I think Jessica will come back and if she doesn't, well, I don't . . . I don't actually mind raising her.' Minnie had settled on the name Jessica one night as she went over her story. Australia was full of Jessicas. Minnie met Lela's eyes and saw some understanding there.

'What if you fall in love with the kid and then your cousin comes back and takes her away?'

Minnie didn't tell Lela how far she had already fallen and she didn't mention that her true worry was the police turning up and claiming the baby the whole country had been looking for. It was old news now but some nights Minnie woke covered in sweat with her arms already reaching for the baby being torn from her.

'I guess I'll just have to cope if that happens,' said Minnie.

Lela nodded. Minnie had never done anything wrong in her life. She had once been mortified over a parking ticket because she'd misread the sign. No one would ever assume that she could commit the terrible, horrible sin.

'Being good has its own rewards,' her mother always said.

'I have so much stuff to give you,' said Lela, who had accepted Minnie's story along with everyone else. 'The most adorable little dresses and stuff—you'll love dressing her up. You have to enjoy it while they're young because when they get older they have lots of ideas about what to wear—and believe me, they don't care what you think.'

'Oh, I will enjoy it,' said Minnie, and she understood that Lela wasn't going to push for answers.

'I don't know what has happened to young people these days,' said June when Minnie handed her the polished gem of a story, and Lou shook his newspaper and nodded his head.

No one would ever guess the truth, Minnie assured herself. No one would ever think fat, placid Minnie capable of such a thing.

Minnie read books at night and fretted over how to get things exactly right for Kate. Some days she barely had time to eat a full meal before it was time for bed. Minnie found herself throwing food away for the first time. She felt full a lot of the time anyway. Kate filled her up and the weight continued to drop off. Minnie didn't notice. She was too busy taking care of Kate and worrying about everything that she had to do.

She met June for a walk every day because babies needed fresh air.

The first time they had walked together Minnie was covered in sweat and chafing after just a few minutes. She had clutched at her chest and sat down on the nearest wall and then looked around dismayed to find that they had only walked a few metres down the road.

'You just catch your breath, dear,' said June. 'It's good to start slow.'

Minnie had smiled gratefully at June and then she had heard the boys laughing from their garden sofa.

'Jesus fuck, look at that—someone gave the fat dyke a root,' said the tall one with the shaved head.

'Who'd want to fuck that?' laughed the one who looked older than the other two.

'You might have a go, Callum,' said spiky haired Brent. 'You'd root anything with a pulse.'

'Screw you, Brent. I would die under that load. Look at her—she can barely move.'

June had crossed her arms and Minnie could see her getting ready to say something.

'Just leave it, June,' she had panted.

'Shut the fuck up,' the one called Brent had suddenly shouted at his sniggering cronies. Everyone fell silent. 'Poor fat cow is trying at least,' he said, and then he led them all back inside and Minnie and June walked home and carried the pram inside without having to deal with their stares.

It was a strange act of kindness from the young man and Minnie thought that if he had been a different sort of person she would have thanked him. Although they always tried to schedule their walks for the early morning when they could be assured that Brent and his friends would still be asleep, they would sometimes have to wait for the day to warm up before venturing out. The next time Minnie and June spotted 'the boys' in their front garden Minnie swallowed the anxiety she felt when looking at Brent's threatening tattoos and attempted a small smile. She meant it as an acknowledgement that she understood that beneath the menace there lurked an altogether different sort of young man. As soon as she met Brent's eyes she realised she had made a mistake. He turned his head to the side and spat onto the sidewalk—right in front of the pram. Minnie felt her stomach turn and June skipped sideways in disgust.

'Savages,' she muttered. 'Disgusting beasts,' she whispered.

Minnie kept her eyes down and walked quickly away. 'Shush,' she told June.

'I bet that pram cost you a fuckload,' called the one with the shaved head.

June couldn't help herself. She stopped and turned and shook her fist at the group. 'You keep your foul mouths shut,' she yelled.

'Fuck you, you old fucken witch,' said Brent and he began to move towards them.

Minnie grabbed June's arm and practically ran her around the corner. She didn't turn back but could hear the laughter that followed them down the street. They were just a joke to 'the boys'.

She and June sat on a bus stop bench, panting at each other.

'Really,' said June, 'I don't know how much longer we can all take this.'

'Hopefully they will leave soon,' said Minnie.

'Perhaps we should sit here for a bit,' said June.

Minnie nodded her assent. She wondered if the man who had spoken did know how much the pram had cost. It wasn't the most expensive pram on the market but it certainly wasn't the cheapest. Minnie always made sure to keep the truth about her money a secret.

It wasn't that much anyway—certainly it was not enough to completely overhaul her life—but it was enough to give her a buffer, enough so that she didn't have to work if she didn't want to, enough so she could give Kate everything she needed. Her father had left her a property, even though they had not seen each other since the day he was thrown out of the house. He had never even tried to contact her. When the news of her inheritance came through Minnie had been determined to refuse it but Charlotte had other ideas.

'Sell it, love. Sell it and keep the money. You don't have to think about where it came from but you'll never have to worry again. The old wanker should at least do something for you. God rest his wicked soul.'

Minnie had swallowed a laugh at her mother's profanity and done exactly what Charlotte suggested.

'Why do you think they would care about the price of my pram?' said Minnie.

'Who knows why they do anything, Minnie. Now, when are you thinking of starting this little one on solid food?'

Minnie swallowed her concern and listened to June's advice on rice cereal.

13

Tara tried to get to the park every day. The dry winter sunshine felt healing. She made sure to always be back before her father got home from work.

Alicia didn't even question her anymore, but she did make sure Tara was always carrying her mobile phone.

'You can text me if you need me,' said Alicia. 'Texting is okay, isn't it, Tara? I mean it's not like you'll tell me anything or actually talk to me and it will only be for emergencies.'

Tara wondered what it would take for her fingers to work.

Alicia looked up from folding the endless washing and Tara saw the brightness in her eyes of tears held back. Alicia cried when she was very angry and Tara knew she was being pushed to breaking point.

Tara nodded at Alicia and showed her the phone. She had been carrying it all along. She thought about typing some words on her phone so that Alicia would feel better. She wanted to give the words to Alicia but it felt like there was a hand inside her pushing everything down into a black silence. If she opened her mouth she had no idea what would come out. If she started typing what would she say?

She walked out of the house, closing the door quietly behind her, and took a deep freeing breath.

In the park she sat quietly on the bench. The park was mostly empty during the week. The swing set pushed itself in the gentle eerie way that unoccupied swings do. There was a large tree in the centre with branches perfect for climbing. It was ringed by a small fence and on the fence was a sign: TREE-CLIMBING PROHIBITED.

Tara sat in the silence and breathed in the lack of expectation.

It had been decided that she would take at least a term off from school. It had been decided by her father and Alicia and her psychiatrist. No one had even looked at Tara when the decision was made. Her silence rendered her invisible when the adults needed to make decisions.

The principal, Mrs Beeches, had been reluctant to allow it. 'Her marks have already slipped this year, Mr Sanderson,' she had told Tara's father, who had put the call on speaker phone. 'We don't want her going into year eleven on the back foot.'

Tara had wanted to giggle when the principal talked about year eleven. Like it had any relevance to her life, like her D for history had any meaning at all.

'I understand, Mrs Beeches,' Max had said slowly and patiently, the way he always spoke when he was talking to someone he regarded as intractable. 'But now we know why her results were so bad, don't we?'

'I suppose,' said Mrs Beeches, although her tone reflected her persistent belief that any failing student was simply being lazy—secret pregnancies notwithstanding.

'Tara will catch up next term and hopefully this will all be sorted out by then and she can regain her former position in the year.'

'One would hope,' said Mrs Beeches.

'Yes, thank you for your understanding,' said Tara's father.

There had been emails after that and work sent home that Tara was supposed to do. Tara read over the English essay question and couldn't imagine ever being able to put pen to paper again. How could anyone care about long-dead poets? How could it possibly be something that she needed to think about?

Everyone hoped that by the start of term four the police would have figured out what to charge her with, if they were going to charge her at all.

Or they hoped that the baby would turn up. Or that she would tell them where the baby was, or she would open her fucking mouth and say something.

•

Once a week now Tara went to visit Dr Adams. Dr Adams looked like a grandmother should. She had tightly curled grey hair and she wore long skirts and a string of coloured beads. Her glasses sat on the end of her nose and she liked to knit. The first hour they had spent together had been spent mostly in silence. Dr Adams talked for a few minutes, explaining how therapy worked, and then she opened a drawer in her large wooden desk and brought out her knitting. 'It's a jumper for my grandson,' she said. 'I'm knitting as fast as I can because he grows bigger every week.'

The jumper was a deep blue and Tara and Dr Adams sat for a while without speaking as the needles clicked.

'Would you like to do a little knitting?' asked Dr Adams, and Tara surprised herself by nodding. The desk drawer was filled with different-sized needles and balls of coloured wool. Tara chose pink. Pink was no longer the favourite colour it had been but she wanted to sit with Dr Adams and knit a pink scarf. Dr Adams showed her how to cast on one stitch at a time and then she showed her how to loop the wool and move the stitches from one needle to the other. Tara's knitting looked very different to Dr Adams' work. 'You'll get the hang of it,' the therapist said.

Each week the scarf grew longer and sometimes Dr Adams was silent and sometimes she talked and looked at Tara, who would nod that she understood what she was being told.

Tara understood that she'd had a baby.

Dr Adams kept telling her she had given birth but she accepted the knowledge as she might listen to a story about herself as a toddler.

'When you were two,' her father liked to narrate, 'you drew all over the walls in red pen. Your mother was having one of her bad days and she just let you. You drew long red lines all over the living room walls. I couldn't get it off so we had to repaint.'

Tara could not remember drawing all over the walls. She could not remember the red pen in her hand or her father's reaction but it must have happened because her father said it did.

She thought of 'the baby' the same way. It must have happened because everyone said it did but she couldn't remember it at all. There had been blood for six weeks. It kept coming and coming and Tara desperately wanted to ask Alicia if it was possible to bleed to death slowly over days and weeks, but then the blood had stopped. If she searched her mind a picture of herself with blood all over her legs flashed behind her eyes, but she couldn't remember when the picture was from or why there had been so much blood.

Her stomach had been dough-like and gross but now it was back to where it had been before—before the pregnancy. Some nights in her dreams there was agony and fear, but while Tara understood that she was the one who was afraid and she was the one in pain there never seemed to be a specific reason why.

She had no idea what to say to the police or Dr Adams or her family and so the hand kept the words down. And always at the back of her mind was the knowledge that if they knew what she felt, if she opened her mouth and told them that she could not remember or believe in the baby, or that she was afraid of the truth of what she had done, then she would end up like her mother. What if she had killed the baby? What if she had smashed its head against the ground or thrown it in the small pond at the park? Was she capable of murder? And if she was, did that make her crazier than her mother or less crazy or just the same?

Once, when she was about twelve, she had Googled: *Is bipolar disorder hereditary?* Five pages later she had still been reading. And every site, every opinion, every doctor said: *yes*. One site suggested that by having one parent with the disorder she had a fifteen to thirty percent chance of developing it herself. When she hit thirteen and the world seemed to go from the most beautiful place filled with endless possibilities one day and this black hole that she couldn't see her way out of the next, Alicia had started suggesting she see a counsellor. Tara was already freaked out by the uncontrollable feelings that writhed through her body, and even though Emma and Jody said that they felt the same way she still found herself spending some days watching her own behaviour and making sure that no cracks appeared, that she gave Alicia and her father no reason to push the idea of therapy.

She knew that the words needed to stay trapped inside. If you never told them how you were feeling and what you were thinking then they could never use it against you.

•

Time drifted by and Tara had just got up to leave when she saw him standing at the back of the park. He was almost hidden by a large gum tree.

She stopped and waited. It was possible that he had been here every day but had remained hidden. The fact that he was visible now was only because he wanted to be. Tara just stood, silent and still, and waited until he was ready to come to her. She was about to give up when he came out from behind the tree and walked towards her. She had waited for him and now he was here, but looking at him in his torn T-shirt and baggy jeans Tara knew that there was nothing Liam could do or say that would make things better or change them. He was a couple of years older than her but he looked like a kid. He still had pimples on his chin.

'H-h-hey T,' he said.

She nodded at him.

'I don't . . . I don't . . . I don't know what to s-s-say,' he said.

Tara touched her throat so he would know that she no longer had the words either. He didn't ask her why she couldn't speak. It wasn't his way. He would simply wait for her to tell him and if she never did then he would accept that as well.

It was almost a joke, really. He could barely get a word out and she had lost the ability to speak.

They walked back to the bench in silence and Liam took her hand. Tara looked down at his stubby fingers and felt her heart slow. He didn't need to say anything—not really.

They sat until she touched her watch and he knew she needed to go.

There was so much they had to say to each other but the silence felt right. The silence felt necessary.

Tara waved as she left the park.

'I'll be . . . be . . . b-back to-to-tomorrow,' said Liam, and Tara nodded.

On the way back to her house and her room and the questions, Tara wished that she could find her voice.

She wanted to sing.

14

June talked and talked and Minnie read the books and made a list of all the things that needed to be done.

The internet said she needed to visit an early childhood health centre. She needed to get Kate weighed and measured and immunised and have her hearing tested. It should be recorded in her blue book. The internet said the hospital where she gave birth would give her a blue book. Kate also needed to have a birth certificate so she could go to school one day. She needed to exist.

Minnie went back and forth over the problem. 'Now what, Mum?' she said.

'Grab the bull by the horns, love,' her mother always said.

Minnie called and made an appointment at her local centre. The cousin story wouldn't work with a baby nurse, who would want evidence of Kate's existence. The nurse would want to meet the mother, wouldn't she?

Minnie needed a new story—one that she could keep forever. 'I hate the lies, Mum, but needs must.'

She bounced Kate in her arms while the television droned on in the background.

A new program was on. It was called *I Didn't Know I Was Pregnant*. Minnie watched women who took themselves to the emergency room with stomach pains and came home with babies. 'Lucky,' she thought.

The women were mostly large. One of them looked like Minnie used to look. There were some angles on Minnie's face now but she remembered being so large and she watched, fascinated, as the huge woman on television explained how she had eaten Mexican food and assumed she had indigestion only to find herself having a baby.

'Well, Mum,' said Minnie, 'I guess that's clear enough.'

She bought some hair dye and coloured away the grey. The boys thought the baby was hers. They knew nothing but she thought there was a chance she could convince someone else.

Fat people could be any age. She would be forty-three instead of forty-seven. You could have a baby at forty-three. You could get pregnant and not know it—especially if your body's natural shape was round. She was smaller than she had been but she was still what Dr Benson called 'morbidly obese'.

She had stepped on the special scales she had ordered from America and found that in the weeks that she had been with Kate she had somehow lost twenty kilos.

She found an old dress made of stretchy fabric in the back of the cupboard. It went around her body nicely. Minnie could feel the empty skin beginning to sag in places.

She did her makeup and looked in the mirror—really looked in the mirror after years and years of not really looking, of only seeing small pieces of herself because the whole of Minnie was too much to look at.

'I think I'll do, Mum,' said Minnie, and then she added, 'God, if you want me to keep this child let this go well.'

She smiled at herself in the mirror. There was no reason why she couldn't twist her prayers to suit herself. 'Right, Katie,' she said, 'let's get this show on the road.'

•

'Hi, I'm Alicia,' said the trim nurse in jeans and a blue striped top.

'I could crush you like a bug,' thought Minnie. She hoped her fear and desperation weren't showing.

'And what is this lovely young lady's name?' asked Alicia.

'It's Kate,' said Minnie, pleased to have dressed Kate in the pink dress with little matching socks. The blonde tufts of hair on her head didn't make her any gender yet.

'What beautiful eyes,' said Alicia. 'One of my sons has eyes the same colour—so dark they're almost black.'

'She is truly blessed,' said Minnie and Alicia nodded.

'Now, let's take a look at your blue book.'

'Well, actually, I don't have one—I gave birth at home, you see.' Minnie launched into her explanation, hoping that she would be able to keep the lies straight. The sins piled up on top of each other but when Kate smiled Minnie pushed them to one side. If she was going to land up in hell then so be it; it seemed a small price to pay for such heaven on earth. In her dreams she was chased by the devil but the morning light bounced off Kate's blonde tufts and Minnie accepted the dream punishments for her sin.

'The truth is, I didn't even know I was pregnant. It was all a bit of a shock and a friend helped me and I don't . . .'

'Didn't your midwife give you a book?'

'There was no midwife. Like I said I didn't know . . . well, I'm a bit of a big girl, you see, and . . .' Minnie indicated her general roundness, humiliating herself for the nurse, humiliating herself so the nurse would only see the round lies and not feel inclined to probe for the truth.

'Well, however she got here she's here now. Have you registered the birth?'

Minnie breathed out slowly. So far so good.

'Um, not yet, I'm just getting used to things. I haven't been to a doctor or anything but I wanted to have her examined. I wanted to make sure that she was okay.'

'She should really have seen a doctor after she was born. There are shots that we give babies in the first few days of life.'

'Oh dear,' said Minnie and she felt herself begin to sweat. Alicia was looking at her with kind eyes but her mouth was firm.

'I seem to have done everything wrong,' said Minnie. She looked at her feet and swiped at her eyes and hoped that the nurse would find some kindness within her.

'Now, now, don't worry about it,' said Alicia. 'We'll get you sorted out. It must be very exciting to have a surprise baby. I can't quite imagine it myself.' The nurse went quiet for a moment and stared at the back wall. 'Did you not have any indications that you were pregnant at all?' she asked.

Minnie shook her head.

'Nothing? I mean no morning sickness, no tender breasts, nothing?'

'They made a program about it,' said Minnie softly. 'It's on the television. It does happen and I lost my mother recently and I have to admit I have been comfort eating.'

Alicia looked at Minnie and looked quickly away.

'Yes, well, Kate looks like she's doing just fine. I'll get you a blue book and you can go online and find out how to register the birth. It's all easily sorted. Now, let's get her clothes off so we can weigh her.'

Minnie was proud of Kate's pink plumpness.

Alicia filled in the blue book and Minnie gave the right answers. She gave an average weight and measurement for Kate's birth and hoped that her weight gain would seem correct.

'She's put on quite a bit of weight,' said Alicia.

'Well, I'm a big girl,' said Minnie again, hoping that Alicia would not ask any more questions she couldn't answer.

'Yes, but we don't want that for the baby. We'll keep an eye on things. You need to get her to a GP for her first shots.'

'I've made an appointment.'

'Good. Now any worries about sleeping or feeding?'

Minnie allowed Alicia to schedule her in for another appointment and she left clutching the precious blue book. The nurse had recorded all the information Minnie had given her. Kate was almost official.

At home she looked up what she needed to do to register a home birth. She would need two independent witnesses to say they had seen the birth occur.

Minnie fed Kate her bottle and wondered where she would get two people from. She could ask Lela, but that would mean telling her the new story, and she wasn't ready to do that yet. She needed to keep her secret but secrets had a way of finding a gap and stretching towards the light.

'What am I going to do about this then, Mum?' said Minnie, but she knew the answer. Charlotte would have told her to pray. 'God answers those who are willing to listen,' Charlotte always said.

God was strangely quiet on whether or not Minnie should tell the police but Minnie had to admit it was possible that he knew she didn't really want to hear His answer.

Minnie wrapped Kate up and put her in her new cot. Kate looked tiny now but Minnie knew it wouldn't be long before the baby filled the space.

She sat in the rocking chair and closed her eyes, humming to herself and to Kate, and she asked God for the answer. This time she really listened.

The phone rang through the silence of the house.

'Hello, dear, it's me,' said June. 'I was just wondering if you fancied another walk today. I know we've already been once but the sun is so beautiful we should get that baby of yours outside.'

'That baby of yours,' Minnie repeated in her head, and knew she had her answer. Kate was her baby. She belonged to Minnie as much as any human being could belong to another. Kate was hers and there was no way she was going to let her go.

'Oh yes,' said Minnie. 'Give me an hour so she can nap and I'll meet you out the front . . . Oh, and June?'

'Yes, dear?'

'I have a favour to ask. I'll tell you about it on our walk.'

'Of course, dear, anything to help.'

Minnie put the phone down. 'Thank you, Jesus,' she said, and she went to grab an apple before her walk.

In the kitchen she chewed her way through two apples and thought about what she was about to do. She wanted to write some of the lies down so that she could keep them straight but she knew that the written word could be dangerous. People couldn't get at the secrets in your head unless you opened your mouth to speak.

'I'm going to hell, Mum,' said Minnie, but she didn't care anymore. She had spent her whole life trying to be a good human being and where had it got her?

'Lonely and fat and stuck to the couch, Mum, that's where,' said Minnie. She was surprised to find that she was angry. 'I've been as good as a person can be. All my life I've been as good as you told me to be. And now I'm supposed to give up the one beautiful thing in my life. I know it's wrong, Mum, but you know what? Fuck that and fuck anyone who tries to take her from me.'

Minnie felt her face heat up at the dreadful words and thoughts. She filled a glass with water and drank deeply to cool herself down.

'What is wrong with me, Mum?' she said, but she knew the answer really. All her life she'd been a meek little kitten, staying out of the way, staying out of sight, but now that she had her own kitten to take care of she needed to be a big cat. Only a big cat could protect her kitten from harm. No one messed with a big cat, no one tried to take away what was hers. Minnie would be a cat, a big cat, a giant cat. And for Kate she would roar.

15

When the police came over to talk to her now they didn't talk about finding the baby and making sure it had a good home. They talked about finding the body.

Tara understood that they thought the baby they were all looking for was dead but she didn't know how they knew that. No one knew where it was so how did they know if it was alive or dead?

'You have to talk at some point,' said the policewoman. 'I know you think that by keeping silent you can avoid the consequences of your actions but that's not the case.'

'That's enough of that,' said Daniel Walters.

Tara sat forward and opened her mouth. She wanted to say something, anything, but all she could do was push the air out. Everyone watched her for a minute and then the policewoman shook her head and got up to leave.

'We'll be in touch,' said her partner, who had eaten a chocolate biscuit while his colleague talked.

'No doubt,' said Tara's father.

'No doubt,' thought Tara, but she didn't say anything.

•

'B-B-Brent has-has-has moved into h-h-his own p-place. He s-says if I-I-I l-l-leave s-s-school and go on the d-d-dole I can l-l-live there too.'

Liam traced Tara's hand with his fingers. The park was cold but bearable.

She gave him a long hard look. If she had her voice she would have used it to yell at him. Liam dropped his eyes to the stone his feet were moving around and around.

'D-don't b-be cross with me, T. I can't t-take anymore. Not f-fucking learning anything anyway.'

Tara turned her face away from his and stared across the little park. On the swing a little girl was singing 'Humpty Dumpty'.

The mother sat on a bench engrossed in a fashion magazine.

Even if she had been able to speak Tara knew there was nothing she could say to him that would make him change his mind.

When they had just started going out—when she had a voice and he didn't; when she was just fourteen years old and nothing else—Tara had refused to spend any time with Liam's friends.

He had met them at the skate park when he was ten and he didn't seem to be able to let go of them. Not even for Tara. They were older than he was. Older and already headed in a certain direction. They skipped school and smoked in the skate park and laughed about stupid teachers. Liam thought they were gods. They did as they pleased without the adult interference that suffocated Liam. They possessed a whole store of lightening quick comebacks for teachers and police, seeming to know they were untouchable.

Liam was awed by the brash way they approached the world. He had spent almost all of his young years dreading any inter-action with the public. He had no idea where his stutter had come from but it haunted his life. His parents came late to the realisation that he was not just being difficult but couldn't actually force the words to come out the right way.

'If you would just think before you spoke,' said his father.

'If you would just talk slowly,' said his mother.

But they both noticed when he stopped talking completely. There were people to see and programs to take part in but nothing helped for long. There were so many rules that needed to be applied before he even opened his mouth that it was exhausting. 'Breath like this, hold your mouth like this, vocalise like this,' Liam was told.

'You have to persist,' said the speech pathologist. 'It will get better if you just persist.' But Liam was too old to be trained. At ten he gave it a go for a few months until he slipped up one day and the other kids noticed and went back to taunting him.

Loony Liam they called him, and there were times when he thought he really was going crazy. The sheer effort to get a word out would sometimes make him sweat. He knew exactly what he wanted to say, he could see the words lining themselves up in a coherent sentence, but when he went to speak his jaw muscles would clench and his breath would judder in and out. Sometimes he would be consumed by rage and his fingers would curl into fists, his fingernails leaving red crescents on his palms.

At night in their bedroom his parents yelled at each other and shifted the blame for their strange son back and forth. They loved him—Liam knew they loved him—but he was conscious that his parents had not signed up for a child with his issues. They just wanted to stand on the sidelines at soccer games and say, 'That's my boy.' Liam hated soccer and when his parents invited friends around he would stand hunched and sweating as they attempted to prise some form of conversation out of him.

Liam's twin sisters had talked early and walked early and doted on their baby brother until they grew bored waiting for him to finish a sentence. All Liam could see when he sat down to dinner with his family were the expectations he had failed to meet. No one was deliberately unkind but Liam felt them waiting for him to get better and do better. He would catch his mother staring at him when she thought he was engrossed in his PlayStation. He could feel her eyes on him and would look up quickly and catch the look of deep concern on her face. It turned his stomach. 'Worry about yourself,' he wanted to shout, but of course the words would only get stuck and cause her eyes to fill with tears so he would pretend he hadn't seen anything and just go back to his game.

At school he was the easiest kid to pick on and he never fought back or complained. He simply accepted it as his due for being the failure that he was. He ate lunch alone. He sat in the library and read his way through primary school. But when he was in high school a visiting aunt had brought him a skateboard. His mother freaked out and insisted on a helmet and knee and elbow pads. Liam agreed to anything as long as he was allowed to keep the red board with black racing stripes and skull-and-crossbones motif. He went up and down on the pavement a few times and then, without even thinking about it, he pushed off and he was away.

On a skateboard Liam flew. He twisted and turned and leapt on and off with the freedom of a bird. On the skateboard he wasn't required to speak. He could spend a whole afternoon in silence and he ruled the ramp.

By the time Brent, Leo and Callum figured out that Liam could barely utter a word they were captivated by his technique with the board.

Brent was the one who approached him. One afternoon in the middle of summer Liam had just managed to pull off a perfect

360 flip and was sitting in the sun while some others boys gave it their best shot when Brent walked up to him.

'That was okay,' said Brent.

Liam looked up to find himself staring at the boy that everyone else knew to steer clear of. When Brent stood at the top of the ramp everyone else moved aside to let him go first. Once some kid who didn't understand the rules had pushed past him and taken his turn and Brent had broken his nose with his skateboard. The kid was wise enough to tell his parents that he had fallen. No one got in Brent's way. Liam had simply shrugged at Brent, conscious that silence was his best option.

Brent sat down next to him and after a few minutes Leo and Callum came and sat down as well. Liam had looked around the skate park and seen that he was now part of Brent's group. Brent and Leo and Callum talked to him and simply required a 'yes' or a 'nah' or 'cool' when someone performed on the board. Liam could manage one word at a time.

At the end of the day he lifted his hand in farewell and Brent said, 'See you tomorrow?' and all Liam had to do was nod. He understood as he rode his board home that he had found his first friends. Brent could be scary but he could never be as scary as the loneliness that sometimes woke Liam up from a deep sleep.

At school, Brent made sure that everyone left Liam alone. One afternoon in the playground a teacher had confronted Liam about the chip packet lying near him.

'Pick it up, boy,' he said.

'N-n-not mine,' said Liam.

'D-d-don't . . . care,' mocked the teacher.

'Aren't you s'posed to help kids instead of make fun of them?' said Brent, who was sitting on the steps behind Liam eating a hot dog.

The teacher's ears had turned a furious red and he had turned and walked away.

'Wanker,' Brent had said to his retreating back.

Liam hadn't said anything but he had been grateful for Brent's words. Brent hadn't made him feel like he was being protected or smothered by someone who saw him as incapable; Brent was just being Brent and the teacher had pissed him off.

Even now when Liam was seventeen and Brent was nineteen they were still a tight-knit group. Now they drank and smoked whatever they could find and Brent declared everything 'crap' or 'bullshit'. Leo and Callum nodded and smiled and agreed that the whole world was 'boring as fuck'. Liam drank too, hoping the alcohol would loosen his stubborn tongue, but it only made things worse. Dope sometimes relaxed him enough to get out a whole sentence but inevitably Brent would say, 'Shut the fuck up, Liam.' Liam didn't mind being told to shut up. After all the years of people trying to force him to speak he appreciated Brent's frankness. Brent hated hearing him trying to stumble through his words and Liam hated hearing it as well. It was a relief to be told just to keep quiet.

•

'They're just scum, Liam,' Tara said when they had first been introduced. 'All that arsehole Brent does is tell you to shut the fuck up. How can you let someone treat you like that?'

'He's m-m-me mate,' said Liam and Tara sighed and let it go.

Now Liam was supposed to be studying for his final exams. He was supposed to be thinking about what he wanted to do at university. He was supposed to be thinking about *trying* to get into university.

Tara knew that if Liam dropped out of school and moved in with Brent he would simply be condemning himself to a future marked only by the emptying of beer bottles and smoking of joints. When she and Liam had been together she had tried to reason with him about Brent, tried to get him to see the damage that Brent could do but she had never been successful. Now she couldn't even say anything and even if she could have, her own problems were so overwhelming she could not deal with anyone else's.

Despite everything she said about him Tara understood Liam's need to be near Brent.

Brent drew people to him. He extended his web and it filled up with lost souls. Callum was always bruised. He had a little boy's intelligence trapped in the squat muscled form of a man. His stepfather found his strength intimidating and basically beat the crap out of him whenever he could.

'He liked me at first,' he told Tara one night when they had all had part of a bottle of vodka and Tara was still trying to fit in with Liam's friends. Brent had passed out.

'Like when you were little?' said Tara.

'Yeah,' said Callum, and Tara had nodded along with him. She understood what it meant to go looking for the second half of a unit that other kids seemed to have.

'I was only six when he and my mum got married and he told me we were going to be best buddies. And we were, kind of. I tried to be a good kid, you know. I always did everything he told me. But then when I got bigger he just seemed not to like me anymore. The first time he gave me a smack I was already bigger than him.'

'Growing up sucks,' Tara had said.

'Yeah,' Callum had nodded and then he had taken another swig of vodka and drifted back into his own thoughts.

When his stepfather hit him, Callum would stand still or lie curled on the floor waiting for the man to run out of energy. He still called him Daddy because his mother insisted he do so.

Leo was in love with Brent and fighting himself every step of the way. Or maybe he was just looking for someone, anyone, to show him a little kindness, a little patience. He had spent his whole life being set aside because his sister needed so much care.

When Tara watched them she could see that Brent knew. The jokes about fags and dykes flew back and forth around the group and Leo always laughed the loudest. He was the most active in hurting those the group deemed to be different.

Tara would have thought that Brent would kick Leo out of the group when he discovered who he truly was but that wasn't the way Brent dealt with people. He would take loyalty in whatever form it came. Loyalty from unrequited love, from someone flailing in the river of self-hate, was very powerful. Brent kept Leo in the group because he enjoyed the adoration. He enjoyed the way Leo looked at him and all the things Leo was prepared to do for him.

Occasionally he would touch Leo gently on the shoulder or run his hand down his back in gestures that could be seen as friendly but Tara knew what he was doing; she had seen Leo pause and grow still when Brent was near him.

There was something about Brent, something deep and wicked. No one knew his full story. Late at night all the boys would talk about their parents. Callum would joke about 'getting the shit kicked out of him' and Leo would talk about his damaged sister, but Brent never mentioned where he came from. No one had ever even been to his house. If there was a gap in the 'fucked-up family' conversation going round with the joint he would simply declare his parents 'arseholes' and the talk would move on.

He was at once incredibly sexy and completely repellent to Tara. Before she had realised just how dangerous he was Tara had wanted to be part of the little group. She'd wanted Liam's friends to like her, because what girl didn't want that?

One night they had all been hanging out at Liam's empty house, passing joints back and forth and drinking beer, when Liam had fallen asleep on the couch.

Tara had stood up to leave. She would rinse her mouth and go outside and call her father to meet her nearby. It was too far for her to walk all the way home. She would tell her father she had decided to walk back from whatever friend's house was closer. 'We had a fight,' she would say and then she would let him lecture her about the dangers of walking alone at night.

'I'll just call my dad,' she said to Brent, aware suddenly that the other girls who had been around had left. Callum had already been dragged home by his stepfather.

'You don't have to go,' said Brent. His voice was slow with dope and alcohol.

'Nah,' said Tara, 'I should get home. I wanted to do some studying tomorrow.'

'You work too hard, T,' he said, and she felt herself shrink from his use of Liam's pet name for her.

'Yeah, well, I want to, you know, do something with my life.'

She had grabbed her bag from the floor and stepped over Leo, who was sleeping on his side with his hand still holding a bottle of beer.

She had been searching in her bag for mouthwash when Brent placed himself in front of her.

'I said you don't have to go, T.'

Tara could remember the shiver that ran down her spine. Close up, his eyes were sky-blue even in the dim light. He wasn't that much taller than she was but he took up a great deal more space. He smelled vaguely of cigarettes and aftershave.

He raised his hand and touched her cheek gently. 'You're so pretty, Tara—so fucking pretty.'

'My dad is waiting for me to call,' she said. It was hard to get the words out over the thumping sound filling her ears.

'So fucking pretty,' said Brent, and he ran his hand down her neck and into her top, where he cupped a breast and squeezed hard. Tara had felt stunned into submission. He kept moving his hand and his breathing grew ragged and she could feel her mind dull as she watched his lips part and felt his eyes on her.

'T-T-Tara,' said Liam behind them.

Brent removed his hand from her top as casually as he removed a cigarette from the packet he always carried.

'I have to go,' Tara called to Liam but she didn't turn around. Her face was on fire and she couldn't catch her breath. She ran a fair way down the street until she could no longer see the lights from Liam's house. That was when she called her father.

He came to get her in his pyjamas and gave her the standard lecture that included telling her how important she was and how devastated he would be if anything happened to her.

Tara had let the words wash over her. Mostly her father sounded like he was reading from a badly written script.

Her body still burned where Brent had touched her.

Her father had no idea what she had just been through and no idea what she was doing on the nights she was supposed to be with one of her friends.

Sometimes the level of deception bothered her. She felt like she was hiding some secret part of herself the same way her mother tried to hide the voices and the delusional thinking. But it wasn't as if he was going to give her permission to spend a Saturday night hanging out with her boyfriend and his older friends. She had it all worked out. If Max ever tried to call Emma's house or Jody's house they knew what to do. 'She's in the bathroom; I'll get her to call you back.' And then they'd call Tara. She kept her mobile phone out in the open all the time so she could answer it as soon as it rang.

Tara waited for the call, waited for Max to check up on her, but he never did. She should probably be flattered that he trusted her, but she knew it wasn't that. Tara always suspected that as soon as she left the house her father's new family took over. She doubted her father thought about her when she was not with him. It was almost as if she and her mother had never existed. Ethan and Michael and Alicia were the straightforward family he had always longed for.

In bed that night she felt Brent's hands again and she knew that he wanted to add her to his list.

She imagined that once he was done with her he would make sure that Liam was done with her as well and she knew that she wasn't ready to lose Liam. She began to refuse to see him when he was with them. Liam fought her a little but she got the sense that he understood what had happened and he knew what Brent wanted and needed. He didn't want to lose her either.

Now, in the park, she wanted to tell Liam what she had been thinking for months.

'I shouldn't have let you go,' she wanted to say, but the silence was easier than any discussion.

When she found out she was pregnant she had told him and he'd just freaked out. Like almost every other boy who had ever been confronted with the consequences of his actions, he turned it on her.

'How the f-f-fuck could that have happened? You were supposed to be looking after things,' he said.

Tara noted that the stutter faded slightly when he was over-taken by emotion and stopped listening to himself speak.

'I don't know, Liam. How do these things usually happen?'

'You'll h-h-have an abortion won't you?'

'I haven't thought about it. I don't want a fucking baby either and thanks for acting like this had nothing to do with you.' She had wanted him to . . . wanted him to what? Be support-ive? Tell her he loved her no matter what? Tell her to keep the baby? The truth was that even now, after everything that had happened, she had no idea what he could have said to make things okay. She knew she was screwed up from watching the crap on television and movies where boys behaved like real men. There was nothing Liam could have said or done to prevent her getting angry with him, nothing that would have stopped her pushing him to say the right thing and then being disap-pointed when he failed her. The situation was completely fucked up no matter what anyone said.

'S-sorry, T,' he said and hung his head.

Tara wanted to run her hands through his brown curls and make him smile. He had a great smile. His eyes were usually dark solid green but when he smiled it was like someone was shining a torch behind them. Even through her anger Tara felt her heart lurch with love for him.

She didn't want to think about her last conversation with him. Abortions cost money, didn't they? And even if she could get it done through Medicare they would need to know her age. There would be questions and forms to fill in. There would be no way she could do anything without telling Alicia and her father. They had gone over the possibilities again and again and finally Liam had tired of the discussion and spat, 'Don't you dare fuck up my life, Tara.' And then he had walked away. Tara had been too weary to run after him and too wrapped up in tremendous fear for her future to call him and make it better. 'Finally a proper sentence and he's an arsehole,' she thought.

That night he changed his status to 'single' on Facebook and just like that they weren't together anymore. Tara had been dumbfounded. She asked Emma to talk to him on Facebook but he wouldn't reply to any messages.

Tara could sense Brent's influence. She'd heard him talk about other girls often enough. 'She's just a whore,' or a dyke or a bitch was the way he described most of the girls he met. They were still attracted to him though. They liked the snake on his muscled arm and the pale blue eyes. She knew that Liam would have told him about the pregnancy and she also knew that Brent would have told him to cut her out of his life. She sent Liam a few messages and chewed on her fingernails all night while she waited for him to reply. He was online for half the night and then all of a sudden he disappeared. But Emma could see that he was still online and Tara understood that he had removed her as a friend. The thought made her burn with anger. Liam was so easily led.

She changed her Facebook status too and then defriended him. She could have called him, could have talked him round. She knew that she should have just told him she would get an abortion. But the callous way he had changed his status rocked her belief in him.

She lay on her bed at home and hated him. She stopped eating and she stopped caring. Her father yelled and Alicia lectured but she didn't listen. She went to school and came home and then went to sleep. Her grades dropped.

She watched her stomach grow and felt removed from it.

Some days when she walked home from school she saw him in the park, waiting for her to come by. He was always there. He would see her and lift his hand in a sad little wave but Tara would turn her head away and walk past. When her belly was so big that she thought everyone could see she started carrying a giant bag around with her. No one noticed—or if they did they didn't say anything.

'You've stacked it on a bit,' said one of the dickhead boys at school.

'Shut the fuck up, you small-dicked wanker,' said Emma, who could be relied on to stand up for her friends.

Emma hadn't been surprised when Tara turned up on the news.

What happened? she had messaged, and when Tara came home from the hospital she turned on her computer and found the message repeated again and again from all her friends.

She deleted everything and for a few weeks Emma had just carried on the conversation with herself. *I thought you might be preggers but I didn't want to say anything. Sorry for being a bad friend. Let me know if you want to talk. I'm here for you, T. We're all here for you.*

Tara didn't doubt their sympathy but she couldn't talk to them.

Eventually they just stopped posting messages and Tara felt the relief of being forgotten. She knew when she went back to school she would have to begin again. She would have to ask for forgiveness, especially from Emma.

•

At the time when her belly grew hard and soft of its own accord she had thought about talking to someone, telling someone her secret.

She wanted to tell Alicia and her father so they could take care of things for her, but whenever she thought about what she would say she could only hear their judgement and their distance.

'When did it happen?' she wondered as she lay on her bed, ignoring her stomach and the alien creature moving around inside her. 'When did I lose them?'

Because it hadn't always been bad. When she was little, Alicia had finally completed the picture for her. She had made them a proper family. She felt like she had spent years trying to get Sasha to fit the mould.

'Why can't you be like Lila's mum?' she had asked Sasha when she was only four. She had shouted the words really. She had come home from a playdate at her friend's house to find her mother silent on the sofa. Lila's mother had made lunch and then helped Tara and Lila make a doll's house out of a cardboard box. She hadn't danced and sung nonsense songs, and she hadn't twirled around the room laughing at nothing and muttering to someone. She had just sat quietly cutting out windows because windows were difficult for small hands. When the doll's house was finished she had given them juice and cookies and then she had talked quietly on the phone to someone. Tara had envied Lila her peace, although she had not been able to articulate it at the time. 'Why can't you be like Lila's mother?' was the closest she could come. When Max had introduced her to Alicia she had seen the possibility of a Lila-like family.

She had loved Alicia from day one, even as a little voice in her head told her not to give up on her mother. Alicia had baked one cake on a Saturday afternoon and she had baked one cake every Saturday afternoon no matter what. Alicia went to work and came home again and she always did the laundry when the box was full. Alicia made her father smile and Alicia read stories at night.

It hadn't changed when the boys arrived. When Ethan was born Tara had been delighted with the new creature in the house. She had helped change his nappies and settled him back to sleep. She had played with him for hours so Alicia could rest and when Michael came along she had been just as entranced even though babies' needs were beginning to bore her by then. It was only later that Tara started to notice a separation between her and Alicia. Her father went to work and left the children to his wife. He had large bills to pay. Peace Hills was expensive and he would never abandon his ex-wife to the state. Alicia kept things going at home. She never said or did anything that Tara could point to, but one day Tara noticed the way Alicia looked at Ethan and Michael. It was a look of intense pure love, and it made Tara feel grateful to be in the presence of such a mother. It was only afterwards that she realised Alicia never looked at her the same way. Alicia looked at her all the time but it was a different sort of look. Alicia looked at her like she was waiting for something. And at that moment Tara mentally took a step back. 'She's not really *my* mother,' Tara thought and she was deeply shocked by the revelation. She had always known it to be true but it felt as though her heart had finally caught up with her brain. Alicia and Max both belonged to Ethan and Michael but only Max really belonged to Tara. Tara was eleven at the time of her epiphany and that was when her behaviour began to exasperate her stepmother. She understood now that she had merely been protecting herself.

•

In the park with Liam, Tara touched her watch again so he would know their time was up.

'I'll . . . I'll w-w-wait for you t-t-tomorrow,' said Liam. Tara reached up to touch his face and nodded. He would wait for her forever if she asked him to. She was completely sure of that.

It was like the pregnancy and the ten-month separation had never happened. It felt like they were back in the middle of their relationship and nothing had changed. Tara wanted to just hold on to that thought. Tara knew she was fifteen and her body had just been through an experience that should have been reserved for the body of a grown woman, and Liam was seventeen and should have been upset about the fact that his girlfriend couldn't speak or remember what had happened to her baby, but in the park Tara felt like a child and so she swept it all away and she didn't think about it and neither did Liam, because it was easier just to sit on the bench and hold hands.

16

'But I don't understand, dear,' said June. 'You said it was your cousin's baby.'

'I know, and I'm sorry I lied—but I was so ashamed, June. It's not supposed to happen at my age, you know, and I've never been . . . well, I've never been very active in that department so I suppose I ignored the signs. And then when I realised what was happening . . . well, I was just so embarrassed. I mean, what would Mum have said?'

'Oh, Minnie, she would have been horrified. But still I don't understand why you didn't tell us. I mean, you never looked . . . I mean, I did notice you'd put on a few but I never suspected.'

'I know and I'm sorry, but I think I just wanted it to go away at first. I didn't want to have a baby on my own. In fact, I didn't think I would ever have kids. You know I'm not one for going out.'

'But where did you meet the father? Who is he, Minnie? Don't you think he should know he has a child? She must look like him. She has your nose, I think, but the eyes must come from him.'

'They do, June. Look, it was someone I met through one of those websites and we didn't exactly get along well. We just met a couple of times and I wanted to . . . oh, June, it's so shameful but I wanted to see what it was like.'

'What it was like, Minnie? Whatever do you mean?'

Minnie met June's pale blue eyes and had to bite her lip to stop a giggle escaping. She was terrified that June would wrangle the truth out of her but she couldn't stop herself from finding the ridiculous conversation funny.

'I'd never really had it, had s-e-x before, June. I just wanted to do it once before I settled into old age.' June didn't have to know about Joel. He barely counted anyway.

'Well I never,' said June, bringing her hand to her mouth.

'There were always boys around when you were younger and I just thought, well, I never really thought about it but . . . oh dear, Minnie.'

Minnie gave her a weak smile. 'I thought I was too old and then when it happened I was mortified and then I just sort of pretended it wasn't happening until the day she arrived.'

'But, Minnie, we would have helped. You know Lou used to be a paramedic. We would have taken care of you. And you should have seen a doctor, Minnie. A clever girl like you knows that you need to see a doctor when you're pregnant. What if something had gone wrong?'

'I know, June, I know. But it didn't. Here she is and I did it on my own. It wasn't very nice but I managed. I'm sure there are plenty of women who do and we've been to the clinic and I'm seeing the doctor but I just need to get a birth certificate and to do that I need you and Lou to say that you witnessed the birth.'

Minnie could feel June moving away. The whole thing was too much. It was too shocking. She was hurt that Minnie had lied to her, hurt that she had not been able to share in every aspect of the pregnancy. Minnie knew that if she had really been pregnant June would have accompanied her to every doctor's visit and on every shopping trip.

June had two boys, one of whom was living in America and married to a young woman that June couldn't warm to. She saw her grandchildren once every few years and never had enough time with them. 'I feel like we have to get to know each other all over again every time we see them,' she told Minnie when she'd returned from her last trip overseas.

June's other son, Benjamin, was on his third tour in Iraq. The whole church prayed for his safe return every Sunday.

'What should I do now, God?' Minnie prayed silently as June worked her way through the betrayal.

'I don't understand, Minnie,' said June, patting at her short grey bob, 'giving birth is not an easy thing. You must have been in pain. Why didn't you call us? How could you have known what to do?'

'I watch those shows on television, June. I watch them all the time.'

June sighed.

'I was going to call you when it was all happening,' said Minnie. 'It was too much for me and I did want you to be there but as soon as I started to move I felt like I wanted to push and then there she was.'

'I was in labour for hours and hours, Minnie,' said June.

'It was only a couple of hours for me,' said Minnie, 'but it may have been longer. I don't really know.'

'We would have helped,' June repeated.

'Yes,' said Minnie, 'but perhaps you could help me now.'

June nodded, and Minnie could see her struggling with forgiveness. She was not one to take being excluded lightly.

'June, I know I've hurt your feelings and I know I should have told you. You're like a mum to me and I'm sorry that I haven't behaved very well. But Kate's here now and I do want to share her with you. I don't know why it worked out so well but Reverend Sam always talks about unexpected miracles from God. Maybe Kate is my one unexpected miracle—and to tell the truth I've been so lonely since Mum . . . well, since Mum . . . you know.'

'Oh, Minnie, I know that. I have tried to get you out of the house and I can see that Kate has made things better. I really can.'

'If you could help me, June, I would never forget it. And I was wondering . . . well, I was hoping that you would babysit Kate for me while I go and get all the paperwork sorted out.'

Minnie watched June's face soften as she had known it would.

'I tell you what—we'll say no more about it. You give me the papers. It's only a little lie and, really, who can it hurt?'

'Oh, thank you, June,' said Minnie. 'As soon as they get here I'll bring them over.'

'Just call, dear. Just call and I'll be there.'

Minnie wheeled the pram back into the house and put Kate on her play mat for some tummy time. The books were very firm about tummy time. She had six of them on her bedside table now.

In the newspaper there was a small article appealing for any information about the missing baby. It was buried right in the middle of the paper and it was just a little square of writing. Minnie was probably the only person in the whole world who still scoured the papers and the internet for any mention of the missing baby.

The public were bored with the story now. It had been months and apparently the young girl was still refusing to give any information. Minnie did not think about the family, did not think about the young girl and whether or not she would be charged.

Minnie had never asked for much. She had never really had friends or a proper boyfriend. She worked from home so she didn't have to endure the stares of her clients and she watched television. She had been hiding in her house her whole life and she had never demanded anything of her life or of the world. The way she saw it Kate was her reward for years and years of prayer. Her reward for a life that she had not really lived at all. If that was a sin then so be it.

'So be it, Mum,' she said, and she flipped Kate over so they could smile together.

•

The papers arrived a few days later in an innocuous-looking brown envelope. They were simple forms. There was no hint of suspicion in them but Minnie made sure she wrote the truth down. The truth as she saw it. If she closed her eyes she could imagine everything. She could see the man with dark eyes who had climbed on top of her once or twice and then never called again. She could picture herself noticing her breasts enlarge and her body change but ignoring it. She made up a rainy night when she had taken herself off to the late-night chemist and quietly bought the pregnancy test. She looked in the mirror and made the shocked and disgusted face at herself that she surely would have made. She watched a recorded documentary about life in the womb twice and placed her hand on her stomach, remembering how it felt to have a small creature moving inside her, and then she remembered giving birth. The pain and the blood and cutting the cord herself. That had happened, hadn't it?

By the time Minnie had finished filling in the papers she knew that Kate had arrived just as she said she had.

Across the road Lou signed without saying anything but June brought out a cake and they clinked teacups.

'You've lost so much weight, Minnie,' said June.

'I had noticed that my clothes were getting looser,' said Minnie, uncomfortable with Lou's grim smile.

'Well, you need to look after yourself now that you're a mum. I'll make a pot of stew and bring some over for you.'

Minnie recoiled at the thought. She preferred light quick meals now. Meals that could be eaten standing up.

'That would be lovely, June,' said Minnie, and she looked over at Lou.

'You'll be a good mum, Minnie,' he said, 'and I really hope you won't be excluding us again.'

'Oh no—no, I promise, Lou, and I am so sorry,' said Minnie, and she squeezed out a tear or two to show how sorry she was. They were tears of relief but Lou wasn't to know.

'Enough now,' said June. 'I told you we'd say no more about it.'

Kate woke up then and all attention turned to the baby. Minnie liked it that way. She didn't mind being invisible because Kate was in the room. Being a mother was, she thought, the best possible way to disappear.

•

Lela asked lots of questions about the birth.

'You mean you were all alone?'

'Yes, all alone. I didn't want anyone to know.'

'But I would have helped you, Minnie. I wouldn't have judged you—you know that. I know how lonely you've been since your mum passed on. I wouldn't have said anything and I would have come with you to the hospital.'

'I know you would have, Lela. June said the same thing and I'm really grateful to have such good friends, I really am—but I was just so ashamed and embarrassed and I just didn't want to think about it. Once she was here and I knew that she was safe and healthy I lied because . . . I don't know why. It seemed a dreadful thing to be my age and suddenly produce a baby.'

'I suppose—but what about her dad? Doesn't he want to see her? You should tell him, Minnie; fathers are important.'

Minnie could feel a headache beginning to take hold. 'It was only once or twice and then he didn't call me again. I don't really know much about him. He could be married with children for all I know.'

'Married? Oh, Minnie,' said Lela, and then she began to laugh.

'What's so funny?'

'I'm sorry, but it is a little bit funny. You've crammed a whole life of scandal into a few months. A married man and sex without marriage and now a baby.'

Minnie smiled. 'Yes, well, I waited long enough. Perhaps I should be in a magazine.'

'Oooh yes, you should. You should give that one that does all the personal stories a call.'

'No way, Lela! What would happen when Kate gets bigger and reads about herself like that? It would devastate her.'

'I'm only joking, love. Look, I'm pleased for you, I really am. You deserve a bit of happiness, Minnie—everyone does. And look at you; you've taken to this whole motherhood thing like a duck to water. You've lost so much weight.'

'Babies take up a lot of time.'

'Yeah, I remember. So now tell me, is she trying to crawl yet?'

On her way home from seeing Lela Minnie felt a lightness in her soul. It was going to be all right. Lela and June believed her and soon Kate would have a birth certificate and she would be official.

She watched her daughter bat at the toy clipped to the top of her pram. Her daughter.

If she hadn't gone to the shops after two cups of coffee and if she had just braved the stares in the bigger bathroom and if she hadn't had to go right there and then and if, if, if. Minnie didn't want to think about the possibility of not finding Kate. She didn't want to believe it was just random. 'God must have had a hand in it, Mum—he must have wanted Kate to be with me. He must have,' she said as she pulled the pram up the steps and into the house.

'Who am I to question God?' she said aloud.

Who indeed . . .

17

'Y-you should come s-s-see Brent's house,' said Liam.

Tara shook her head. She had no desire to see Brent and the others. There was no way she could leave the park anyway.

Her time with Liam was the only time she felt she could breathe properly. If she returned home even a minute late Alicia would make sure she was never allowed out again. Logically Tara knew that Alicia was scared for her, that she was worried about her and that she had an idea of what Tara was doing. But it felt like cruelty.

Alicia had never met Liam and her father had only met him once when he drove past the park one afternoon and caught them sitting together. The whole thing had been horribly awkward, with Liam stuttering and blushing and her father standing up tall and not giving Liam a chance to answer his questions. They were disparaging about the relationship from the first moment Tara started talking about him.

'Don't let it affect your grades,' said her father.

'Who exactly is he anyway?' said Alicia.

Then they started calling him That Liam. As in 'You are too young for That Liam,' and 'I hope you're not seeing That Liam at Emma's house tonight.' They knew she was. Tara could see they were protesting more for the look of it. If they had really wanted to stop her from seeing him they could have made her stay home, could have taken away her computer, could have paid more attention. Tara had seen other parents do it. She would have hated them for it but at least it would have seemed like they gave a fuck.

She talked about Liam on and off but they never really wanted to meet him properly and she hadn't wanted to subject him to their scrutiny. It took him weeks to stop blushing when he talked to her and there was no way she was going to torture him by making him spend time with her parents. She had never met his family either, although they sounded a lot like hers. Kind but concerned about their horribly flawed children.

Of course now Tara wasn't just a pain-in-the-arse teenager anymore. Now she had disappointed them on a whole new level. If she could find the words she would have loved to have said,

'See? And you thought I was bad before.' The thought made her smile.

•

At home she sat at the dinner table and watched as Alicia and her father and the boys talked about their days. The conversation went round and round the table and they didn't even look at her anymore.

Tara wanted to speak. She tried to force some words, *any* words, from her mouth. When she was alone in her bedroom she turned up her music and tried to make herself say her own name aloud but nothing came out.

Every night her father would knock on her door after the boys had gone to sleep and go through the same sad routine, trying to get her to say something or write something that would let him and the rest of the world into her head.

Step one: A quiet knock.

Step two: He held the pen out.

Step three: He pushed his notebook under it.

'You can text me, you can email me, you can write me a letter. You can communicate any way you want, Tara, but you have to give us the answers. You have to tell us what happened.'

'The police are waiting, Tara,' Alicia would say. 'If you would just tell us what happened then we can figure out how to move on. Your father and I will do everything we can to help you. Just tell us what happened so we can get on with the rest of our lives.'

Tara understood that she was causing her family pain, but when she closed her eyes and tried to force herself to remember she could only summon a black brick wall behind which she knew was the memory everyone wanted her to find. The wall was high and thick and she couldn't see her way around it. The images that did come to her arrived when she least expected it. She would be standing under the shower and the swollen feet in blue canvas shoes would appear in her head. Or she would bend down and her body would remember bending down but wracked with pain. Nothing made sense, nothing fitted together. Tara wanted to howl in frustration but she couldn't even make that sound.

•

Usually the conversations about Tara's lack of communication were conducted after the boys had left the table for a bath and some television time, but one night they had come back late from soccer, wet and covered in mud, and the whole family sat down together for takeaway pizza after Ethan and Michael were showered and dressed in pyjamas.

The boys were silent as they enjoyed the midweek treat and Max seemed to forget they were there. Tara was shocked that her father brought up the subject at all. Neither Alicia nor Max had ever said anything about protecting the boys from what had happened but it was understood that they didn't need to know anything. It may have been that her father had found his day at work difficult or it may have been the latest bill from the lawyer that Tara had noticed lying open on the kitchen table. Her father's tone was aggressive, his shoulders up around his ears as he spoke.

'Have you checked your Facebook, Tara? Have you talked to any of your friends? Can you talk to us, Tara? Can you tell us something, anything? Can you just tell us how you're feeling? Please?'

Tara shook her head and ate the crust of her pizza, letting the questions wash over her.

Alicia kept clearing her throat, trying to signal to Max to be quiet. The boys had stopped eating and were watching to see what would happen. Her father wasn't even asking the questions with the expectation of an answer, he was simply going through his usual list, but Ethan and Michael had never heard it before. They didn't ask any questions about their silent sister. She was a mystery to them anyway, being so much older than they were and from a different mother.

When Max fell silent Ethan darted from the table and returned with his own solution. 'You can use my Magna Doodle,' he said, thrusting the toy at her. Like that had been the solution all along.

'Yeah,' said Michael. 'Write on that and tell us a joke, Tara.'

Tara had always been good with knock-knock and poop jokes.

She smiled at him. The one-way conversation meant nothing to the boys. They knew she was in trouble but they had no idea what it was about. Tara wished she could remember being that young and innocent but she knew she never really was.

Even at four years old she had drifted off to sleep wondering what Mummy would be like in the morning. The good mummy liked to bake and sing and play games. She would talk fast and throw Tara in the air and push her high on the swing. Sometimes she pushed her too high. The good mummy could be scary but she was better than the bad mummy. The bad mummy wouldn't talk to her. Her eyes looked dark and she slept all day. The bad mummy didn't give her breakfast and she was too small to reach the cereal on her own. The bad mummy made Daddy sad. The bad mummy was always talking to someone else and not to her. Tara could never see the other person; only Mummy could.

When she got older and thought about her mother Tara decided she was like water. The good mummy was the sea—changing colours, rising and falling waves, loud and crashing. You approached the sea with excitement, with joy, but always at the back of your mind there was a small amount of fear because you never knew when a wave was going to dump you under a suffocating wall of water and sand. The bad mummy, on the other hand, was a lake on a day mired in heat. Stagnant and flat, hiding things that could bite and scratch underneath the glass-like surface.

Tara envied Michael and Ethan their unquestioning acceptance of their own safe little world. Sometimes she envied them so much she hated them. Mostly, though, she loved them for showing her what it looked like to be a kid.

At the dinner table she took the toy and held the special pen in her hand. Usually she just let her father's pen and notebook slide to the floor but she held on to the Magna Doodle, knowing that she could write the words and a minute later they could be erased and it would be like she had never written anything at all.

She could feel the stillness that had suddenly overtaken Alicia and her father as they waited for her to finally communicate. She was a zoo animal. She was a circus monkey. Dance, monkey, dance.

The plastic pen stuck to her sweaty palm. It had been months since she had done anything other than nod or shake her head. They had talked and asked and begged and pleaded and threatened. It had been months, but that night she wanted to tell them something. She wanted to let them know the truth. And so she held on to the pen and she listened to them holding their breath and then she wrote. She wrote about the black wall.

I don't remember.

I don't remember.

I don't remember.

I don't remember.

I don't remember.

She wrote it over and over again and she pressed harder and harder on the grey surface. She wrote it in large letters and she wrote it in tiny letters. She kept going until she felt her father place his hand over hers and gently remove the toy.

'It's all right, Tara. Hush now. It's all right.'

It was only then that she felt the wetness on her cheeks and when she looked at Michael and Ethan she saw they were open-mouthed with shock.

She didn't remember but the tears told her that her body held some knowledge. Her body knew enough to cry.

She left the table and went to her room. On her bed she opened her mouth in a silent scream.

She could not remember the baby but at night there was blood and pain and terror in her dreams.

Some days she would jump out of bed filled with a restless energy that had nowhere to go and some days she could barely move.

She knew that this must be what her mother felt like. The urge to lie still and wait for time to pass was overwhelming some days. She only forced herself to get out of bed and eat and dress and shower because she could not be her mother. Of all the terrible things people were saying about her, the one thing she could not be was her mother.

'Tara,' said her father. He knocked at her door and then knocked again.

Tara turned down the music and got off the bed.

'Oh, Tara, love, I know this is terrible for you. I wish I could help you. I wish I could make this all go away but there are too many people involved. You see that, don't you?'

Tara nodded.

'I don't know how long Daniel will be able to keep the police at bay, Tara—do you understand that?'

Tara nodded again and then she sat down on her bed. On her bedside table her mobile phone shone in the glow of the lamp. It was covered in pink crystals. At school last term all the girls had covered their phones in coloured stones but Tara had been away so long now that all that could have changed. Things changed overnight sometimes, overnight or over a day, after a few hours or a few minutes, or they could change when you breathed in. You could breathe out and find your whole world was different.

Tara picked up the phone and pushed the Create Message button.

I know that you are trying to help, Dad, she typed. *I know how hard this is for you and for Alicia but I can't remember the baby. I can't remember anything at all.*

Her father took the phone from her and read her message. She saw him wipe at his eyes and she knew he was grateful that she had at least tried to talk to him. She couldn't find her voice but she could give him the gift of some words. She had held the Magna Doodle and breathed in, and when she breathed out she wanted to give them some words. They weren't the right words and they wouldn't solve the problem but they would have to do for now.

'Do you remember being pregnant? Do you remember getting pregnant? Do you remember who got you pregnant? Was it that Liam? Was it him?'

Tara shook her head and cleared the screen.

Please, Dad, just leave it. I know I was pregnant, I can remember that, but I don't remember what happened on the day I went to the hospital. I just can't remember and I really want to. The last sentence wasn't completely the truth. Tara wasn't sure she really *wanted* to remember.

'Why didn't you tell us, Tara? We would have helped you. If you wanted to terminate the pregnancy I would have helped you and if you wanted to keep the baby we could have . . .' He stopped.

Could have what, Dad? Tara typed.

Her father put his head in his hands. 'I don't know, love, I just don't know. I have no idea how to handle this, Tara. I don't know what to do. Daniel calls every day and the police are pushing to have you committed and Alicia is . . . I just don't know what to do, Tara.'

Tara could see that her father was going to cry and she felt her stomach flip with fear.

I'm sorry, Dad, she typed.

'I know you are, love, but if you could just write down all you know, if you could . . .'

If I had the answers I would give them to you, she typed, and then she handed her father the phone.

Her father nodded. 'I know you would, but if you can't find them, if there is something else we could be doing . . . Maybe we should get you some proper help.'

I like Dr Adams, Tara typed.

'I think you may need more than Dr Adams, Tara.'

Tara looked at her father, at his tired eyes and slumped shoulders, and she saw the same look he had given her mother when he had not been able to take anymore.

Please don't give up on me, Dad, typed Tara.

Her father shook his head and stood up.

Tara grabbed him and showed him the phone again.

But he didn't want to see her message. He shook his head and closed the door softly behind him.

Tara lay down on her bed and studied the black wall. It was solid and strong and when it came down she knew it was going to fall on top of her.

•

In the passage Max stood with his hand on Tara's door and tried to banish images of Sasha from his mind. Tara couldn't be like her—she just couldn't be.

Tara had his dark eyes but everything else came from Sasha. Sometimes he caught sight of his daughter's profile and felt his heart lurch with recognition.

Did this silence come from Sasha too? He wanted to burst back into her room and shake her by the shoulders until she opened her mouth and told him what had happened and where the bloody baby was. Normal people didn't have a baby and forget about it. Normal people remembered giving birth.

He wanted to force her to speak, to answer, to just be an average sullen teenager, but there was nothing he could do. Just like there had been nothing he could do for Sasha.

Sasha had spun into his life one hot night on the beach.

Literally spun.

Max had gone out with friends on New Year's Eve and after many parties and more drinks than he could remember he found himself on a beach as the sun rose. A large fire was just burning down and music blared out into the dawn. People were huddled in groups or fucking under towels or dancing. Max had stood watching the embers, waiting for his head to stop feeling like it was going to fall off, when someone careened into him from behind. He turned and caught the girl just before she fell into the fire.

'I was spinning,' she said and Max felt the world stop. She locked eyes with him and Max noticed how green they were even in the dim light of dawn and then she stood up on her toes and gently bit his lip. Then she laughed and Max laughed and then they were drunk on something else altogether.

Her blonde hair hung all the way to her waist. He held on to her even though she had stopped moving and he knew in the way that people sometimes know that he would never want to let go of her.

She was studying art and he was studying accounting and he couldn't stop thinking about her. Every day with Sasha was an adventure. She liked to sleep naked under the stars and climb on a plane when the flights were cheap. She swam with the old guys in the sea in the freezing cold of winter and she took dance classes at the seniors centre. She dressed in flowing skirts and tight little tops that made men stop and stare. They ate and drank and fucked their way through their final year of uni and Max had to force himself to go home for a few weeks so he could study and get through his exams.

He proposed when he got his first job offer. His mother wasn't the only person to sound a note of concern. 'She seems restless, Max—like she's looking for something more. She's always running.'

'She'll settle down, Mum. She'll be fine once she gets a job and we're married.'

His friends found her difficult to talk to. She jumped from subject to subject without listening to anyone else.

'She's amazing,' said his friend Jake, 'but just fuck her and be done with it, Max. You can't actually spend your life with someone like that.'

Max laughed at everyone and shook his head. They didn't understand Sasha like he did.

Max didn't want to hear what anyone else had to say. He felt like Sasha coloured his life. She painted their small flat and covered the walls with rainbows and unicorns. There were clouds in the bathroom and stars on the ceiling. He liked coming home to it after a day watching the numbers on his computer. He liked the way she told him to ditch work and spend the day at the beach.

She was always happy and always laughing. Sometimes they got a little drunk and she laughed longer than he thought she should. There were moments when he noticed an edge of hysteria to her happiness, but he put it down to alcohol or lack of sleep or stress.

He only started to notice the down days once they'd been married for a few months. When they had lived apart she would tell him she needed time to complete a project or see a friend and he wouldn't see her for a couple of days, but then he was almost grateful for some time to catch up on his own life. Once they were living together he couldn't explain away the days when she didn't want to get out of bed. When she didn't get the job teaching art that she wanted she took it really badly. She spent a few days in bed until he managed to coax her out of her depression with a good bottle of wine. He couldn't explain away the down days but he tried. He told himself that she was adjusting to married life, that he was difficult to live with, that there needed to be some down times for someone so filled with energy.

With hindsight Max understood that he had chosen to ignore the truth about his beautiful wife. Sasha couldn't keep a job even when she did get one. Her classes were always over the top. The children were scared of her or she would get upset about a meeting with her head teacher and not go into school for a week. Now he knew the incredible highs and black lows were just part of the disease. Then he had thought that if he could just keep her happy, just do whatever it was that she needed done, she would be okay.

When she fell pregnant with Tara he hoped that it would solve some of the problems. She wouldn't have to work anymore, wouldn't have to deal with people who upset her.

But according to all the doctors Sasha had seen since then, having a baby was the final straw for her. She came home from the hospital and took to her bed for weeks. Max had to call his mother in to help. Sasha never really talked about her parents. Her father lived across the country and her mother lived across the world. Neither of them had made it for the wedding. When his mother had to go home again, Max hired a nanny that he couldn't afford and waited and hoped and eventually Sasha did get out of bed, but then it became a pattern. She would be up for weeks and then down for days and then up again and finally he told her she needed to see someone. She agreed and they began what he now thought of as the medication merry-go-round.

This pill made her sick and that pill made her fat and another one didn't work. This one worked but she couldn't paint when she was on it and that one made her worse.

'Can't you just take the one that works and focus on being a mother for now until we can find something else?'

'My art is everything to me, Max—are you asking me to give up everything?'

'No, Sasha—I'm asking you to put Tara first.'

'And I'm asking you to put me first.'

'You can't come first anymore, Sash. We have a child.'

'Fuck you, Max!'

The medications clashed and she seemed completely detached from reality on some days. In her sleep she muttered about the 'black angel'.

He agreed that she needed a break from the medication. They needed to try something else.

And so they tried electroshock therapy and cognitive behavioural therapy and special herbs and more therapy and different pills.

Max had been overwhelmed with guilt when he asked her for a divorce. She hadn't known what he was asking for. She had looked at him uncomprehendingly. She hadn't been home for a year and he couldn't take it anymore. Alicia was part of his life. She fetched Tara from school and made dinner and sat at a restaurant table with friends and listened and talked like everyone else did.

He had called in the therapist to help her understand what he was asking for. The medication and the electroshock therapy made her spacey. She had nodded that she understood but he knew she had no clue what he was talking about. She spent her days painting, deeply absorbed in mixing colours. Sometimes she didn't even manage to get any paint on the canvas.

'The act of mixing the paint soothes her,' said one of her doctors.

She hadn't been able to sign anything because the new medication made her hands shake.

'Are you sure she won't be able to come home?' Max asked the doctors one last time.

'You need to get on with your life,' said Dr Lawrence. 'Today is a good day but there are many bad days. More than good really. Don't worry. We'll take care of her.'

And Max understood that he was being released. He needed to keep paying but that was all he needed to do.

And then, just a few months after he and Alicia were married, the doctors had declared her sorted. 'She's doing really well on the new drugs,' they told him. 'She's in charge of art therapy and she wants to come home and go back to her old life.'

Max couldn't believe what he was hearing. He shouted at Dr Lawrence for misleading him. She just shrugged her shoulders. 'We're not gods. New drugs are invented all the time. We didn't know that this drug would work on her a year ago.'

They were divorced and she was no longer his responsibility but there was no way he was going to let Sasha live on her own until he knew she was safe. When he looked at her then he saw the girl she had been and he felt so old around her. He needed to protect her. He picked her up from the hospital and she wound her arms around his neck and stuck her tongue into his mouth. Max felt his body melt but he pushed her away and spent the ride back to his house explaining about Alicia.

'I understand, Max—I really do,' she said after he had gone over it a few times. 'You had to move on for your own sanity. Tara needs a mother in her life. I'll stay for a few days and then I can move to the halfway house. I want to get back on my feet, Max.'

She was so present, so lucid, that Max began to regret his marriage to Alicia. At dinner he watched how Sasha and Tara connected and he imagined taking them away—to Europe or somewhere—and just being together as a family. He didn't look at Alicia even though he knew she was looking at him.

In bed that night he moved himself as far away from Alicia as possible as he worked through what he was going to do. Alicia kept silent and he could feel her just waiting for the whole thing to be over.

In the middle of the night Alicia got up to get some water and found Sasha slicing up their wedding album.

She was incoherent and violent.

When Alicia called him he tried to talk Sasha down. He spoke slowly, like he had spoken to her in the car. He thought that if he could just get her to calm down they could discuss how she was feeling. He moved towards her to get the scissors out of her hand and she lunged at him, catching him on the arm with the blade.

It wasn't a huge wound but there was a fair amount of blood and Sasha freaked out completely and started screaming about him trying to murder her.

Alicia summoned the paramedics and the police and they got Sasha sedated and into the ambulance.

From her bedroom doorway six-year-old Tara watched in silent horror as the men wrestled her mother down and pumped her full of drugs. Max didn't even have time to go to her. He had to go to the hospital and when he returned Alicia told him that Tara had locked herself in her room and refused to talk.

'I think that we are no longer just dealing with bipolar disorder. I think your wife is now suffering from schizophrenia,' said Dr Lawrence.

'But how is that possible?' said Max.

'They can overlap.'

'They can overlap?' said Max. 'What sort of a fucking answer is that? How do you know she wasn't always suffering from schizophrenia?'

'We don't know for sure, but her symptoms have not been consistent with it.'

'So how do you know she has it now?'

'Look, Max, it's not an easy thing to deal with. Sasha says the black angel told her to cut up the photographs. She says the black angel wants to hurt you and Tara. It's not something we can just dismiss. She is now a real danger to you and your daughter.'

'Is it because I remarried? Has that sent her over the edge?'

'We doubt it, but we will never know. It was traumatic for her to find out about your marriage. I know you told her but it's possible that she didn't really comprehend it until you brought her home. It could have been coming anyway. No use in blaming yourself. We're just lucky she didn't hurt anyone.'

The doctors couldn't explain what had happened. Sasha moved in and out of reality and they couldn't reach her anymore.

Now she sat in a chair at Peace Hills and everything they had tried had led to her losing her grip on the world. Max stretched his back and stood up straight. He wiped his eyes and stroked Tara's bedroom door. His little girl was in trouble and he had no idea how to help or what to do. An image of her sitting next to her mother flashed through his mind and he shook his head.

'No way,' he whispered into the empty passage. 'No way am I going to let that happen.'

Downstairs Alicia switched on the dishwasher and Max heard her turning off lights as she locked up the house.

Tomorrow was another day. He would get up and do it all again.

Fuck, but he was tired.

18

Minnie pushed the pram over the road to June's house. Kate had kept her up all night and June asked every day when she could babysit. Minnie didn't want to let Kate out of her sight but June had signed the papers and so had Lou and they deserved some time with the baby. June was leaving for a visit to America soon and Minnie felt she would regret not allowing June a little time with Kate.

'On eBay that pram costs six hundred bucks,' came a voice behind her.

Minnie stopped and turned. Her heart missed a beat and her hands were instantly clammy. She had not heard Brent come up behind her.

She had noticed him watching her more and more as the days passed. Whenever she came outside he seemed to be there. But, then, he was always outside during the day. She doubted he ever really left his house except to restock on alcohol.

He was standing in the garden when she went for a walk and staring at the engine of his foul van when she packed Kate up for an excursion to the shops. She assumed that she was simply seeing him more because she was out more, but with one sentence he had confirmed her fear. He was watching her.

She had never really had a conversation with him. She wanted to keep walking but felt trapped by his dead-eyed gaze.

'I got . . . I got it second-hand,' she said, and cursed her stupidity for engaging with him.

'Looks brand new to me,' he said, smiling.

She shook her head in a vicious denial, conscious of Kate wriggling awake in the pram.

'Where'd you get that kind of cash from, I wonder?' said Brent. His voice was level. He could have been asking her about the weather.

'I have to go,' she said.

'I reckon I could sell that for a lot on eBay,' said Brent.

'I need to go,' Minnie repeated, and she walked on towards June's house.

'I reckon I could sell that for a fortune,' he called after her.

She knocked and when June opened the door she almost fell inside.

'Minnie, what's wrong?' said June.

It took Minnie a few minutes to get the story out.

'Those little bastards,' said Lou. 'We should call the police.'

'And say what exactly, Lou?' June asked. 'It's not like he said anything that could be considered a threat—and even if he did there's not much we can do about it. Mary said that as long as they're paying rent there's no way she can get them out of the house until their lease is up.'

'When will that be?' asked Minnie.

'A few months from now. We'll just have to hold on till then. Unless we can prove they've actually done something apart from just being awful neighbours, there is nothing we can do about them. Now, why don't you go and have a rest, Minnie? Lou will walk you back to your house, won't you, Lou?'

'Oh no, June, don't worry about it. I'll be fine. I'm sure he's gone now anyway. He was probably just making his version of conversation. I'll be fine.'

Minnie didn't see Brent until she was opening her front door and then she just heard him.

'Everyone reckons you've got millions hidden under your floor,' he said. His voice was so low she could barely hear it.

Minnie stopped and waited for him to say something else. She felt frozen to the spot at her front door.

'Someone like you doesn't need all that money. What do you do with your time? You look after that baby and you go for a walk once a day. You don't need all that money.'

'I don't have any money,' said Minnie softly. She didn't turn around; she didn't want to look at him.

'Oh, I reckon you have money. You got loads of stuff for the baby. I know you cut the boxes up but you can't fool me.'

Minnie didn't reply. She slammed the door and went to sit on the couch.

Who were the people who thought she had millions of dollars? Was it possible the whole neighbourhood was discussing her? Did they know about the property her father had left her? And who would speak to Brent and his disgusting friends about it anyway?

Minnie felt a shadow settle above her. Brent wasn't just a noisy lout. Brent was a thinker, maybe a planner and a plotter. All these months she had been wrapped up in taking care of Kate, she hadn't noticed that she was being studied by the boys. She hadn't noticed anything really. Some days, when Kate was fussy and it was raining outside so there was no reason to walk with June, she found herself still in her dressing gown at five in the evening. Your world became really small when you took care of a baby. You could almost forget anyone else existed.

Brent and his friends were watching her, had been watching her for some time. It was a shocking thought. And if they were watching her then the whole neighbourhood had been underestimating them. Lou called them 'young louts' and Sarah at the top of the street sometimes smiled indulgently at them and said, 'Boys will be boys.' Minnie had been afraid of having her television stolen and June thought they were 'little animals'. But what if they were more than that? What if they have moved into the neighbourhood for a specific purpose? Because, somehow, they knew about the money hidden under the floor. It wasn't a lot really—a few thousand dollars in a box under the floorboards in the living room—but still . . . how did he know?

All her real money was in the bank. She wouldn't be stupid enough to keep all her money under the floor.

But how did he know?

Minnie got up and went to make herself a strong cup of tea.

'I'm just being silly, aren't I, Mum?' she said. 'They know I work from home—I mean, everyone knows that. They probably just assume that I have money. That Brent is probably just teasing, trying to scare me to entertain himself.'

She took her tea to the front window and pushed aside the heavy lace curtain, noting that it was time to wash it again.

'I'll have to call that nice Marlene to do all the curtains in the house again, Mum,' she said.

She peered up to the top of the road and then turned her head a little to look at June's house.

Brent was standing at Minnie's front gate. He wasn't walking past and he wasn't waiting for anyone. He was just standing at her front gate and staring directly at her.

Minnie dropped her cup of tea and let go of the curtain. Her heart felt like it was trying to leap out of her throat.

She dropped to her knees and crawled over to the couch.

She pulled herself up onto the soft fabric and stayed there. For an hour she sat stiffly on the couch, too terrified to turn on the television or go to the kitchen for something to eat. She sat and waited until it was time to fetch Kate.

Before she left the house she took the large golf umbrella from the laundry. 'At least I can swing it at him if he comes too close and maybe get him to leave me alone,' she thought but really she had no idea what she would do if he attacked her. He wasn't going to attack her, was he? The thought was at once absurd and terrifying. She opened the door and looked up and down the street. Brent was gone.

She hurried across the road and had a cup of tea with June and Lou before pushing the pram quickly home.

Only once she had triple-locked the back door and locked the security gate at the front and touched the button to bring down the shutters did she feel safe.

In bed that night she strained her ears to every creak and sigh. She lay awake and listened as Kate slept through the night. Only when she heard the first dawn birds was she able to sleep, comforted by the security of daylight.

Spring

19

I can't come tomorrow, Tara wrote on her phone.

Liam studied the screen. 'Wh-why?' he said.

I have 2 go 2 work with Alicia. I'm not allowed 2 b alone.

Liam grabbed his own phone; his typing was quicker than his speech. *Y didn't u tell me you were keeping da baby?*

Tara shrugged. She hadn't meant to open up a discussion. She didn't want to have to answer questions from anyone else, especially Liam. She knew he must have seen anyway. All those afternoons when she had ignored him as he stood and waited in the park he must have seen. He had been physically closer to her than anyone, so he surely would have noticed her getting fatter and fatter. She didn't want to talk about it but she was pretty certain that, like Alicia and her father, he hadn't seen, hadn't noticed, because he hadn't wanted to notice. Tara could remember longing for someone to say something, longing for someone to take the problem away from her. But no one said anything. Not her parents, not her teachers and not her friends.

Now it was over and she didn't want to think about it anymore—and she didn't have any answers for Liam, either.

But the police were still demanding answers and Daniel Walters was not having much luck holding them off.

'The wheels are in motion now,' he told her father when he came over to update them.

'What are they going to charge her with?' Alicia had asked.

'I'm not completely sure. The worst-case scenario is murder.'

'Jesus,' her father had said.

'But she's a minor,' said Alicia. 'And she can't remember.'

'I don't know exactly what the Director of Public Prosecutions has in mind, but I think they'll demand she be assessed at a psychiatric facility.'

Tara had got up and left the room after that. She didn't want to hear yet again how she had fucked things up for everyone. It didn't really sound like they were talking about her anyway. If she could have made her voice work she would have agreed that the girl who had given birth and then left the baby to die was a horrible human being. She had to remind herself that it was her they were discussing.

She had started texting her answers to Alicia and her father after she had written on the Magna Doodle. She didn't text much but she did answer questions. She answered questions about where she was going, 'the park', and what she wanted for dinner, 'don't care', and if she had done the homework they were sending home from school, 'Yeah'.

She didn't answer the only questions they really wanted answers to.

In the park with Liam she had been hoping just to let it all go.

Dnt want 2 talk about it, she wrote.

Liam nodded but he didn't seem to want to let it go.

'Wh-what's going to h-h-happen to you?'

Don't know, Tara typed. *They want to throw me in the nuthouse.*

'Wh-wh-why?'

I can't remember what happened and I can't talk.

I would have helped. We could have got married, typed Liam.

Tara snorted. *Yeah right.*

I'm serious, T. It would have been ok.

Leave it alone Liam. U r just talking crap. What would Brent and the other dickheads have said?

U r more important than they r. They r not so bad u know.

Whatever.

Brent's got a plan 2 make us all rich.

I'll bet.

It's true. There's dis fat dyke who lives in his road. Brent says she's loaded.

And?

He reckons she hides money in her house.

Great so now u r a thief as well.

Brent said my share will be massive. We could go away together. Go to Queensland and get married and leave all this bullshit behind.

Sometimes u sound like a kid.

'F-f-fuck you, Tara,' said Liam aloud. He got up and walked away.

Tara wanted to run after him but she stayed put on the bench. She didn't have the energy.

Liam hated being called a kid. She knew his parents treated him like he was a child. They thought that his slow speech somehow translated to his whole life. But if they were over-protective and smothering sometimes, at other times they were just a little cruel.

'They s-said that . . . that if I wanted t-t-to get a licence then I would h-h-have to call and b-b-book myself,' he told her before she had found out she was pregnant. They wanted him to wait until he was eighteen to get his licence and this was their way of stopping him.

Tara had raged against the unfairness of it with him but she had to stop herself from treating him the same way. At school Liam had been the quiet kid who spent lunchtime drawing or sitting in the library. One lunchtime when Tara had felt unable to face her friends she found herself sharing a table with him.

'Draw me,' she had said, not expecting a response. But he had. He was good. Not as good as he was with a skateboard but good enough for Tara to recognise herself. She liked that he was quiet. She felt that beneath the stutter was a complicated human being. She brought him out of the library and included him in her lunchtime circle. After a while she noticed that she had begun answering questions for him and speaking for him. He didn't mind it at first but after a while he would shake his head at her and make her give him time to answer. By the time he got to the end of the sentence her friends would be discussing something else.

Now, watching him leave the park, she wondered if she had been wrong about Liam.

'Tara thinks her boyfriend's got hidden depths,' said Emma.

'Whatever he's got it's definitely well hidden,' smirked Jody.

'Shut the fuck up, both of you,' said Tara.

'Oooh, Tara's in love,' said Emma.

'Maybe.' Tara smiled.

She had thought that there must be something more to him but it was possible that there wasn't. He had dumped her when she got too difficult to deal with. Now he was going to do something stupid because Brent told him to.

Part of the reason she hadn't told anyone about the pregnancy was to protect him. She had been giving him time to stand up and be a man, to tell her what to do or to help her. Giving him time to come back and apologise.

But what if that had been a mistake? What if Liam was just as much of a dickhead as his idiot friends?

Who was Liam anyway?

Tara walked home in the sunshine, wondering if she could blame Liam for everything that had happened. Dr Adams told her she had to accept responsibility for her own life and her own choices.

Dr Adams didn't make her write her answers to the questions she posed but she did keep asking Tara how everything felt.

'How does it feel when your father is angry at you?'

'How does it feel when you get messages from your friends on Facebook?'

'How does it feel when people mention the baby?'

'How did it feel when you knew your mother was not coming home again?'

'How did it feel when your father married Alicia?'

'How did it feel when your brothers were born?'

'How do you feel, Tara? How do you feel?'

Tara had nothing to give the doctor. 'Some days I don't feel at all,' she wanted to tell her.

Dr Adams seemed to have the answers to the questions she continually asked. She would say things again and again in different ways as though she was hoping that Tara would pick up on the clues.

'The pain you felt when you gave birth was more than just physical, Tara—it was deeply emotional.'

'It hurt to have to keep your secret and when you gave birth it was like giving birth to all the pain inside yourself.'

'The issues with your mother and the loss of her in your life is a pain as great as that of childbirth. You have to get past that so you can heal. You have to talk to me so I can help you get past it. Only by confronting the pain can we get rid of it.'

What pain? wrote Tara in thick black texta.

What pain? Because it was hard to know where to start.

She felt like she was standing on one side of a river looking across at a field filled with flowers. She knew that she wanted to get there and she knew that she had to cross the river to get there, but whenever she thought about putting her toe into the river she could see how much mud and water she would have to wade through. It seemed easier just to sit on the bank and look at the field opposite. It felt easier just to give up.

•

Liam waited behind a tree in the park until he couldn't see Tara anymore. He didn't want to go home. It didn't feel like home anyway. He didn't want to go to Brent's, either. He wished he could have told Tara what he really thought, what he really felt. 'How many times have I wished for that in my life?' Some days he wanted to rip his tongue out so at least he would have a valid excuse for why he couldn't speak.

He wanted to tell Tara that Brent was getting weirder. Every day Liam told himself that he wasn't going to go over there. He got dressed for school and did everything he was supposed to do but then he would get to class and some wanker teacher would make some remark like, 'Well, we're all delighted that Liam could join us for this lesson—I mean it's only his final year of school.' And all the other dickheads in the class would laugh and he would hold on until the bell and then find himself on a bus to Brent's place. Brent always chucked him a beer as he arrived and he would drink away the arsehole teachers and idiots at school.

But now Brent only seemed to have one topic of conversation. He was obsessed with the woman and her baby. Liam couldn't understand why. Brent had heard a neighbour mention in passing that the woman—Minnie was her name—never had to worry about working. He hadn't even been part of the conversation; he'd just overheard it one night as the old man and woman walked past the house. It was the same old couple who had owned the cat. The cat thing had really bothered Liam. Brent had made Callum break into the house on the night they got their big new television. Callum could break into anywhere—although he was worried about getting into the fat dyke's house.

'There's fucken security everywhere,' he said to Brent.

'I'll figure it out,' Brent had replied.

It had been easy enough for Callum to break into the old couple's house. They came from a generation when everyone left their doors unlocked. Their back door had been locked but, according to Callum, 'a fucken kid could have picked it'.

'If you happen to see the cat bring him over as well,' said Brent.

Callum had only managed to get the TV, but then the old man had sent the police over to look for it. It was long gone but Brent had been jumpy all the same and then a few days later the old man himself had come over. He had started out by saying, 'You look like decent enough blokes,' and after that Liam knew that even while Brent was agreeing to keep the noise down he was plotting. That night he made Callum go back for the cat. It was so fat and so old it didn't even try to escape.

'We could just drop it off a few streets away,' said Leo. 'It'll probably get run over.'

'Nah, mate,' Brent had said. 'I want to have some fun.'

Liam hadn't been there at the time and Leo had told him the story in that way he had—like he was trying to make it sound like fun but you could tell he had actually hated every minute of it.

Liam's parents had always had cats in the house. They were funny creatures. Sometimes they would come to you and want to be stroked, but they ran away if you came to them. Cats were smart. The old cat had probably had a good life. Liam was sure that he wouldn't have had a good death.

Liam wondered if, had he been able to get the sentences out, he would have said anything to Brent if he'd been there. Leo and Callum could talk and they kept their mouths shut. They just accepted whatever Brent did. But Brent was not the same person he had been when Liam first met him. Then he had just been someone who was almost as good as Liam with a skateboard. He hated school and his parents, but who didn't? His father smacked him about but he never mentioned his mother. But then, while hanging around at school one afternoon for parent–teacher interviews, Liam had spotted Brent and his mother.

The woman was fat—not just regular fat, but gigantic. She was bigger than the dyke who lived down the road from Brent, bigger than any human being Liam had ever seen. As they walked through the school everyone stared. The woman was dressed in a purple tent thing and Brent was holding her hand tightly. He was sixteen then—too fucking old to be holding his mother's hand—but he was holding it tightly and speaking to her quietly as they walked from classroom to classroom. Every now and again he would look around and try to catch someone staring, daring anyone to say anything. All the other kids dropped their eyes or turned away. No one wanted to piss Brent off. He had once bashed some kid's head against the climbing frame because the kid was quicker than he was and that was when he was ten. Afterwards he claimed it was an accident, that he was actually just trying to get the kid to back off, and even though no one had believed him there wasn't anything the school could do. The kid with the bashed head moved schools and everyone else knew to keep well away from Brent. It wasn't the only thing he'd done; Liam was sure there must be a whole file of similar incidents. He missed school when he felt like it and swore at teachers. He pushed and shoved and fought but he always had an explanation, always had a way of getting out of trouble.

His father usually came to parent–teacher meetings or no one came at all. Seeing Brent with his mother was bizarre. He seemed like someone who had never really been a little kid. But that afternoon Brent had looked different; he had looked almost proud of his mother and like he was trying to protect her as well. Liam had been far enough away to watch the pair without Brent noticing, and when his mother turned her head he had seen how fucked up her face was. Brent's father obviously did more than just give his son a good smack.

A few months later Brent had been absent from school for a few days and Callum had whispered to him and Leo over lunch that he was testifying against his father in court.

'Put the fucker away for at least five years,' Brent had boasted when he returned to school.

'Bet your mum was happy,' said Leo, and Brent had nodded slowly.

'Yeah, she's fucken happy.'

'She can't work, you know,' said Callum to Liam and Leo when Brent had gone to grab something from his locker. 'She can't work and now the old bastard's gone to jail there's no money coming in except for welfare, and that's never enough. Brent thought he was doing the right thing but I know that my mother would rather have my stepfather in the house than me.' Liam knew that he didn't have the same problems his mates did. His parents were morally against hitting him and his sisters. They were just an ordinary family—a family he should be grateful for he supposed but it didn't always feel like that. His parents were just trying to help him, he knew, every time they sent him to a new clinic or therapist or program, but he hated how disappointed they were when, yet again, some miracle cure failed to work.

Leo lived with an aunt and uncle who handed him fifty dollars every week to buy his own food. 'They don't like me eating with them at night,' he explained. 'My aunt reckons the piercings and the shaved head scare my little cousin but I don't think she cares. The kid laughs every time she sees me.'

Leo's parents had enough trouble looking after his sister, who had some sort of disease that made her arms and legs stiff. Leo was supposed to visit them every week but mostly he spent the night in the park with Brent and Callum. 'I can't stand looking at that freak,' he said. Now he was living with Brent and Liam was sure he hadn't been home for months.

Brent had become obsessed with money. He was always talking about how unfair everything was.

'All those fuckers living in big houses with their fancy cars and their fancy clothes—what have they ever done to deserve lives like that? Someone needs to show them that their money can't protect them from everything.'

'They do like, you know, work,' Callum had said and Brent had stood up and punched him just like that. Leo and Liam had laughed but Liam had known that Brent was sending them all a message. He had a plan and he needed them to follow him without question.

When Brent and the others had first moved into the house Liam had imagined that it would be a little like a holiday. It would be a place he could go when all the bullshit at school got too much for him. The first few weeks of ditching school had been bliss. He had loved the freedom. He didn't have to think about the HSC, didn't have to worry about talking to teachers and other students or delivering stupid oral presentations. He could just be completely silent. No one expected or wanted anything from him except that he drink his beer and keep quiet.

At home his parents didn't usually ask about his day because it took him forever to tell them. He went to school just enough to stop any calls home.

But Brent's house was no longer a sanctuary. After the cat thing, Liam could feel a constant churning in his gut whenever he went to visit.

Home sucked and school sucked and now going to Brent's house sucked too. Maybe if there was money in the dyke's house he could use it to piss off.

He went to sleep at night comforting himself with pictures of a beach and a small house that was his alone. He liked to place Tara in the house. They could be together and just . . . just be.

His parents probably wouldn't miss him at all. They could be a perfect family without the stuttering weirdo messing up every day with his spitting and shuddering.

Brent had said that in the dyke's house there was so much money none of them would ever have to worry again. But Liam didn't know how he knew this or what would happen if there was no money. He was worried for the woman and her kid. Once she had walked past him with the kid in the pram and Liam had looked down and the baby had seen him and just like that she had given him the biggest smile. Like she was happy to see him even though she didn't know anything about him.

Brent watched the woman all the time. 'She used to be fatter than my mother, but not anymore,' he had said yesterday as he watched the woman walk past with the baby in the pram.

'Wh-wh-why do y-y-you care?' Liam had asked, risking being told to shut up.

'Stupid fucken fat bitch,' Brent had muttered.

Liam wondered if Brent had any idea who he was actually talking about.

20

Alicia seemed stiff and unfriendly when Minnie dragged herself into the clinic to have Kate weighed. Minnie was almost too sick to notice. The cold had crept up on her suddenly. Her whole body felt clammy and her muscles ached as though she had run a marathon.

She longed to be able to stay in bed with some tea but Kate was sick herself and would not settle or sleep.

Minnie had spent the night walking up and down with Kate in her arms, wondering if this was to be her punishment for the terrible, awful sin. Kate wailed and cried and arched away from her bottle and Minnie shed a few tears herself. Dawn brought the relief of the rest of the world having to be awake as well. 'I've never been this tired, Mum—never. I can see why they use sleep deprivation to torture people.'

She looked in all the books and she tried to pray—'Please, God, make her be quiet for an hour'—but Kate would not settle. She wanted to be held all the time. She didn't want Minnie to stand still or sit down. She wanted to be moving. Minnie walked despairing laps around the house, stopping only to dose herself up on cold medication.

Minnie called the doctor and made an appointment for both of them and then she went to the clinic to see Alicia because she had to get out of the house and the doctor couldn't fit them in until that afternoon. Minnie liked Dr Sing—he had given Kate her shots and listened with rapt attention to the story of Minnie's home birth—but he was a popular doctor and she didn't feel as though she would survive until the afternoon.

'I know I'm just being dramatic, Mum,' said Minnie as she listened to Kate wail while she stood in a scalding shower, 'but I feel like death.'

'I wanted to ask if you had any advice as well,' sniffed Minnie. 'I haven't slept at all because she's so unwell. Is there anything I can do for her, anything that will help her sleep?'

'It's just a cold,' said Alicia. 'She'll get over it. Keep her warm and try for extra fluid. You can put a little bit of Vicks under her nose to help her breathe and there's some over-the-counter stuff you can get but the less you use of that the better.'

'Oh,' said Minnie as she felt her misery compound. The

inference was that a good mother would simply ride out the cold with her child. Minnie felt her body crying out for rest.

'You look like you could use a break,' said Alicia. 'Can't you call in your neighbour to help?'

'She's gone to visit her son in America. I don't really have anyone else.'

'Well, it will be over soon.'

'Oh, Alicia, but I'm so tired. I feel like I'm going to die. I haven't slept in days.'

'Poor love, it can be difficult. What you need is a babysitter to help out. A nice young girl who's looking to earn some money. You could put a notice up at your local school.'

Minnie heard a sound from the corner of the room. It sounded like a cross between a snort and a laugh and she focused on the young girl sitting in the chair behind the bookcase. She had blonde hair and dark eyes and was curled up on the hard chair. She hadn't noticed her when she entered the room, overcome as she was by her own misery.

'That's my stepdaughter,' said Alicia. 'She has a day off school today.'

'Maybe she could help me,' said Minnie. Once the words were out of her mouth it seemed a perfect solution to her problem. She just needed a little bit of sleep. 'I would pay her. I'd pay you,' she said to the girl, who was grim-faced in her chair.

'Oh no, Minnie, I'm sorry but Tara is just here for the day and I think she's not feeling very well anyway. She's lost her voice.'

Again there was a snort-laugh from the chair and Minnie locked eyes with the girl.

She was angry about something, that much was clear. Her hands were jammed into the pockets of her jacket.

Minnie tried a small smile but the girl didn't smile back. She kept looking over at Alicia as though she wanted to say something.

Ordinarily she wouldn't have allowed someone who was unwell anywhere near Kate but the child already had a cold, she reasoned.

'Are you sure?' she asked Alicia.

'It's really not appropriate, Minnie.'

The girl looked hard at Alicia again and seemed to nod her head.

She wanted to come with her. Minnie could tell. She didn't want to spend the day watching babies get weighed and measured. And it seemed obvious to Minnie that she didn't want to spend the day with Alicia either.

Minnie could glimpse the relief an hour of sleep would bring. She craved it as she had once craved food.

'Alicia, I know it's a strange request but I don't have anyone else I can trust and I just need an hour's rest. Please, Alicia—I'm going crazy.'

'Minnie, I'm sorry, but I can't just let Tara go with you. We don't know each other very well and she's only fifteen. She has to stay with me. I can give you the names of some nanny services or you could call in a mothercraft nurse. They're a little expensive but they're very good.'

Alicia was adamant. Minnie could sense her impatience as she leafed through a folder and wrote down some names for Minnie to call.

'Oh,' said Minnie. 'Okay, thank you.'

The girl got up and showed Alicia her mobile phone.

'No,' said Alicia.

The girl showed Alicia the phone again.

'Enough,' said Alicia, raising her voice a little. 'Sit down, Tara.'

The girl would not sit down. She took the phone away and furiously typed something and then showed it to Alicia again.

Minnie could feel the tension in the room. Alicia locked eyes with the girl and Minnie could feel a whole conversation going on behind their stares. In the silent argument going on between the two, Kate grizzled her dissatisfaction. Minnie rocked her back and forth in her arms.

And then Alicia broke away from her stepdaughter and sat down at her desk again. She dropped her head into her hands. It seemed to Minnie that she was about to cry. Minnie picked up her large bag and started to back out of the room.

'Fine,' said Alicia. 'Go with her, Tara.'

'Oh, don't worry about it,' said Minnie.

'No,' said Alicia. 'Tara wants to go with you. She wants to get out of here and away from me. She wants to be with anyone except me. Even a complete stranger is preferable. Isn't that right, Tara?'

Tara shrugged. Minnie felt her face colour at having to witness so intimate a domestic scene. The girl, Tara, looked at her and nodded slightly.

She didn't want to take the girl with her now. She had no desire to get in the middle of whatever was going on between Alicia and her stepdaughter. But she had asked and now she was getting what she'd asked for. Minnie felt a small prick of smugness at Alicia's inability to deal with the girl. She wasn't perfect after all.

She knew that she should refuse to take the girl with her now, but it felt like God himself was offering her a solution. She was too tired to think properly.

'In for a penny, in for a pound,' her mother had always said.

'You have my numbers and my address, Alicia. I'll bring Tara back in two hours, I promise.'

Alicia nodded but she said nothing more. She opened the door for them and looked around the waiting room to find the next mother and child.

•

'Do you have much experience with babies?' said Minnie as she and Tara walked to her car.

The girl typed on her phone and held it out. *A lot.*

Minnie could feel the exhaustion of relief creeping into her bones. She knew she should worry about who this young girl was and why she couldn't speak but she was nauseous with fatigue.

'Please, God, just give me an hour,' she prayed.

'Look out for us, Mum,' she thought.

It will be fine, typed Tara.

And Minnie accepted that it would have to be.

The girl could be a complete lunatic for all she knew but Alicia was a nurse and she would have said something if she thought Tara would be a dangerous choice.

'It's not like I'm leaving them alone, Mum,' whispered Minnie as she loaded the pram in the boot.

She could hear Kate working her way up to a howl of protest at being strapped into her car seat.

'Oh, God, what if this is the wrong thing to do?' Minnie thought.

In the car Kate was suddenly quiet.

Minnie opened the driver's door, climbed in and turned around to see why Kate had ceased her crying.

In the back seat the girl was rubbing one finger slowly down Kate's face from the top of her forehead to her chin. Kate's eyes kept closing as she struggled against sleep.

'Shhhh,' said the girl each time she ran her finger down Kate's face. 'Shhh.'

Minnie turned around and started the car.

'It's going to be fine,' she said to the road ahead of her.

•

Minnie carried Kate into the house and Tara followed, carrying the nappy bag.

Minnie felt her face colour at the mess. She gestured around the living room, where crumpled washing lay on the couch and tissues filled a plastic bin. 'I'm sorry about the mess—we've just been so sick,' she said.

The girl shrugged and gave Minnie a blank look.

Minnie felt an immediate rush of alarm. What on earth was she doing trusting Kate to this strange silent child?

Tara took out her mobile phone and Minnie watched her tap at the screen.

I can tidy up and I can hold the baby.

'Kate,' said Minnie. 'Her name is Kate.'

Tara smiled at Kate, who was slumped against Minnie's breast, red-eyed and snivelling.

'Well, she might not . . . I don't know,' said Minnie, regretting ever having asked Alicia to allow Tara to come with her.

Tara stretched her arms towards Kate and to Minnie's surprise the baby allowed herself to be taken. Kate dropped her head onto Tara's shoulder and Minnie watched as Tara began the rocking bounce that she had seen thousands of mothers do, that she had learned to do herself.

She was so grateful she wanted to weep.

'I just need an hour, but there's a bottle in the fridge and if you put it in the microwave for forty seconds she may drink it. Remember to shake it up and if you can get her to go down in her cot it's the bedroom down the hall. If there's anything you need to know just come and wake me, and if she seems to get hot or starts crying or . . .'

Tara took her phone out of her pocket and with one hand typed a message. *I've got her. Go to sleep. I have two little brothers. I know what to do.*

Minnie nodded and stumbled off to her bedroom, where she lay on her bed.

She spiralled instantly into a heavy sleep. In her dreams Kate was snatched from her arms but she could not move or run after her.

She woke up sweating and shaking to find she had been asleep for well over an hour. Her head felt a little clearer.

The house was silent.

She jumped off the bed and ran to the living room. Tara lay on the couch with her eyes closed. Kate lay on top of her clutching her pink blanket. Her sleeping breaths were slow and even but a soft snore was evidence of the cold. Tara's body was completely relaxed. One arm was wound around Kate's body and the other rested on the couch.

'Oh,' said Minnie, and Tara opened her eyes.

She picked up the phone lying on the couch and typed a message. *She fell asleep and I didn't want to move her. Is that okay?*

'Yes,' whispered Minnie. 'It's okay.'

21

'Are you completely insane?' said Max that night at dinner.

Alicia looked at her plate, grateful that the boys had finished their dinner and were watching television. She hated it when Max spoke to her like that. Every time she did something he didn't like he would question her sanity, as though a lack of mental competence was the only reason anyone ever made a decision that he couldn't fathom.

She assumed it was something left over from his first marriage. She assumed and she forgave because his first marriage had been so difficult. His marriage to the certifiably crazy Sasha who cost them thousands every month.

'Am I insane?' wondered Alicia as Max waited for an answer.

The two hours that Tara was gone had been agony for Alicia. One of the mothers had even rebuked her for being distracted, but Alicia barely noticed, consumed as she was by imagining the catastrophes that could occur. She had sent Tara home with a stranger. If she allowed herself to think about it she almost could not believe the level of stupidity, but she couldn't think about it because that would mean admitting that she had just wanted the girl to go away.

Tara had been sitting in the clinic all morning playing games on her mobile phone and occasionally snorting with derision when Alicia gave one of the mothers some advice. All Alicia could feel was Tara's judgement and contempt, and in a place where she was usually in control, usually the expert, admired and needed by the women who came to see her. It had felt like a terrible invasion of the only part of her life that was hers alone. When she had first returned to work after Tara had been released from the hospital she had waited for one of the other clinic sisters to say something, waited for one of the mothers to point at her in recognition, but the clinic had proved a place of safety. The other nurses had kept their questions about Tara to themselves. Meg had touched her on the arm when they crossed paths making tea and said, 'You know we're all here for you should you need us,' but that was all. Alicia had nodded gratefully and got on with her work.

Outside of the clinic it had not been as easy to separate herself from what was happening at home.

When the story was front page news she had tried keeping her sunglasses on and her head down whilst she waited for the boys at pick up time but the other mothers were not likely to let the smallest scandal go without investigation. When Belinda, who barely gave her a glance most of the time, sidled up to her as they waited for the bell to ring she knew she was talking to the anointed one. Belinda had come for information so that she could disseminate it amongst the other curious women.

'We are all so sorry,' she began and Alicia had to bite down on her lip to prevent herself from swearing at the woman with long dark hair and a weird orange tan.

'Oh, thank you,' she had replied instead. 'I am grateful for everyone's support and I do hope that you will understand that this is a private family matter.' What the hell, if all the famous people could say something so ludicrous why couldn't she?

Belinda had swallowed the neatly parcelled phrase and not known where to go from there, so she had simply drifted away to the waiting pack of other vultures. Alicia knew she was guilty of the same behaviour when rumours of failed marriages or bankrupt businesses surfaced but she couldn't indulge anyone with her misery.

She had neglected to return calls from her real friends for a couple of weeks and then she had simply told them they were coping with the situation and changed the subject. She hated the idea that people were looking at her with pity, that they might want to sympathise with her, to take care of her. That was her role—she didn't enjoy having things turned around.

Today it had felt like she was losing the only oasis of peace she had left. Tara could not be alone and for the first time in weeks she and Max could not juggle their schedules. They had both agreed that Tara's hour long excursions to the park were probably good for her but to leave her in the house with no supervision was not possible. Alicia's workplace seemed a better option for Tara.

When Sylvia had seen her come in followed by Tara this morning she had simply raised her eyebrows and Alicia had shrugged to indicate she had little choice in the matter. She had assumed that Tara would sit quietly and page through old magazines until it was time to go but Tara was annoyed at being dragged out of the house. She made her displeasure known with noises and sighs and by tapping her feet and hands on the chair where she sat. She turned the pages of a magazine loudly and she dropped it at her feet when she was done.

As the morning progressed Alicia had felt a hot white anger burning its way through her and she occasionally had to clench her fists to keep herself from actually hitting Tara. She and Max had never struck the children—never.

She should not have let Tara go but she had felt at the time that she was saving herself.

When she wasn't worried about what could happen to Tara she allowed herself a moment of concern for Minnie and Kate. Tara had abandoned a baby somewhere—possibly just left it to die. Was that the sort of person who should be taking care of someone else's child? It was surely morally and legally wrong of her to have sent Tara with Minnie. But she could remember how Tara had been with the boys. Even at eight years old she had seemed instinctively to know how to settle and soothe a baby. Surely she wouldn't hurt Minnie's child?

When Minnie and Tara had returned two hours later she had almost wept with gratitude that everyone was okay.

She had poured herself a large glass of wine when she got home and resolved not to think about the matter again, but Tara had told her father about it.

'She can't communicate but she can still fuck things up for me,' thought Alicia when Max confronted her.

Now she was three glasses of wine into the evening and she knew that Max was waiting for an explanation. She grimaced to herself as she imagined what he would say if she simply said, 'Yes, Max, I am insane—put me in the room next to Sasha's and absolve me of all responsibility.'

Instead she took the sane route. 'Please don't talk to me like that, Max. I felt that there was nothing I could do to stop her. I had to work and I repeatedly told Minnie—my patient—that Tara couldn't help her, but Tara wanted to go.'

At the table Tara was piling her macaroni and cheese into a mountain and smoothing it out again.

'Why on earth would you want to go home with a woman you've never met before?' said Max to Tara.

Tara shrugged.

'Not good enough, Tara,' said Max.

Tara grabbed her phone and typed. *I just wanted some space. She's a nice woman. She needed some rest. She gave me twenty dollars and I said I would help her two afternoons a week. I can walk there.*

Max read the words and handed them to Alicia. The whole conversation felt ludicrous and one-sided.

'You're supposed to be supervised at all times, Tara,' said Max.

She can supervise me, typed Tara.

'Do you really want us to tell this woman that she has to supervise you and why?' said Max.

Tara typed furiously for a minute and handed the phone to Max, who shook his head but didn't hand the phone to Alicia. 'No, Tara, love. I don't hate you. You just have to understand that this is a difficult situation. I can't have you taking care of this child until we've sorted out what happened.'

Tara shrugged and went back to her macaroni mountain.

'When is this going to end, Tara?' said Alicia.

'Jesus, Alicia, do you really think she's going to give you an answer?'

Tara slammed her hand down on the table.

'If you don't want to be treated like you don't have a voice then open your mouth and say something,' said Alicia. The wine flowed through her, pushing her to say things she knew she shouldn't.

Tara shifted her chair back and typed on her phone again.

'She says she going to spend two afternoons a week with this woman until she goes back to school,' said Max.

Alicia looked at her husband but bit her lip and said nothing. He looked drained. Only a few months ago they had been planning a summer holiday riding rollercoasters and sitting on the beach and now they were trapped in this nightmare with doctors and lawyers and the police breathing down their necks.

'If Minnie knew the truth about you she wouldn't want you taking care of her baby,' said Alicia.

'Jesus,' said Max, and dropped his head into his hands.

Tara stared at Alicia open-mouthed.

Alicia topped up her wine. She had no idea who the fuck she was right now. She knew she was going to regret everything she had said in the morning but the words kept spilling from her mouth. 'The poor woman was so desperate for a little sleep that even you, Tara, even you with your sour face seemed like a Godsend. Imagine if I told her that somewhere out in the world is the body of a baby that you gave birth to and killed or left to die some terrible death.'

'Alicia, what the fuck?' yelled Max.

Tara dropped her fork onto her plate and closed her eyes. Then she sniffed and Alicia watched her fingers dance over the screen of the phone.

Tara handed her the phone and Alicia took it, resisting the urge to hurl the thing across the room.

Would you really do that? Tara had typed.

Alicia sighed. She could feel tears pricking her eyes. Alicia felt her rage drain away as suddenly as it had appeared. A sad weariness settled over her as her husband and stepdaughter waited for her to respond.

'No, Tara, I wouldn't really do that—but it is a concern. If you could just tell us where the baby is, if we just knew that it was safe or that it had been stillborn, we could get back to our lives and get on with things. This is killing us—all of us. Have you looked at your father, Tara? Have you really looked at him?'

Max said, 'I'm fine, Tara. Alicia, I think it would be best if you just went to bed now. I'll see to the boys. I don't understand what's going on with you, I really don't. You're not a cruel person. I would never have imagined you even had this in you.'

Alicia let her tears fall and nodded her head. She stood up to get herself away and into her bed before she did any more damage.

Tara pushed the phone into her hand but Alicia batted it away. She didn't want to have to respond to anything else. Tara pushed the phone at her again.

Alicia looked at the screen.

I'm sorry, Alicia. I'm sorry. I want to remember but I can't. I would never, never hurt a baby. I would never hurt my brothers. I'm sorry.

Alicia looked at Tara and noted the tears and for a moment the girl was six years old again and sobbing in her arms after a particularly damaging visit to her mother. Back then Alicia couldn't imagine not loving her wholly and completely. She lifted her hands up and wiped away a tear that had run down Tara's cheek. 'I'm sorry too, Tara. I'm just . . . I'm sorry.'

She leaned forward and kissed the top of Tara's head. And then she went upstairs and left everything to Max, even though she felt guilty about it, even though he was completely worn out and desperate, even though she loved him and she knew that she should have been standing behind him, holding him up, she left everything to Max.

•

In bed the wine sent her mind into overdrive. She had had too much to sleep. She could hear Max getting the boys into bed and the television going on in the living room. Ethan and Michael, with the insight that children sometimes had, didn't even ask where she was.

Alicia lay on her back and stared at the ceiling. Was she insane? Would it be easier to be insane?

The myth of the damaged Sasha loomed over their marriage, casting shadows over everything Alicia did.

Sasha's needs appeared, at times, to supersede everyone else's. It didn't seem possible because she was mostly only a whispered name but it happened. Max would never cease paying the enormous cost for Peace Hills, would never give up on his monthly visits to someone who barely recognised herself in the mirror, would never give up trying to drag Tara down there even though the girl refused month after month.

Alicia had gone with Max once or twice but had been unable to engage in a nonsense conversation with the ravaged Sasha, who insisted there were men trying to rape her in her room at night. Max would hold her hand and tell her about Tara and remind her of the good days they could hold on to. 'Do you remember when you baked that castle cake for Tara when she turned two? Do you remember how she just walked up to it and grabbed pieces with her hands and I was so angry because I knew how hard you'd worked but you just laughed and said, "It's her cake." Do you remember that, Sash?' Alicia had watched Max play with Sasha's fingers and occasionally stroke her hair, only to be greeted by the vacant look of the drugged. Her eyes were green and in pictures from before Alicia had seen how they lit up her face, but now they were dull and vacant.

'Why do you go, Max?' Alicia had asked in the car on the way home.

'I don't have a choice—she's my wife,' said Max. 'I mean my ex-wife. She's Tara's mother. I have to go. I couldn't bear for her never to have a visitor.'

In bed that night Alicia had held him tight so he would stay on top of her even when he wanted to move away from her and into sleep.

'Stay with me,' she whispered.

'I'm not going anywhere,' said Max, and he kissed her again, but Alicia knew there was part of him that would always be gone.

Alicia was not allowed to bring up the money it cost to keep Sasha off the street. Whenever Max and Tara discussed her there was an unspoken agreement that they would not bring up her illness. Instead they focused on craft projects Sasha had devised or days she had spent writing silly plays. They focused on her few perfect moments, polishing them up until they shone with the gloss of a photograph.

Sasha was suffering and because of that Max and Tara would always be suffering as well. Tara's bedroom was filled with happy family photos. Max and Tara and Sasha dressed up to go to a party. Max and Tara and Sasha standing around a perfectly iced pink birthday cake. Sasha holding Tara close and looking at her the way Alicia knew she looked at Ethan and Michael. Max and Tara blowing bubbles on the lawn with their eyes on the photographer.

Max looked so young in the photos. Sasha had his youth.

'But I have him now and for the rest of our lives,' Alicia would comfort herself.

She had been completely against having Sasha come and stay when Tara was six. She had tried to get Max to see it from her point of view, but even before he had picked up his ex-wife from the hospital she had felt her husband distancing himself from her.

Sasha's blonde hair flowed down her back and she was rail thin. She looked like she could float away on a strong breeze.

She thanked Alicia continually for letting her come to stay and she did her best to help with dinner and taking care of the house. Her hands shook and her mouth was always dry. She spent hours in Tara's room and Alicia would pass the closed door and listen to the squeals and giggles and pretend that Tara was simply with a friend.

She had seen the way Max looked at Sasha, seen the longing he still had for her and she had tried not to let it bother her. She had watched Max all the time, hoping that he would look up and catch her eye and then they could smile at each other and know that they were in this thing together. As the days passed Max clung to his side of the bed—afraid to touch her—and he looked through her and past her but not at her and Alicia realised that this would be it. She was grateful that they hadn't had children yet, grateful that she was still young enough to start again. She felt the ache in her heart extend to her throat and she couldn't push food past it. She mentally started to pack her bags.

But then one night she got up to get herself a glass of water and found Sasha cutting up her wedding album.

She hadn't meant to yell but they didn't have copies of the photos and she had been frightened by the weird rocking and singing that Sasha was doing as she gouged out eyes and cut off arms.

Max and Tara had come running and then of course it had all become chaotic.

If Sasha had been stable, if she had stayed on her meds, then Max would never have sought a different life. Would a competent Sasha have known how to deal with Tara, with what Tara had done? Would it have even happened if Sasha was still being a mother to Tara?

Alicia tried to imagine the kind of life she would have had if she had never met Max. If she had just met an ordinary man with no baggage and no child. When things had been good they had been really good, but had they been good enough to keep her here? What would happen to Ethan and Michael if they stayed and Tara was sent to jail?

The press had lost interest in the story for now, but not before they had found Sasha and tried to interview her.

When the story broke through their private lives and onto the news Alicia had been terrified to turn on the television. The first few weeks there had been some sympathy for Tara and for everything she and her family were going through but then the press got bored with feeling sorry for her and went on the attack. Alicia had picked up the paper one morning and seen an old photo of Sasha in some community drama production. Sasha had looked at the camera with a measure of defiance, just daring anyone to judge her or her daughter. The public would have to read the article to find out that Sasha was institutionalised and hadn't seen her daughter for years.

The article talked about how Max was refusing to allow the state to assess Tara and it just went on and on. Alicia had assumed that it would be easier when the rest of the country lost interest in her family tragedy but now that it had happened she sometimes wanted to shout, 'Hello out there, just in case you were wondering, it's all still a horrible mess in here.'

But she had no idea who would listen. They had, as a family, effectively cut themselves off from everyone.

None of Tara's friends had been over to visit, and even though Max had left Tara unsupervised with the computer in the hope that she would at least tell someone the truth, her Facebook account was dormant.

Tara wasn't talking.

She was not the child Alicia had met ten years ago. Not really a child at all now, of course. Alicia could feel Tara pushing her and Max apart with all her might. Max didn't want to face the fact that his daughter might be suffering the same affliction as his first wife. He was determined to see the innocent little girl who had found herself caught up in her mother's mania. He was still paying for leaving her alone with Sasha, for having to go to work. He was paying for asking Tara's mother for a divorce and then getting one granted because Sasha was incompetent. He was paying for having made a new life for himself, and even though he had included Tara in that life he still thought it wasn't enough. Max was so busy feeling guilty about Tara's childhood that he refused to acknowledge the adult she was becoming.

Ten minutes later the door opened and light from the hall sliced into the room.

'Are you awake?' whispered Max.

Alicia thought about keeping quiet. He would go away if she didn't answer and she could deal with all of this tomorrow. But he sounded like Ethan did when he came to wake her to tell her he was feeling sick. 'Are you asleep, Mum?' he would say, standing over her full of hope and fear.

'I'm not asleep, Max.'

Max came into the room and closed the door. 'The boys are in bed. Tara is watching TV but I told her to turn off all the lights.'

'And what did she say?' said Alicia.

Max took a deep breath and then he coughed a little and then a little more and Alicia realised he was laughing. And then she was laughing as well. It was a terrible, sad laughter but they were laughing nonetheless.

Max lay down next to her and ran his hands through her hair. 'I know you're doing your best, Ali. I am sorry I'm being such a prick. I'm sorry but—Jesus, I don't feel like I can keep going through this. Daniel called me this morning to tell me that the police are going to get a court order and have Tara committed. I don't know how to stop them and I don't know what more Daniel can do.'

'Oh God, Max. God, it's all such a fucking mess.'

'It is—and I can't let them put her in a hospital, Ali. I just can't let that happen to her.'

'I know, Max. I understand. But maybe some time away will help. Maybe if she's in a safe place she will feel that she can talk.'

'This is the only safe place for Tara. I have to keep her here with us. I have to keep her home.'

'It doesn't feel very safe anymore. It feels as though we're one step away from complete chaos.'

'I don't think we're one step away, Ali. It feels like we're in the eye of the storm. I think it's all going to get much worse before it gets better and when it does I know I can't do it alone. Please say that you'll hang on to me for a while longer. Please, Ali. I can see that this is all getting too much but I can't lose you. I can't lose the boys. Tell me you'll hang on, Ali. I need to hear you say it.'

'Oh, Max,' said Alicia, grabbing his hand and squeezing. 'I'm not going anywhere.'

Max didn't reply but he covered her body with his and for a short time they lost themselves to the physical sensation of being together.

Afterwards Alicia stroked Max's back, tracing the muscles she knew so well.

'Maybe some time with Minnie will do her the world of good,' she said.

'Who's Minnie?' said Max. He was only moments away from sleep.

'Minnie is the woman she went home with today. The woman with the baby.'

'Oh.'

'Maybe it will be good for her to be around a baby. It might help her to remember.'

'Or it might send her over the edge.'

'At this stage anything could send her over the edge, Max— why not give this a try? It's not like the police are watching her every move.'

'Not yet, anyway.'

'So we're agreed. I'll drop her at the house for a couple of hours twice a week, okay?'

'Yeah, all right. Doesn't this woman know who Tara is, though? I mean, hasn't she seen the story on TV or read about it or something?'

'I think she's having a bit of a hard time adjusting to motherhood. It's her first baby and from what she says she had no idea she was even pregnant. She's a rather large woman. Or she was. She tells me she barely has time to eat these days.'

'Tara doesn't need to be with someone who's not coping with life. She had more than enough of that with Sasha.'

'Minnie is perfectly sane, Max. She's like every other new mother I see. A good night's rest makes the world of difference and Minnie will benefit from a little time to herself, that's all. I wouldn't allow Tara to go home with someone if I had even the slightest concern about her.'

'What if she figures out who Tara is?'

'They haven't shown a picture of her in the media. People associate your face with the story more than anyone else's. It was months ago now. I'm sure if she suspected something she wouldn't want Tara in her house. She doesn't even know my surname. Everyone just calls me Alicia.'

'It seems like an odd thing to do—to ask a complete stranger to take care of your kid.'

'Well, we all do it at one time or another. I never knew anything about Kathy before I found her ad offering babysitting at school and she worked out really well.'

'I can't even remember going out on a Saturday night.'

'Yes, well . . .'

'Yeah.'

•

Tara watched television until she couldn't see straight. She wanted to fall into bed and obliterate the whole evening but when she got upstairs she was wide awake again. She had never heard Alicia say such things before. Her father had called her 'cruel' and the words had felt hateful and sharp but they were also a relief. Her father was always so careful with her. He spoke softly and gently and even when she fucked up he tried to stay calm, like he was a bomb diffuser and she might blow any minute. Like she was her mother.

Now that this thing had happened he danced around it, trying so hard not to say, 'Did you kill your baby?' because that was what everyone wanted to know, wasn't it?

Had she given birth to a living creature and then taken its life or just left it to die?

'Could I have done that?' thought Tara. 'Could I?'

Alicia was the first person to actually say what everyone around her was thinking. Tara had watched her drinking one glass of wine after the other and she had been interested to see what would happen. She knew that Alicia would have wanted her to keep quiet about going to Minnie's house but she had told her dad anyway, even though she knew it was going to mean a heap of shit for Alicia.

'Why did I do that?' she wondered.

At least she knew now for sure how Alicia felt. She wasn't imagining it. It wasn't just hormones or being a teenage girl, it was reality. And it was possible that Alicia had felt that way even before all this stuff happened.

Or maybe not? Maybe this was all just too much for her. It looked like it was too much for her dad. He looked so old and tired. Oh, why couldn't she remember anything?

She walked around her bedroom once and then she started to open her drawers and take out her clothes.

She picked up each item of clothing and then either folded it neatly or tossed it on a growing pile to be thrown away. Some of the stuff just seemed so stupid, so childish. She felt the need to get rid of the clothes right now. She knew that she would probably regret throwing away the tight skirts and small tops that she would one day want to wear to a party, but she couldn't imagine ever going to a party again. The idea of standing with her friends and talking about nothing seemed completely absurd.

Next week she would get to babysit again and right now that was the only thing she could anticipate with any pleasure. She had been so bored sitting in the room with Alicia whilst she droned on and on about babies and tried to calm hysterical mothers.

She had no idea how anyone could discuss poo so much and not laugh themselves sick. And then Minnie and Kate had come in and Tara had felt . . . what? She had felt something. Maybe it was because even though she could see how sick the baby was the little thing had still caught her eye and given her a smile. She was the first person other than Alicia to even acknowledge that Tara was in the room. She had looked into Kate's dark brown eyes and for the first time that day she had actually wanted to hold one of the babies.

She had looked at the mother and wondered how old she was. Did women just keep on having babies? Wasn't there some sort of cut-off date? Minnie looked too old to have a baby, but then all those movie stars kept popping them out. When Minnie had started asking about getting help Tara had felt her fingers move by themselves. She knew that if the woman had any idea who she was there would be no way she would be allowed to be in charge of the baby, but suddenly she desperately needed to hold the child. She had to clamp her arms to her sides so that she didn't open them up for the baby. Of course Alicia said no, but Tara knew how hard she was finding it to have her in the room. Alicia was pretending Tara wasn't there but Tara could see from her scowl and the way she spoke to the patients that she knew she was being watched. It wasn't Tara's fault. She'd asked Alicia to let her stay home. She let her go to the park alone, didn't she? So Tara had typed it in capitals: *LET ME GO WITH HER*. She could see that she was wearing Alicia down. That's mostly what she counted on, even before the whole baby thing. Alicia and her father got tired of arguing a lot quicker than she did.

In the car next to the baby she had felt a small jolt of triumph at doing something she wasn't supposed to be doing, and then when Minnie had finally left her alone with Kate she had walked up and down with her because she didn't seem to want her to sit. Finally she had stopped by the window and looked out onto the street and she had felt her body begin to sway in the way she had seen other mothers sometimes move when they were holding babies. She had felt Kate relax and get heavier and heavier. Her little head had dropped onto Tara's shoulder and she had heard the deep breathing of sleep but she had kept moving because she loved the way the baby felt in her arms. Kate smelled sweet and a little sweaty. Tara had finally sat down still holding her, even though Minnie had said she could put her down in the cot when she was asleep. In Minnie's house holding her baby Tara had felt an amazing sense of peace—like she was exactly where she was supposed to be. And she was going back to Minnie's to see Kate again, no matter who tried to stop her.

22

Minnie kept jumping up to look out of the window every time she heard a car go past. Alicia was dropping Tara over for two whole hours. She wasn't sure what time Tara's school got out but Alicia had said that three would be a good time for Tara to come over.

Minnie knew that Alicia would want to come in and spend some time first. She had cleaned the house all morning, singing and talking to Kate as she did. She'd baked a sponge cake and put out her mother's best china teacups. 'It's for a good cause, Mum, and I know you like to see them used, don't you?'

After her shower she had stood in front of the mirror in her bedroom and tried to find something to wear. The woman in the mirror was shrunken inside her large folds of skin. Minnie hated looking at herself even more now than she had when the hanging skin was filled with fat. Her face sagged as well. All these years she had imagined that the key to true happiness was losing the weight. In her dreams there had been admiring glances and men who wanted her attention. She would imagine herself travelling the world and blending in with crowds in Europe.

'I guess I left it too late, Mum.' She forced her eyes away from the disappointment in the mirror and reached to the back of her closet to find a dress she had bought many years ago after an ill-conceived liquid diet. The weight had crept back on the moment she went back to solid food but Minnie had enjoyed a couple of months of feeling less noticeably gigantic. The dress was made of a soft rust-coloured material and it hid all the things it needed to hide.

She was surprised to find that the dress fit her so well and was even a little loose. Her clothes were all much too big for her now. She wasn't consciously trying to lose weight; she was just trying to get through her days with work and a baby. She considered giving up work every now and again but she could see a time in the future when Kate would go to school and then she would have nothing to do with her days. She understood that Kate was everything to her. And right now she was everything to Kate. But the love she felt for the child was scary and overwhelming. She could not imagine ever being parted from her but she knew that babies grew up and children didn't need you quite as much and young adults just resented their parents.

She could imagine being one of those mothers who helped out in the classroom and was the first one at the school gate and the last one to let go when her teenage daughter chafed at her. And there was also the thing she didn't want to think about: the truth about Kate and the terrible sin she had committed and what would happen if the world came knocking at her door.

Some nights the thought caught her off guard and she would vow to end her life if Kate was no longer in it. It seemed the simplest solution. But at other times, when the sun filtered through the living room window, she understood that she would miss the beauty of the world and so she tried to retain some things from her old life so that she could go back to them. If she was allowed to go back to them.

'I'm not going to think about all that now, Mum. I can hear Kate waking up and it's nearly time for Tara to arrive. She's a lovely girl—I'm sure you'd like her and Kate seems to love her. We were so lucky to find her.'

She had planned to work while Tara was babysitting Kate. She wasn't ready to leave the house with Tara in charge but she would take her laptop and her mobile into her bedroom and pretend to be away and that would have to be good enough.

Finally she heard a car stop outside and footsteps approaching the front door.

Minnie opened the door before Alicia could ring the bell.

'Come in, come in, Alicia. Hello, Tara. Please sit down. Did you want some tea? I've just boiled the kettle. And would you like some cake? I made a sponge—a recipe from my mother. I make it with a touch of lemon.'

Minnie watched Alicia look around the room and take everything in. All Kate's toys were neatly in the pink toy box and the washing was hidden in the laundry. All the surfaces gleamed and there were fresh flowers in a vase on the dining table. Mothers were a little like the canary down the mine: they were the first to spot potential danger. Minnie could see Alicia checking things off in her head and then she breathed out and smiled at Minnie, and Minnie felt her own exhalation of relief. She had passed.

'Please, Minnie, don't worry about it. I just came to drop Tara off and then I'm going to run a few errands. Your home is lovely. I can see that Kate has really taken over.'

Minnie smiled and looked around the room. On the mat Kate was trying to catch her feet. There was a highchair in the corner for when Kate was ready to use it.

'I guess she has. I put things away at night but then somehow everything gets used during the day.'

'Oh, I remember that stage of things. You're doing such a wonderful job with her. I hope Tara can be of help.'

'Oh, she is,' said Minnie. Tara had already got onto her knees next to Kate and was helping Kate to grab her foot. 'It was such a relief last week to have her. She just walked Kate up and down for the whole hour. I got some sleep so I was able to deal with

Kate that night. I was so grateful to have her, Alicia. I really was.'

'Yes, she's wonderful with kids. She's always helped with her half . . . with her brothers.'

'Are you sure you won't stay for tea?'

'Oh no, really, I must get on with my errands. Um, you know that Tara . . . well, she's still not talking.'

'Oh, the poor dear. I didn't think she would still be ill.'

'She's not ill. I wouldn't have let her come if she was. She's just . . . look, it's complicated but she doesn't talk at the moment. We've had some—she's had some emotional issues and . . .'

Minnie waited for Alicia to say something else, to explain why Tara didn't speak, but Alicia seemed to have run out of words. She stood next to Minnie, watching Tara play with Kate. Minnie could see Tara concentrating hard on pointing out shapes to Kate.

Minnie had not known that the girl would still not be talking. She had assumed it was an illness that would be over, but if the girl was—what did they call it, selectively mute?—then what did that mean for her ability to take care of Kate? Babies needed to be talked to. Kate was reaching for Tara's face and she was smiling. Surely an hour or two wouldn't hurt and she did have so much to do . . .

'Maybe this was a bad idea,' said Alicia.

Minnie saw her much-needed time slipping away. 'I'm sure everything will be just fine. Kate doesn't mind if she speaks or not, do you, Kate?'

'Bah,' said Kate.

'Yes, but Minnie, I don't want to mislead you—Tara is just . . .'

Minnie saw Tara shoot her stepmother a look that clearly meant 'shut up'.

'Alicia, I'm sure you wouldn't have brought her over now or let her come with me last week if you didn't think I could trust her with Kate.'

Tara nodded at Minnie.

'Oh God, of course not, Minnie. I would never put Kate in danger. Tara is an excellent babysitter. She's just . . .'

'I understand. Right now she doesn't speak and that's okay with me. We all have our bad times, don't we?' Minnie hoped that she sounded confident. She had never met a person who chose to be silent, but perhaps it was the girl's way of dealing with life. She could have chosen to eat or take drugs or something. Minnie was aware that she was hardly in a position to judge anyone for their strange behaviour.

'Yes, I suppose we do.'

'I know about those difficult teenage years, Alicia. I remember them very well. Now, I don't want you to worry about her. We'll get along just fine, won't we, Tara?'

Tara looked up at Minnie and Alicia and smiled. Minnie could feel the warmth behind the smile. Alicia seemed a little taken aback to see it.

'I'll be back in two hours, then,' said Alicia.

Minnie walked her to the door and then watched her sit in her car for a minute staring into space before driving off.

She closed the door and resolved to think well of Tara until Tara proved her wrong.

'People in glass houses shouldn't throw stones,' her mother always said.

'Would you like something to eat or drink, Tara? A cup of tea and a piece of cake, perhaps?'

Tara nodded yes to both and Minnie went into the kitchen to put some things on a tray.

'What do you think, Mum?' she whispered. 'Can I trust her with Kate?'

Minnie's mobile rang and she picked it up to find a panicked Mr Peterson on the line. He had lost his tax records. Minnie had never met Mr Peterson in person. Everything had been done by phone and email. At first he had wanted to meet her but she had pleaded a broken leg and then by the time the leg was supposed to have healed she had proved herself capable and he never suggested meeting her again. Mr Peterson had a high squeaky voice and Minnie imagined him as short and bald with a rounded stomach and stooped shoulders. He ran a small company but seemed to be perpetually in crisis mode.

Minnie went into the living room and pointed to the phone. Mr Peterson's squeaky voice was loud enough for Tara to hear.

Tara nodded and got up and went into the kitchen. When she came out with a cup of tea and a piece of cake, Minnie watched her look around for somewhere to balance the cup and plate.

'Not near Kate,' thought Minnie but she didn't say anything. Tara found a space on the mantle and then stood far away from Kate watching the baby whilst she sipped the hot tea.

Minnie smiled. 'Don't worry, Mr Peterson—we'll sort it out.'

'Time to get this show on the road,' she thought.

She waved at Tara and went into her bedroom. There was work to be done and Kate was in good hands. God and Mum would watch over both of them.

23

Tara lay next to Kate on the rug batting at toys with her. Kate was a beautiful baby. She had dark eyes and the beginnings of blonde curls. She did not need Tara to talk. When Alicia had told Minnie that she didn't speak, that she chose not to speak, she had seen Minnie's face and readied herself to stand up and leave. She wouldn't have blamed Minnie. Who would want a crazy person taking care of their child? Because that's what she was, wasn't she? She was crazy. People called you crazy when they couldn't understand the choices you made. When Tara was eight years old she had been singled out for having a crazy mother. She had never mentioned her real mother, preferring to let everyone think that she belonged to Alicia, but parents had a habit of talking in front of their children. Even now Alicia and her father would say things without realising that Ethan and Michael were in the room. Children heard everything and a boy in Tara's class had arrived at school one day armed with the knowledge that Tara's mother was crazy.

At lunchtime she was waiting in the line for her chance at the skipping rope when Vincent had sidled up to her and announced, 'My mum says your mum's got something wrong with her brain.'

Tara had stared at him for a moment, taking in his black-framed glasses and rabbit-like front teeth.

'Go away, boys can't skip,' she said.

'My mum says that your mum is crazy and that she lives in a place with other crazy people.'

By this time the others had stopped skipping and were observing the exchange with interest.

'Go away,' said Tara again, and she turned to find Emma and Jody watching her. She was hoping for backup. She was hoping that someone would step forward and push stupid Vincent to the ground so that he would fall on his stupid butt. But no one said anything. Emma and Jody seemed frozen in place as the secret that they themselves had known for a while was spewed out in the playground.

Tara felt her ears burn and the threat of tears.

'Crazy mum, crazy mum, crazy mum,' said Vincent, hopping up and down on one leg like a demented creature.

Tara had reached out and pushed with all her might. Vincent had fallen to the ground and his glasses had cracked on the asphalt.

'Aah,' screeched Vincent. 'You're crazy too.' And then the teachers had come running.

Alicia arrived an hour later looking harassed and Tara would not tell her why she had pushed Vincent.

Vincent had hurt his wrist when he fell and proudly displayed a thin fiberglass cast for a few weeks. Emma and Jody had compensated for not supporting her by being extra nice and always giving her the first turn at the skipping rope. Alicia and Max had held whispered conversations for a few days, casting sidelong glances at Tara.

After that Tara started telling her father she didn't want to go and visit her mother. Some months she would drop to the floor at the front door and refuse to get in the car. Some months she pretended she was sick. Her father would reason and plead with her but she would cross her arms and refuse to listen.

'Leave her with me, Max,' Alicia would say and Tara would love her then for rescuing her from her crazy mother.

'And look at me now,' thought Tara. 'I'm proving what everyone has always suspected—I'm as crazy as my mother.'

Minnie could have told her to go but Tara had seen something cross her features as Alicia talked. There was a tilt to her head and a set to her mouth that seemed to acknowledge that there could be crap days when you had to choose a way to get through the pain. Minnie's face told Tara she knew something about suffering.

She was so grateful that she was still allowed to babysit Kate. Being with Kate felt right. She wanted to hold the baby tight and kiss her soft skin.

Outside the sun was bright and Tara wished she could take her for a walk to the park but she knew she would have to earn Minnie's trust first. 'And how would I ask, anyway?' she thought ruefully.

She picked Kate up and took her over to the window to show her the garden.

'Oooh,' said Kate.

'Oooh,' whispered Tara close to her perfect little ear. She felt her breath catch as the soft, husky sound came from between her own parted lips.

'Oooh,' said Kate again.

'Oooh,' said Tara feeling the sound come from somewhere deep inside herself.

Kate touched her face and smiled. Tara felt like she was being congratulated.

'Oooh,' she said again and she felt a small giggle make its way up from Kate's stomach.

Together they looked out at the garden and giggled at their ability to make sound.

Summer

24

'I don't know, Tara,' said Minnie. 'Perhaps you should just come with me and walk Kate around the city in the pram?'

Tara shrugged. Minnie kept talking to her like she would open her mouth any minute and say something, but Tara had learned early on that Minnie was quite happy talking to people who never replied.

'Yes, I know, the city is not really a place for a baby—but are you sure you'll be all right here with her? I've never left you alone with her before, not really. I mean I'm always in the other room, aren't I?'

Tara watched Kate grasp the coffee table and pull herself up to stand. It was her new trick and Tara clapped and praised her for it when they were alone.

She wanted to tell Minnie to watch her daughter but Minnie was pacing the room muttering, and Tara knew that meant she was either praying or talking to her mother.

She had noticed Minnie's habit of talking to her mother the third time she had babysat Kate. Minnie had been in the kitchen making tea when Tara heard her ask, 'So do you think I should tell him about the missing money, Mum? I don't want to get anyone into trouble but I am the bookkeeper and I need to tell him what I've found.'

Tara hadn't heard the doorbell ring or anyone come into the house. She knew Minnie lived alone with Kate because there were only two bedrooms.

She checked Kate's position on the mat and then got up quietly and went to the kitchen to see Minnie's mother. At the door she glanced quickly around the small room and then focused on Minnie's back.

'I suppose it is my job, Mum, isn't it?' said Minnie.

Tara looked around the room again and she even glanced under the small round wooden table in the centre.

'Oh,' said Minnie, flushing and smiling slightly. 'I was just, you know . . . I lost my mum some time ago and, well, you get used to people being around, don't you?'

Tara felt a flash of panic. Was Minnie like Sasha?

'I know she's not here, but people are never really gone, are they? I still feel her here. She lived here her whole life so I know she's still here.'

Tara had nodded and smiled. Lots of people talked to the dead.

Minnie talked to her mother and she prayed. She didn't preach at Tara or anyone else; as far as Tara could see her mother and God were just part of the family. Lots of people talked to God. Talking to the black angel made you crazy but talking to God and your dead mother made you . . . eccentric.

Neither Minnie's dead mother nor God told her to cut up photo albums and stab people.

Tara didn't find Minnie strange anymore even though she looked a little crazy in her giant clothes. Minnie seemed a little thinner every time Tara saw her. She claimed not to have time to eat and Tara thought that was just bullshit, but she was always starving when she got home from babysitting Kate. For such a small person she took up an enormous amount of time and energy.

Even Minnie's shoes were too big for her. At home she walked around in a pair of stretched blue canvas flats that made her look like a child trying on her mother's shoes. Tara wanted to laugh at the way she looked in those shoes but found the image comforting somehow.

Today Minnie was wearing old-lady heels and the same brown dress she had worn the first time Tara babysat. It was probably the only thing she had that still fit her smaller body. Tara wanted to take her shopping and get her hair done but Minnie wasn't her mother or part of her family.

'Oh God,' whispered Minnie. 'Please tell me what to do.'

Tara had tried praying. In her bedroom at night when the house was silent she pulled the covers over her head and asked God to help her. She whispered into the darkness, hoping that God would take pity on her and give her the answers everyone was looking for. She could whisper to God. She could barely hear the sound she made but she knew her lips were moving.

Kate didn't care if she spoke or not and Tara was willing to bet that God didn't care either. She prayed with her hands held tightly together and she begged and begged for the memory to return, but the idea of the lost baby was still just a bunch of words everyone kept repeating. Some days Tara thought they might have made it all up, that they might be trying to drive her completely insane. That they wanted her to be like her mother.

Tara felt a small tug inside herself and knew it to be a longing for Sasha. She shook her head and went over to sit down next to Kate on the floor. She worked hard to avoid thinking about her mother as anything except the lunatic who had lunged at her father with a pair of scissors, but memories had a way of rising out of the darkness and pulling you in. Still, the idea of a mother who would worry over her and protect her was sometimes so sweet she could taste it on her tongue. 'What would it be like to be loved like that?' she sometimes wondered as she watched Alicia grab Ethan on his way through the kitchen and plant a kiss on the back of his neck despite his wriggling protest.

She waited while Minnie twisted her hands together and whispered to the unseen presence in the room and she drifted into a memory of her mother on the good days.

She could smell the scent of vanilla that greeted her when she opened her eyes and knew that today was a day for the good mummy. She would run downstairs and find the kitchen filled with treats. Her mother would have been up for hours already. 'Good morning, sleepyhead,' she would say, even though the sun had barely made its way over the horizon.

And then there would be pancakes for breakfast and collage-making and painting and more baking. But at some point during the day her mother would begin her pacing— usually when it was nearly time for dinner, and Tara knew it had to do with her father coming home. Another adult was a threat. Children could inhabit a make-believe world along with you but another adult would stand at the kitchen door the way Tara's father did and shake his head at the sight of three cakes and plates and plates of pink-frosted cupcakes.

Sasha would pace back and forth and talk to the unseen presence. She would whisper and giggle and Tara could remember feeling excluded from the conversation and angry about that exclusion. She never told her father about the whispering because she had no idea it was significant. Only after Sasha had come to stay and had cut up the wedding album, blaming the black angel, had Tara remembered about the whispering. It was never clear to Tara who her mother was talking to.

She loved the activity, loved licking the bowl and helping pour the cake. She would watch in awe as intricate doll houses appeared from random junk as if by magic.

There would be times when her little hands frustrated her mother. She would break something or spill something and then there would be agonised screaming and more muttering.

Tara would find a space in the kitchen and wait for her mother to notice her and include her again. She would wait for her mother to come back to her. She longed for the arrival of her father in those moments, understanding that he would make the world safe again.

By the time he arrived home the conversation would be over. Her mother would become stiff and careful, protecting the voices in her head from another adult. 'We've had a lovely day, haven't we, Tarakins, just lovely,' her mother would say and Tara would nod enthusiastically, pushing the fraught moments out of her mind.

Even at four Tara knew she had to protect her mother from her father.

'He wants to take me away, my little bird. He wants to steal me away from our nest.'

Tara closed her eyes and breathed away the memory. Minnie's muttering didn't bother her as much.

She knew that if she just opened her mouth and told Minnie that she and Kate would be fine Minnie would feel a lot better, but the secret of her returning voice was something Tara was not ready to share. Only Kate heard her speak. When Minnie was home she always worked with the door closed and Tara would whisper songs and stories to Kate, who would watch her with her deep dark eyes. Kate didn't care if she talked or not. Kate held out her fat little arms when Tara arrived on her babysitting afternoons and smiled her gummy smile.

Tara watched Minnie for a few more minutes then pulled out her phone and typed. *We'll be fine. I'll take her for a walk and then give her a bottle and then put her down to sleep. I'll have my mobile so I can text Alicia if I have a problem. She can be here in five minutes. I won't let anything happen to her. I love her too!!!!!*

Minnie read the message and nodded. 'I guess I have to leave her some time, don't I? You know I wouldn't if I didn't absolutely have to, but Mr Chalmers needs me to come in just for a short time so I can understand the business better.'

Tara nodded. Minnie talked about Mr Chalmers like he might explode if she didn't do exactly as he asked. She was terrified to tell him 'no'. Minnie's clients were a bunch of schoolchildren who needed her to keep them in line. She indulged them and protected them.

Tara showed Minnie the phone again and Minnie nodded and went to find her bag.

'Right,' said Minnie, standing at the front door, 'let's get this show on the road.' Tara smiled. Minnie was forever getting 'the show on the road'.

Once she had watched Minnie pull out of the driveway, holding Kate up to the window and making her wave goodbye, Tara breathed deeply and relaxed.

'Now, my little Katie,' she said, 'what about a walk?' She coughed because she had only ever spoken to Kate in soft whispers. Her voice sounded strange to her.

A voice was how you told the world you were there. Tara felt her body click into focus when the words rushed out of her mouth. 'Here I am,' she thought.

'Here I am, Kate. Here is Tara. My name is Tara and you are Kate and I have not been allowed to speak for such a long time.'

Kate flapped her arms like a bird and said, 'Ba, ba, ba, baa.'

'Exactly,' said Tara.

•

Out in the sunshine Tara made sure the pram was facing the right way to keep Kate's face and arms from being burned. She pushed the pram along the sidewalk in silence. No one except Kate was allowed to hear her speak. She knew the time was coming when she would have to say something to her father and Alicia, but for now it felt like her silence was the only thing she could control.

Soon it would be time to go back to school. She should have gone back already but Dr Adams had suggested some more time off. She had missed the last two terms of the school year but her father was convinced she would be ready for year eleven after the summer holidays. 'You're not going to get put back a year,' he told Tara after she had listened to him argue with her principal about Tara repeating Year Ten. Tara was worried about catching up on maths and science but she had started doing some of the work that was being emailed to her. Alicia and her father looked pleased every time they came upon her working.

Dr Adams also suggested a speech therapist so she could learn to speak the same way she had done as a baby and Tara had laughed at that.

'A smile and a laugh,' said Dr Adams. 'Progress, I think.'

Tara meditated with Dr Adams and together they searched for the missing hours and her missing voice. There were moments when her body felt light enough to float over the black wall and find the answer but she never quite got there. She would feel herself falling back down to earth and her eyes would fly open.

'Perhaps you do not want to know the answer,' Dr Adams had said last week, but she had said it kindly. It was not an accusation, merely an observation. Tara had nodded and found herself reaching for the ever-present box of tissues.

'We'll get there, Tara, I promise.'

She had started replying to the messages her friends sent on Facebook. The first time she posted something there had been a flood of messages in return, mostly words of support. Emma had not sent a message until Tara had privately sent her one word: *Sorry*. She couldn't think of anything else to say.

The language of the internet was easy. She didn't have to say anything. An emoticon was enough to let them know she thought something was funny or sad. No one asked any questions except *When are u coming bk 2 school?*

Dnt know, she had posted.

She felt like she'd been checked out for months and had finally returned. Kate was dragging her back into the world. She had no idea why but she was. She felt happiest when she was with Kate.

The houses they passed all had neat gardens full of summer flowers. The scent of jasmine hung heavy in the air. It was going to be one of those scorching summers where television presenters lectured about sun safety and air conditioning. A light haze seemed to hang permanently over the city from all the frantic back-burning that was taking place.

At the end of the block someone had knocked down one of the small houses and crammed a massive one onto the land. Minnie's friend June called it an eyesore. Tara liked the fountain out the front where water spilled over glass stones. She knew Kate would like to look at the fountain too. The smallest things fascinated Kate. When Tara whispered 'Incy, Wincy Spider' to her and made the spider go up the drainpipe with her hands Kate would watch attentively.

'T-T-Tara?'

Tara yelped in shock. Liam was standing right in front of her.

'Wh-wh-what are you d-doing here?'

Tara pointed to Kate.

'Whose b-b-baby is that?'

Tara almost smiled at how panicked Liam looked. She hadn't seen him for a few weeks. Alicia didn't let her go out to the park anymore. Tara had tried pushing her father to let her have more freedom but it was difficult to argue in writing.

'I agree with Ali, Tara. We agreed that you would not be allowed out unsupervised. If the police caught us I have no idea what would happen. But you know you can change all this if you want to.' Tara understood her father was pushing her. Taking away the park was the first step. She didn't want to think about what was next.

Tara had stomped off to her room and let Liam know that she would no longer be able to meet him. Anyway, he didn't like the way she kept telling him to try to get his grades up and she was getting tired of hearing about Brent's plans to steal some lesbian woman's money. And if it came down to choosing between seeing Liam and seeing Kate, there was no contest. Kate dragged her forward, while it felt like Liam wanted to drag her back to who she had been before. He only wanted to talk about their time in the park. Tara knew what he wanted and she couldn't even think of giving in to him. It would just not be possible.

Tara pointed vaguely down the road. She took out her phone and typed. *I babysit her. What are you doing here?*

Liam turned and pointed to the only house in the street not surrounded by a well-kept garden. An old couch was on the front lawn, and sitting on the couch was Brent with his hands around a can of beer and a crooked smile on his face.

Tara felt her heart slow. This was where Brent lived? This was the road that held the house Brent was planning to rob? She looked around trying to identify where a lesbian might live. Liam said the woman had a child but the only one young enough to have a baby was . . . 'Oh God,' she thought.

This was only the second time she had been allowed to take Kate out for a walk. The first time Minnie had tagged along behind them talking on her mobile phone and they had gone the other way. But today she had wanted to show Kate the fountain in the front garden of the big house.

Now she wished desperately that she had gone in the other direction. The urge to turn and run was overwhelming.

'C-come and s-say hello,' said Liam.

Tara shook her head and started to turn the pram around.

Liam put his hand on her arm. 'Please.'

Tara shook her head again.

Liam didn't let go of her arm. 'J-just . . . just hello, T.'

Tara sighed and walked towards the house.

'Hey, Tara,' said Brent. Leo and Callum nodded in her direction.

'Come inside, Tara,' said Brent. 'Come and see our palace.'

Callum and Leo laughed like idiots.

Tara shook her head and pointed at the pram.

'What?' said Brent. 'Sorry, Tara, I can't hear you. What did you say?' And then he laughed. 'Hey, I'm just fucking with you. Come inside and have a drink. Get the fuck up, Leo, and help her with the pram.'

'I c-can do it,' said Liam.

Tara started to shake her head again but Liam was already working out how to lift the pram. Brent kept his gaze on her and slowly moved his eyes up and down her body. Even in a loose T-shirt and jeans Tara felt exposed. Her face burned and she could feel his hand on her breast again. His grin widened and she felt like he had read her mind.

She knew she needed to turn and walk away. She put her hand on Liam's arm and shook her head again but he was lifting up the pram and carrying it over the cracked front step into the yard.

Kate lay wide-eyed in the pram as Liam and Leo lifted it up the steps into the house. Tara followed, her palms beginning to sweat. She was placing herself in a dangerous position by entering the house and she wasn't alone—she had Kate.

Inside she sat gingerly on the couch and held the can of Coke that Brent had opened for her. The walls were tinged yellow and the carpet was covered in stains. Brent and Leo and Callum were living just the way she'd thought they would, surrounded by filth and chaos. She felt her stomach turn a little at the thought of how dirty the house was. She needed to get Kate outside.

Brent sat down on a peeling fake-leather recliner opposite her and opened another beer for himself. When he had handed her the Coke he had brushed her breast with his hand as he stepped back and Tara had felt her heart rate speed up. Now his eyes never left her.

'So, is that the baby everyone's been looking for?' he said.

Tara shook her head and Liam said, 'T-T is just b-b-babysitting.'

'Just b-b-babysitting, is she?' said Brent.

Tara nodded.

'Is it for the fat dyke down the road?'

Tara shook her head. 'No, no, no,' she thought. 'It can't be.'

Brent took a long swallow of his beer.

Tara felt the urge to run. She stood up.

'Sit the fuck down,' said Brent, but he said it with a smile on his face. Tara felt herself sit. Even Liam, who had been standing up, dropped back down to the floor.

'You know what I think?' said Brent.

Tara stared at him. He didn't want an answer; he just wanted an audience.

'I think it *is* that dyke's kid,' said Brent. 'I recognise the pram. I've seen her pushing it. We've seen her pushing it, haven't we, Liam?'

Liam nodded but he didn't look at Tara.

She rose again to leave, but Brent stood up too and pushed her back down onto the couch. She spilled some of the Coke on her jeans and he leaned forward to brush some of the liquid away. His hand made contact with her breast again.

Tara looked over at Liam, who was busying himself with a cigarette. His stupid pretence that he had seen nothing made her sick. His weakness was nothing new but it crystallised something for her. If the baby that everyone was talking about did exist, then it was better off with someone else or dead. Liam would have made a crap father.

All this time she had tried to think of Liam as a sensitive soul who was overwhelmed with love for her, but seeing how he pretended not to notice Brent touching her made her want to spit at him. Leo and Callum also found other things to do with their eyes and Tara felt the knowledge that they would do nothing to help her creeping over her skin.

She was in jeopardy, which meant Kate was in jeopardy. Tara couldn't stand the thought.

She wanted to scream and run, but she knew she couldn't get Kate out of the house quickly. Brent was just playing with her. She would have to ride it out and then she would tell Minnie . . . What would she tell Minnie?

If Minnie knew she had been stupid enough to allow herself to get into a situation like this there was no way she would ever allow her to see Kate again. And that would break her heart.

'She's a cute kid,' said Brent, leaning over the pram, where Kate was sucking her fist.

Tara stood up again. This time she planted her feet wide and braced her body. She didn't want him anywhere near Kate.

'Sit down,' said Brent.

Tara felt a flash of real fear. The words were a command. But she didn't sit down. She stood and waited. She looked around the room, trying to work out exactly how she was going to get Kate and her pram out of the house. If she grabbed her and ran she could just leave the pram. Prams could be replaced.

Brent leaned into the pram and undid Kate's safety buckles. Tara felt her skin crawl at the thought of him touching Kate. She stepped forward to stop him and he looked at her with his cold blue eyes and she stopped. She understood his look was a warning.

'It's okay, little baby,' he said. 'Uncle Brent's here. You like Uncle Brent, don't you?'

Kate smiled and kicked her legs.

'She's a real cute kid, Tara,' said Brent. 'Real cute.'

And then with one movement he grabbed Kate by her ankles and swung her out of the pram, holding her upside down. Kate screamed and kept screaming.

'Jesus, Brent,' said Leo. 'That's not how you hold a kid, you fucken idiot.'

Still holding the screaming baby, Brent rounded on Leo. 'I know how the fuck to hold a baby, you stupid cunt.' He swung Kate back and forth a little. Her face was blood-red. Tara wanted to vomit.

'Now, listen here, Miss High and Fucking Mighty Tara. You're going to help us get into that dyke's house. You're going to do whatever I tell you or I swear to fuck I will cut this kid up and then I'll cut you up too.'

Tara went rigid with fright. Her arms were open to Kate, whose screams were drilling through her head.

Liam stood up but one look from Brent made him sit down again. The room was enveloped in a tight, greasy feeling. Round and round went Tara's stomach.

'Do you fucking get me, Tara? Do you understand?' said Brent.

Tara nodded and opened her arms wider. She stepped towards Brent. She opened her mouth intending to scream, intending to roar, but all that came out was a hiss. A long strange hiss.

Brent laughed and took a step back with the screaming baby.

'Someone's going to hear that kid,' said Callum.

Brent lifted Kate up and down by her feet and then he flipped her upright and held her in his arms. 'Shhhh, little baby,' he said.

Kate continued to cry. Her body was stiff and her face was an alarming, burning red.

'Jesus, what a lot of fucking noise,' said Brent, and he pushed Kate into Tara's arms.

Tara held her tight and then began bouncing her up and down to try to quiet her. Her cries subsided a little, though she kept grizzling. Tara turned towards the door.

'You're not fucking going anywhere,' said Brent.

'B-B-Brent, let . . . let . . . let her . . . go,' said Liam.

'Shut up, spaz,' said Brent. He sat down on the recliner and lit a cigarette. 'We need keys to the back door, Tara, and you're going to help us get them,' he said.

Tara bounced Kate up and down. She didn't look at Brent or Liam. She looked at the floor. Her head was filled with a ringing that sounded like the fire alarm at school.

In her pocket the keys Minnie had given her grew heavy and burned her skin.

'Don't let him know,' she thought but she shifted her head just a little and even though afterwards she was absolutely sure she had given nothing away, Brent leapt off his chair and came towards her. She started to back away but he grabbed her arm and jammed his hand roughly into her pocket.

'Well, just look what we have here,' he laughed. 'Stupid bitch. You think you're so much fucking smarter than everyone else. I told Liam you were a waste of space.'

Tara looked up and met Liam's eyes but he just shook his head.

Everyone in the room was silent. Kate was quiet now, safe in Tara's arms. Tara could hear her breathing; she could feel the little shudders through the baby's body as she recovered from something she wouldn't remember a minute from now.

'I think you're going to have to visit with us for a little while, T,' said Brent. 'What time will the dyke be back?'

Tara shrugged.

'Give me some sort of answer, Tara, or I swear to fuck you'll be sorry. One hour? Two hours? How long will she be?'

Tara held up one finger.

'That should be enough time. We have to get some copies of these keys quick-smart and then it's all over and you don't have to do another thing. How lucky are you?'

Tara bounced Kate and stared at the wall. Callum and Leo were perched on the sofa, waiting to see what would happen.

Once Tara had watched a program about what to do if you were attacked by a man. The presenter demonstrated a whole lot of self-defence moves and talked about the power of screaming. When a member of the audience asked about being attacked by a group of people, the presenter had said, 'Then just do what an animal would do in that situation—play dead.'

Tara couldn't move because she was holding Kate, she couldn't fight because she had to protect the baby. She couldn't just run because they would stop her and she couldn't scream. So she chose to play dead.

She didn't look around and she didn't think. So she let her mind clear and her body go numb and she waited for it to be over.

'We need to get this done now,' said Brent. 'How long will it take?'

'I can drive up to the shopping centre and get it done in a few minutes,' said Callum.

'I'll . . . I'll . . . I'll go,' said Liam.

Tara looked at his crumpled face. He didn't want to be there. He didn't want to watch what they did to her or try to protect her. Tara hated him anew.

'You can't even tell the bloke what we want,' said Leo.

'F-F-Fuck . . . you,' said Liam.

'Ah, just shut it, you wankers. Callum, you drive and send Liam in.'

'But he—'

'I didn't fucken invite an argument, just go. Sit down, Tara. It's going to be a long wait. Don't make it feel any longer.'

Tara sat down on the disgusting couch. She looked in the baby bag that Minnie always kept packed for some water and a rusk for Kate.

When Liam and Callum had left Brent opened another can of beer.

'Why did you send the retard?' said Leo.

'Dumb fuck. If we get caught—and I'm only saying if—the retard is our insurance policy. Anyone tries to figure out how we got the keys, who do we want the bloke in the centre to remember?'

Leo laughed and opened up a beer for himself.

Then there was only silence and the sound of swallowing.

'You and I could have a little fun while we wait, T,' said Brent.

Tara studied the top of Kate's head.

'We could all have some fun,' said Leo.

'Come on, T, what do you say? I promise you'll enjoy it.'

Tara would not look at Brent, would not meet his eye. If she didn't look at him then she wasn't here and if she wasn't here then this couldn't be happening.

Brent took a long sip of his beer. 'Stupid useless cunt—like I'd want to fuck that anyway.'

Tara swallowed some acid in her throat and waited for it to be over.

25

Fifteen minutes later Callum and Liam were back. Callum held the keys aloft—the returning general proud of his successful campaign.

'Good one, mate,' said Brent.

While they were gone he had finished two beers and smoked three cigarettes. Tara had counted. It was the only thing she could allow herself to do.

The smoky room made Kate cough and Tara kept giving her water and feeding her, hoping to keep her quiet.

With the copies of the keys in his hands Brent relaxed. For a moment he looked little-boy happy. He threw Minnie's original keys at Tara and they landed on the floor by her feet. She leaned forward and picked them up.

'Why don't you toddle along now?' said Brent, like he was bored with her.

Tara nodded at him, too shocked to do anything else. She stood up and walked out, Liam followimg her with the pram.

'Oh, and Tara?' said Brent.

Tara stopped but didn't turn around.

'If you think your boy can protect the dyke and that kid, you're wrong. He goes home to Mum and Dad at night but I have fuck all to do but watch her. I see her whenever she goes out and I see her when she comes home. I know where she is all the time. Think about that.'

Tara took a deep breath and started walking again.

'And if I see the police round here I'll just say you made it up. Everyone thinks you're fucked in the head anyway, and if fucking cops come round here I'll make sure you and that stupid stinking kid are sorry. Understand?'

Tara nodded. She understood. She bounced Kate up and down to keep her calm, keep her quiet.

Out on the street she put Kate back into the pram, tucking her light blanket around her.

Then she looked at Liam, who was standing quietly, looking past her. She wanted to turn and go, to take Kate back to Minnie's house where it was safe, but she was glued to the spot by the anger that was quickly replacing her fear.

Standing in the heavy summer heat, she saw that nothing had changed. Her time in the house had not altered the rest of the world at all and yet everything was different. She leaned down into the pram and pulled on the safety straps, making sure they were tight and Kate was secure, and then she stood up again and without making a sound she shoved Liam so hard he stumbled backwards.

'T-T-Tara, please,' he said, walking back towards her with his arms open.

When he was close enough Tara hit her hand hard against his chest. She could feel a burning rage coursing through her body. She had never felt such fury.

He didn't move so she swung again and again and then she was hitting him everywhere with both hands. She hit him harder and harder until she was breathing heavily.

He just stood with his hands by his side and his head lowered, taking the blows.

Finally he raised his arms, stepped forward and grabbed her in a bear hug that trapped her arms by her sides. Tara struggled but Liam held her tight and then he put his mouth by her ear and for a moment Tara thought he was going to try to kiss her; but he just whispered, 'G-g-get . . . them out of . . . of the h-house before we c-c-come. I'll t-text you when. H-he won't leave them alive.'

She felt his hand at the back pocket of her jeans and the prick of another set of keys being slid into the pocket. Tara went limp and Liam stepped away, giving her a small smile.

He looked like Ethan had the day he had snuck into her room and broken a glass box that sat on her desk. He had tried to glue it back together and had cut himself in the process, but he was so proud of himself for managing to reassemble it into a slightly box-like shape. Alicia had lectured him on not going into Tara's room and not touching her things, but Tara hadn't been able to stay angry at him. He had messed up and he knew it but he thought he had solved the problem by fixing the box.

But Liam wasn't six years old. Liam was seventeen, almost a man. She looked at him for a moment and then she spat at him, hitting his cheek. She heard the loud guffaws of Brent and Leo and Callum, and for a moment regretted humiliating Liam. Then she felt the burn of fear return. Brent could have killed Kate, just like that. He could have swung her small precious head against a wall and smashed it and he would have felt nothing.

Her whole body felt cold, like she was freezing inside. Brent was capable of anything—*anything*—and the child that she and Minnie worked so hard to protect was in danger.

'Oh God,' she whispered aloud as she walked. 'Oh God, oh God, oh God.'

Tears spilled down her face. 'Oh God, oh God, oh God.'

She walked quickly to Minnie's house and pushed the pram around the side to the back door. She turned the corner too quickly and it nearly tipped over but she saved it with her shin and felt the pain of her bone being hit.

When she got inside she went to the front door to make sure

it was bolted. She pushed aside the curtain and looked down the street towards Brent's house.

Liam was still standing in the street. His shoulders were shaking.

Tara let the curtain go. She didn't want to look at him. She lifted Kate out of her pram and gently placed her on the floor.

Kate spotted her hanging toys and smiled. She was no longer scared or uncomfortable and the past minutes had simply disappeared for her.

'Ba, ba, ba, ba,' said Kate.

'Yes—ba,' said Tara, and then she fell to her knees beside the baby and felt anger and despair and dread rip through her body. She felt something open up and spill out. She was stuck in the tilt-a-whirl at some amusement park and she couldn't find a way to make the spinning stop. She couldn't find a way to take control.

'I had a baby, Katie,' she said. 'I had a baby and I don't know where she is.'

She grabbed a pillow from the couch and screamed into it. The muffled screams filled her ears until they were the only things she could hear and she kept going until she had exhausted her newly found voice.

•

Minnie returned home from the city to find a tidy house and a happy baby.

'You are the best babysitter ever,' she said, bouncing Kate on her hip. 'Isn't she, Katie? Aren't we lucky to have Tara to look after you?'

Tara could not return Minnie's relieved smile. 'If only you knew what I've done,' she thought.

Tara kissed the baby goodbye.

'So I'll see you in a couple of days,' said Minnie, and Tara nodded.

On the walk home she tilted her face to the sun. The park was filled with children dressed in shorts and T-shirts thinking of nothing but the thrill of the slide and the heart-stopping flight of a swing. Tara wanted to be five again, or seven or nine or any age where she did not have to deal with this terrible place she was in.

'I will have to tell,' she thought.

'I will have to tell.'

'I have to tell.'

'I will tell.'

'I will have to open my mouth and talk to my father and then I will have to tell Minnie about Brent and even though I cannot tell them where the baby is, I can at least save Kate and Minnie.'

The closer she got to her house the more determined she became to open her mouth and talk, just talk and talk and talk. She would spill all the words she had been holding on to for the past months. She would talk and shout and scream and she would make them listen and pay attention so that she could keep Kate safe.

'This is me,' she thought. 'I am Tara and I am going home to tell everyone what I know. Here I am. Finally, here I am.'

At the front door she pushed her key into the lock. 'Here I go,' she whispered into the air. And then she took a deep breath and, using the voice she remembered, she said, 'Here I go.'

26

Inside Michael was throwing a tantrum in the way that only Michael could, lying on the floor on his back and yelling at the ceiling in some strange parody of a tantrum he had once seen in a cartoon. Ethan was filling a backpack from the box of toys kept in the living room. Alicia came down the stairs with a suitcase in her hand.

Tara's father was sitting on a recliner with a full glass of bourbon on the small table next to him and his head in his hands.

He looked up when Tara entered.

'Alicia and the boys are going to stay with her mother for a while,' he said. His voice was low and bitter.

Alicia dropped the suitcase at the front door.

'It's only for a few days or so. We're going to have a holiday at Nana's house, aren't we, boys? Michael, just stop it now and go get your blanket. Ethan, please can you just help me with your brother?'

Ethan went over to Michael and gave him a half-hearted kick, which made Michael jump up and push him. Ethan ran upstairs followed by Michael, who was giggling. Michael didn't understand how to have a proper tantrum but he did like to add to the chaos around him when he sensed things were getting out of control.

Tara watched the boys go. She felt the tilt-a-whirl start to spin again.

'We have to be away from here for a few days,' said Alicia.

'You don't have to leave,' said Tara's father. 'This will all blow over in a day or two. You don't have to let people push you out of your home.' The conversation had obviously been had many times that afternoon.

Tara touched her father on the arm and looked at him questioningly. He shook his head and took a sip of his drink.

'One of the parents at school must have said something to a child,' said Alicia. 'I thought we had managed to get through this whole thing without it affecting Ethan and Michael, but people are obviously still talking.'

Tara turned to face her.

'One of the children told Ethan that his sister was a baby killer,' said Alicia.

Tara gasped, feeling the sharp stab of the words as Ethan must have felt them.

Tara's father stood up out of his chair. 'You don't have to go, Alicia—please just let the school sort it out. Please don't run away.'

'I have to take care of the boys, Max. I can't let them be subjected to this kind of abuse. It's only for a few days until the principal has had time to deal with it. You understand, Tara, don't you? I'm not abandoning you and your dad—I'm just taking a few days away.'

'Don't fucking ask her if *she* understands, Alicia. *I* don't understand. I know it's been hard, I get that, but I also know that you're walking out that door and that you may never walk back in.'

'Please, Max,' said Alicia. 'Please.'

'I don't know how to be without you, Ali,' he said. He sat down in his chair again and took a large slurp of his drink.

'It's just a few days,' said Alicia. She walked over to Tara and took her by her shoulders. 'It's just a few days, Tara, I promise.' She held on tight, looking at Tara, and when Tara met her gaze she could see the weight Alicia was carrying.

She stepped right into Alicia's arms and hugged her. At first Alicia didn't move, and then her arms went around Tara and held her tight. Tighter than Liam had held her, tighter than her father held her. Alicia held her tight and then she let go and stepped away. Tara could see she was crying. 'Just a few days, Tara, and then I'll be back and we'll sort this all out.'

Tara nodded, sniffing.

'Ethan, Michael, it's time to go.'

The boys came running down the stairs, tripping over each other's feet.

'Why do we have to go now?' said Ethan.

'You just do, buddy,' said his father. 'But you two are going to have a great time. I bet you can get Nana to take you to the big park with the giant climbing frame.'

'Yay,' said Michael, hopping backwards and forwards. 'The big park, the big park!'

'I'm going to miss school, you know,' said Ethan. 'It's not time for a holiday because Mr Leith didn't say. He said, "See you tomorrow, you rowdy animals," and then we all had to be animals and I was a monkey and I screeched louder than Ryan, who was a lion. When it's time for holidays he says, "See you later, alligators," and we have to say, "In a while, crocodile." He didn't say the alligator thing so it's not holidays and so I don't want to go and stay at Nana's.'

Tara smiled at the stream of words that Ethan unleashed on the world without worry or thought. She took out her phone and typed, *See you later, alligator*. She showed him the screen and watched as he mouthed the words as he read.

Ethan sighed. 'In a while, crocodile.'

Tara gave him a quick hug and then she gave Michael a hug too. Together they all loaded the car and then Tara and her father stood in the driveway and watched as Alicia pulled out and drove off.

'I guess it will be just us for dinner then,' said Max.

Tara nodded.

'Just us,' said Max again, and Tara could hear his heart break.

Inside, Tara grabbed a bag of chips from the kitchen and started up the stairs.

'Wait, Tara,' said Max. 'We have to talk.' He laughed at his own words. 'I mean *I* have to talk. Come sit with me in the lounge.'

When they were sitting he handed her a document; it was a court order. 'I'm afraid this is it, love,' said Max. 'I've done everything I can and Daniel too. It's only for two weeks and then they'll make a further decision from there. I haven't told Alicia. It only came today and I was going to tell her but then . . . well, then there were other things to think about.'

Tara sat with the paper in her hand, thinking, 'I could tell him now. I could just open my mouth and speak. I could let him know that my voice has returned and then I won't have to go and stay in a hospital.' But she kept quiet. Her resolve to speak had disappeared along with half of her family. If her father couldn't even save his own family, how was he going to be of any help with Minnie and Kate? Even adults could only handle so much.

When do I have to go? she typed on her phone.

'Tomorrow. I'm sorry, but it's tomorrow.'

Tara nodded, then typed, *I'm going for a run.*

'But . . .' Max began, then he waved his hand at her. 'Okay. Don't be long.'

•

Tara left the room to change and Max drained his glass.

The bourbon settled in his empty stomach, warming him and shooting acid into his throat at the same time. He would wait until she left the house and then he would get up and pour himself another drink. Perhaps at the bottom of the next glass he would find the calm that would allow him to think his way out of this mess.

He didn't want to let Tara go. It was getting late and even though it would be light for a while longer he didn't want her out on the street. He couldn't hold on to anyone anymore. Alicia had said it would only be for a few days, but days had a way of turning into weeks before you knew it.

He watched Tara walk past him on her way to the front door. She was holding so much inside, so many secrets. With her hair scraped back into a high ponytail she looked the same age as when she started school. She had held his hand in a fierce grip and refused to greet anyone. Alicia had told him to let her find her own way and he had. He had stepped back and watched her grow up and somehow he had lost sight of who she really was. Now he had a feeling that soon his wife and sons would be lost to him too. He got up and poured himself another drink. Well, maybe not at the bottom of this glass. Perhaps the next one . . .

27

Outside in the late-afternoon sun Tara didn't start slowly. She went from stretching to sprinting. She needed to run. She needed to burn, to feel her lungs become concrete, to hurt.

She got to the park in record time and then she kept going around and around.

Her lungs wheezed and her eyes streamed but she kept going until she tripped over her own feet and hit the ground hard.

She was going away. They were going to pump her full of drugs and turn her into her mother. They would push and push until she snapped and she knew she would never be the same. It was too dreadful to think about but the worst thing about it was that she would not see Kate, not for two weeks and maybe not ever again.

How could she protect Kate from the hospital? How could she stop the terrible things that Brent had planned?

She lay there for a moment, panting and crying, and then she stilled her mind. There was a light, warm breeze in the park and she felt it kiss her face. 'Let go and breathe,' Dr Adams said when they meditated together. 'In and out slowly, Tara, let go and just breathe.' Tara felt her body relax completely. She closed her eyes and she counted as she breathed slowly in and out. She pictured the black wall—high and solid. She saw herself step up to it; she watched her hands push against it, saw the muscles in her arms tense and strain and whilst she watched she could see the black wall begin to crumble. She could see the flashes of light and so she lay quietly and watched as it tumbled to the ground and the memory came charging through.

There it was.

The answer she'd been hiding from.

Suddenly the images were clear.

She remembered giving birth.

She remembered the baby.

She remembered the pain and her desperate desire to hide herself away from everyone until it all passed.

'I had a baby,' she whispered. 'I gave birth to a baby. I had a child.'

After she had left the house, leaving Alicia complaining to her mother, she had just started walking. Her feet felt disconnected from the rest of her body, which was racked with a pain so intense she couldn't imagine it ever ending. But it did end, and when it was over she could not imagine going through the same pain again until it surged through her once more.

She knew that she should get herself to a hospital, but she also knew that hospitals were not always places of safety. They hadn't been for her mother, whose brain was now just mush. So she had walked around the park for an hour, stopping to hold on to a bench or a tree as the pain came and went, and then when she was so cold she thought she might die she found herself at the shopping centre.

She hadn't known where she was going but, driven by a need to hide, she had walked all the way to the far end of the centre where some of the shops had closed down and there was hardly anyone around.

She had found the toilet just as the pressure on her bladder made her feel like she was about to burst.

She was grateful to find the bathroom empty and she had ripped down her pants and sat on the toilet and then she had felt nothing but agony. She clamped her mouth closed; the need for silence was more important than the pain.

The pain changed after minutes or hours—she had no idea which. It went from an all-over agony to a burning, ripping feeling and she had to get the pain out of her so she pushed and pushed.

At some point the pain stopped and she heard a soft little sound, like a kitten mewling, and she knew that it was over but she also knew that she could not look.

Must not look.

She stood up and felt something slither out of her body. And then she felt free. She looked down and saw that the bloody thing in the toilet had its head down near the water and without thinking she lifted it up and turned the slimy thing around. She didn't want its head to be in the water. It looked cold and lonely but she couldn't pick it up again. She didn't feel like it was happening to her. Despite the pain and the blood she felt separated from everything. She watched herself touch the thing and thought, 'I wouldn't touch that.'

There was blood all over her legs and she left the toilet and went into the next cubicle and cleaned and wiped herself, and then she stuffed paper into her pants and washed her hands and left. The mewling sound had continued but she did not look and she did not go back.

She opened the door of the bathroom and walked quickly towards the exit and all she remembered was a glimpse of a pair of large feet spilling out of stretched blue canvas shoes.

On the way home she had felt free and light, despite the radiating pain, and she had prayed that it was all over. She would go back to school the next day and just get on with the rest of her life.

Now she felt a lot older than she had been then. Now she knew that you couldn't walk away from your mistakes just like that. Mistakes followed you around, demanding restitution.

She had spent the rest of the day in her bedroom trying to ease the pain with headache tablets. She had replaced the wad of paper in her underpants with a sanitary pad, but she had had to replace it after half an hour, and then even that wasn't quick enough and eventually she had just gone to sit on the toilet as the blood flowed out of her.

'This can't be good,' she thought when it wouldn't stop, but she had no idea what to do so she just sat on the toilet, and when she started feeling really tired, too tired to even stand up, she thought about yelling for Alicia and then it was all just black.

She had woken up in the hospital with no voice and no idea of what had happened.

She was ashamed of herself now when she thought about it. Ashamed to have caused so much trouble and to have freaked Ethan and Michael out, and she felt her face burn when she thought about her father crashing through the bathroom door and finding her with her pants down.

She had given birth to a baby and then left it in a shopping-centre toilet to die.

She had left it to die.

She had left it to die.

She had left her to die.

That was months ago—but it felt like years ago and like it had happened to someone else. She had left a baby in a toilet to die but the baby wasn't in the toilet anymore. Someone had found her . . . her . . . her.

'How do I know the baby was a girl?' said Tara to the empty park. She hadn't looked at it then. Had she?

She stood up.

'How do I know?' she said again.

She moved her legs and pumped her arms and sprinted towards home.

She arrived back sweating and panting and heard her father shout, 'Dinner in five minutes, Tara.'

She bounded up the stairs and grabbed her phone from beside her bed and opened her image gallery.

Minnie was always telling her to take pictures of Kate when she babysat. Tara took hundreds so that Minnie would see she was treating Kate well. Kate smiled a lot. Sometimes Kate liked to chew on Tara's phone and then Tara would take it away and say, 'Smile, Katie,' and take a picture just for her. She scrolled through the gallery and found one of her and Kate together lying on the play mat. She had taken a picture of the two of them for Minnie and then she had taken one for herself.

Kate was such a pretty baby. Her hair was the same colour as Tara's hair. Her eyes were darker—not much, just a little. They both had dimples on their chins. Her smile was . . . was . . .

Tara felt her heart jolt. 'Oh,' she said. 'Oh . . . oh . . . oh.'

She understood now.

She went to her chest of drawers and searched frantically under her socks and underwear for the small pink plastic album that she only looked at sometimes—only sometimes because it was filled with pictures of a happy family and Tara knew the pictures told the wrong story. They told an outside story and they were hard to look at when Tara knew the inside story—the real story.

She opened it up to the first page and touched her mother's smiling face. Cradled in her mother's arms was a newborn Tara. She was just a tightly wrapped pink bundle. All Tara could see was the tip of a tiny nose. She turned two more pages, searching each picture, watching baby Tara grow.

And then she turned another page and there was the picture she had been looking for.

There was Kate.

There was Kate sitting on Sasha's hip. It was Tara but it was Kate as well. There was no question about that.

It was true. She had not known it was true and she had always known it was true. Ever since that first day, that first moment when Minnie had walked into Alicia's office, she had known that she needed to go with her, that she needed to be near Kate. It was the only time she was happy, the only time she felt safe. It was the only time she could speak—when she was with Kate.

Kate loved her too. The first time she held her the baby found a space to fit into.

She figured that bodies must remember each other. Kate was part of her. She had grown inside her body for nine months and her body remembered. Kate probably remembered her voice. Kate remembered.

She compared the picture in the album with the one on her phone.

'That's my baby,' she said aloud.

'That's my baby,' she said again.

'Come and eat now,' shouted her father from downstairs.

Tara put down the phone and pushed the album back under her socks.

Minnie was forty-seven. June had said something to her about being nearly sixty when Kate was twelve. 'You'll have to be strong through the teenage years, Minnie,' she had said when she popped over for tea one afternoon when Tara was baby-sitting. Minnie had laughed but Tara had worked out in her head that it would mean that Minnie was forty-seven when she had Kate. She supposed it was possible, but didn't women get too old to have babies?

Tara had heard Alicia tell Max that Minnie had given birth alone. There were no pictures in her house of a pregnant Minnie and no pictures of a man and Minnie never talked about Kate's father. All that stuff could mean nothing—or it could mean everything.

Minnie must have gone into the bathroom right after her.

They must have walked right past each other. They may have bumped shoulders. You breathed in and you breathed out and just like that your life changed. You walked one way instead of another and your whole world was different.

Stretched blue canvas shoes. There had been stretched blue canvas shoes. Fat feet spilling out of stretched blue canvas shoes.

Minnie still wore them.

They were too big for her now but she still wore them. It was Minnie. Many months and many kilos ago, but it was Minnie.

What would she have thought when she found Kate? Why didn't she go to the police? It would have saved months and months of anguish. 'I found this baby in a toilet,' she could have said and they would have replied, 'Thanks, we've been looking for that.'

So why didn't she tell anyone? All these months she had been lying about Kate. She'd lied to her friends and to Alicia and to the world.

She got thinner every time Tara saw her and she said she didn't have time to eat but maybe Minnie was being eaten up from the inside.

Tara understood how a secret could consume you. Her secret had stolen her voice. Her mother's secret conversations with the black angel had taken her mind and Minnie's secret had melted her flesh.

Minnie had stolen Tara's child. She had lifted the baby out of the toilet and taken her home to hide her away. 'How could she have done that?' thought Tara.

'What kind of a person does that?' she said aloud. What kind of a person was Minnie? What kind of a person was Minnie? Minnie was . . . Minnie was . . . Minnie was a mother.

Minnie loved Kate. She loved her with everything she had. Tara saw the way her eyes lit up when she looked at the baby. It was the same when Alicia looked at Ethan and Michael. Had Minnie always loved Kate? Had she loved her from the moment she found her in a toilet? How hard was it to give up something you loved completely?

Tara compared the pictures again. Not everyone had the right to call themselves a mother. Sasha didn't have that right and neither did she, but Minnie was a mother. Minnie was Kate's mother.

'Thank you, God, for Minnie,' she said.

She was grateful to Minnie for rescuing Kate. Grateful to her for taking care of something that she couldn't deal with. Grateful that Kate had not died a sad, lonely, cold death.

Minnie was a good mother and she seemed to have her own mother and God on her side, which was more than Tara could say for herself.

Tara stared at her own dark eyes in the mirror. She couldn't keep this secret. Now that she knew she had to tell. She would start with her father. She would explain everything over dinner. And she would tell him about Brent's plans for Minnie and Kate. For Minnie and her daughter—his granddaughter.

Her father would help. He would go to the police with her and they would sort out this whole mess and then Alicia and the boys could come home and they could all get on with their lives, just like everyone wanted.

She took off her sweaty T-shirt and pulled on a clean sweatshirt.

Her hand was on the door when her phone signalled the arrival of a text message.

It's tonight, said the message.

She stared at the screen. Liam had done what he'd promised; the rest was up to her.

It was tonight.

Round and round went the tilt-a-whirl and Tara could not get it to stop.

She wanted to cry. She wanted to lie on her bed and just cry until her body was drained of feeling.

It was too late to get help. Too late to stop what was going to happen.

If she went downstairs and sat at the table with her father she could open her mouth as wide as a canyon but she knew nothing would come out.

There was too much to say. There were not enough words in the universe and not enough time for her to speak them.

That was why her voice had disappeared in the first place.

The story was too long, too complicated and too painful.

Some stories were like that. The story of her mother and the disease that ate her brain was too much to talk about so she just didn't say anything, and the way her mother still lived in the house but didn't live in the house was too much for Alicia and her father to talk about so they just didn't say anything.

Her relationship with Liam and the way it made her heart swell at first but shrivel later on was too much as well. There were no words for some things.

She could not tell her father. It would take forever to explain. And she didn't have forever because it was tonight.

Round and round and up and down went the tilt-a-whirl.

She had to make it stop.

28

Minnie finished cleaning up the kitchen and parked herself in front of her computer. She was longing for her bed but she didn't want to be one of those mothers who took hundreds of photos of her child but never sorted through or displayed them. She wanted to download some for her digital photo frame. Before Kate she would have slumped in front of the television with a packet of biscuits and the anticipation of a whole evening of numbing her mind with food and television.

'How things have changed, hey, Mum?'

Now she caught herself staring at her cheekbones in the mirror, marvelling at the woman who had been hiding underneath the layers. Her skin hung off her body in loose folds. There were people who had the skin removed. She'd watched the transformations on the health channel. Enormous Americans had their stomachs cut into tiny pouches and then lost gross amounts of weight, leaving them looking comical in their own skins. They allowed cameras to follow them through the bizarre and humiliating doctor's visits where their skin was weighed and lifted, exposing vulnerable flesh. Saggy breasts were displayed and covered in thick blue marks. And finally there was the surgery and the reveal at the end, and the women became glamorous dolls.

She briefly imagined what it would be like to book herself in for plastic surgery and change her body forever, but she knew she would never do it. She would need weeks to recover and for what? There would never be another person besides Kate who would see her body. Children didn't care what you looked like. Maybe one day, though, when Kate was older . . . Minnie smiled as she projected herself far into the future and into Kate's wedding. She gave herself a tight black dress to wear and dressed Kate in cream silk.

'I'm just being silly, Mum, aren't I? Let's have a look at these pictures then.'

She had given Tara the camera and told her to take a quick photo whenever Kate was doing something particularly cute— which, according to Tara and to Minnie herself, was pretty much all the time.

At seven months Kate was crawling nicely. She got up on all fours whenever she could and rocked back and forth on her knees as though she were trying to start her engine, and then off she went. Minnie never tired of watching her. She babbled constantly to the world, always sure of a smiling response from those around her. Minnie looked at her sometimes and felt her love for the child weigh down her heart. She was almost giddy with devotion for Kate. She had never been in love, but she imagined that it must feel something like this.

'There's our little girl, Mum,' she said as she opened the first photo. She clicked through photos of Kate smiling and Kate laughing and Kate surprised and Kate rolling over one way and then the other. Between her and Tara they had hundreds of photos. Tara had even taken a few of her and Kate together. In one photo their heads were together on the play mat. Both were looking up at the camera that Tara was obviously holding in one hand. Minnie could see Tara's lips formed into a word.

She knew that Tara spoke to Kate. The first time she had heard her she had wanted to rush out of her bedroom and acknowledge that Tara had broken her silence but something held her back. She stood quietly with the door slightly ajar and listened to Tara sing to Kate in a whisper.

When she came out of her room an hour later Tara was silent once more, communicating with shrugs and text on her phone. Minnie understood that she was not meant to know about Tara having found her voice. She considered telling Alicia but decided to leave things alone. Tara looked happier these days. Perhaps the silence was a healing silence. Whatever had happened in the family—and Alicia would never tell Minnie, except to say that Tara had been through a lot and had a less than perfect biological mother—silence was perhaps for the best. Perhaps Tara needed the silence. At some point she would decide to speak to the world again and then it was possible that she would go back to the life of a teenage girl and lose interest in babysitting. Minnie felt bad for hoping that she would stay silent, but now that she knew she could trust the girl with Kate she couldn't imagine being without her.

Minnie clicked through a few more photos and then went back to the one of Tara lying on the mat with Kate. Something about the picture bothered her, though Tara and Kate both looked happy enough. It wasn't a particularly good photo either. The photo had been taken inside with a flash and made both Tara and Kate look washed out and pale.

She got up from her computer and went into the kitchen to make a cup of tea. First, as was her habit, she checked in on Kate. The baby was on her stomach in the cot with one hand curled around her pink blanket. Minnie put her to bed on her back just like she was supposed to, but now that Kate moved so much it was impossible to keep her wrapped and in one place.

The room was cool despite the heat and held the heavenly smell of baby powder.

Minnie stood and gazed at her daughter. 'Did you feel this way about me, Mum?' she whispered.

She felt her eyes well up with sadness that her mother never got to meet Kate.

She continued on to the kitchen and made her tea then resettled herself in front of her computer. The picture filled the screen and Minnie stared at it.

Tara's white skin seemed to match Kate's complexion. Their hair was such a similar colour. Tara's long hair was mingled with Kate's and made the baby look like she had long hair. It should have looked odd but it didn't. For some reason Minnie had the feeling that the long hair made it easier to see what Kate would look like when she was older. They both had dark eyes but with the same shine of happiness to them. In fact, their eyes were exactly the same colour and shape and their chins looked . . .

'Ah,' breathed Minnie as the certainty of what she was looking at became clear. The absolute certainty of what the image meant. The two faces smiling up at the camera were not just similar. They were the same.

'Ah,' she said aloud and she felt her throat close up.

No sin ever went unpunished.

God had been watching her all along, just waiting until the time was right.

She had been looking at her punishment for months now and she hadn't seen it because she didn't want to see it. She was a stupid woman who had stumbled into a world she didn't belong in. There was no question that she was seeing the truth, no question at all.

According to June, her son Charles had looked exactly like Lou from the moment he was born. Now, when he occasionally came to visit, Minnie would be startled by his likeness to his father. There were children who combined aspects and features of both parents, and then there were children like Kate who emerged from the womb looking exactly like one parent.

Minnie dropped her head into her hands but couldn't find the words for a prayer.

She looked at the picture again. There they were, smiling at the camera—laughing, actually. What had Tara said to make Kate laugh?

She touched the screen, tracing Kate's face and then Tara's.

There they were.

Mother and child.

She turned away from the computer and went to find the whisky that she and her mother kept for special occasions. She hoped the stuff didn't go off. She poured herself a generous glass and swallowed it in one gulp. It burned and the coughing brought tears to her eyes. It allowed her to concentrate on the physical pain.

How could she have been so blind? How could she not have seen?

She went back to the computer and typed in: *Teenage girl won't reveal where the baby is.*

The headline had haunted her for months. She had followed every article, every tweet and every discussion on the topic. Only a month ago there had been a few lines stating that the father of the girl was using a high-priced lawyer to keep the authorities from committing his daughter. 'There is nothing wrong with her; she's working her way through a traumatic experience,' the father had said. The article had mentioned that the girl wouldn't talk but Minnie had understood that to mean that she wouldn't give the police the information they were looking for. She hadn't understood then that it actually meant that the girl would not open her mouth and allow words to come out.

Now she understood Tara's silence. She understood—and it was too late.

The media had not been allowed to mention the name of the girl or show pictures of her. The father looked nothing like Tara—except for his eyes, which seemed dark like Tara's, like Kate's—but it was possible she looked like her mother. What had she read about the mother? She searched through the old articles again. Bipolar disorder, that was it. Minnie got up from the computer and went back to the whisky. Her head was swimming already but Kate would sleep through the night. Her stomach rolled in a wave and she knew that the next glass would make her throw up. It was what she wanted.

How could Alicia have allowed Tara to babysit? Did Alicia know? Did Tara know?

She poured the whisky down her throat and then ran for the bathroom, where she vomited her terror into the toilet bowl.

Afterwards she stood shaking in the shower, letting the hot water mingle with her tears.

How could she have been so blind?

'There are none so blind as those who will not see,' her mother used to say.

'I know, Mum,' said Minnie as the hot water warmed and then burned her skin. 'I didn't want to see. But how could this have happened?'

She dwelled for a moment on the destruction that coincidence could bring and then she realised that this was no coincidence; God had a hand in everything that had happened.

The clinic where Alicia worked was near the shopping centre and Alicia and her family obviously lived in the area. She had probably passed them before as they made their way around the supermarket aisles, but you could live right next door to people and never know who they were. The world was at once absolutely enormous and incredibly tiny.

She didn't want to believe that God would have sent Kate to her only so she could fall in love and then have the child ripped from her arms, but then she wouldn't have believed that He would take her only companion from her or that He would sentence her to a life of misery. 'The Lord works in mysterious ways,' her mother would have said. Once that had been good enough for Minnie, but now she could only feel the rage building up inside her. She would not let this happen. She would not let Kate be taken from her.

Before Kate became part of her life she would have simply stood by and accepted the punishment that was handed to her. The old Minnie would never have stood up for herself. The old

Minnie would have known that she could not have so much joy in her life. But whatever the world thought was right, whatever God wanted, meant nothing to Minnie now. She would not give up so easily now.

She got out of the shower and threw on an old bathrobe, tying it tightly at her waist. Then she got a pen and paper.

It was easy enough to disappear. If you had money it was easy enough to do anything. As Minnie wrote her list she thought about her life before Kate. She remembered waking up each morning and wishing for, hoping for, praying for something in her life to change only to find herself sitting on the same old sofa at the end of the day with the certain knowledge that she would be there for the rest of the week and the rest of the month and the rest of her life.

'Let's get this show on the road, Mum,' said Minnie as her list of things to do grew longer.

Tara would come again on Wednesday and by then Minnie and Kate would be gone.

'It's a terrible thing to do, Mum,' Minnie said. 'But it cannot be more terrible than what I have already done. I like Tara but I love Kate and I can only take care of her. I can only take care of her and take care of myself. I think God would understand— don't you, Mum?'

But her mother was silent and God had little to say as well. Minnie didn't care anymore. She wrote her list and made her plans and she didn't ask anyone else what to do.

29

It was one in the morning but Minnie could not sleep. She was still woozy from the whisky. The room spun in a lazy circle and Minnie thought about what June and Lela would say. Once she had disappeared and she and Kate were safe she would write to them and explain. She wanted to believe that they would understand. They were mothers as well, weren't they?

But the more likely reaction from both of them would be . . . what? Disgust? Anger?

She could imagine their incomprehension and hurt. They would regret ever being friends with her.

'Glad you're not here to see this, Mum,' Minnie whispered to the ceiling. 'I wonder what you would have done. If you had never had me and you had been given the opportunity to steal a life for yourself, would you have done it?'

She listened to the darkness, hoping for something from her mother or even from God, but she was alone. She could no longer comfort herself with food or television. She could not call on her friends or her God against whom she had sinned. She was alone except for the small precious being in the next room.

'You need sleep, Minnie,' she told herself.

In the morning she would finish packing and she would take the money and she and Kate would just disappear. First they would leave the state and then, when Kate had a passport, they would leave the country.

'I hate to leave our house, Mum, but what choice do I have?' she said.

'I can't lose her. I would rather die. I know I said I felt like that when you left, but being a mother is different, isn't it? I can't imagine breathing if she's not in my life.'

She mentally went through everything she would need to take in the morning. She couldn't just walk out of the door with her purse. It was a lot harder to run away when you were a mother.

She had known, had always known, that she would be punished for her sin. How could she not be? She had stolen a child. True, the child had been abandoned. And what kind of person could dump a baby in a toilet? To think that same person had been looking after Kate! Did Tara know that Kate was hers? Was that why she had wanted to babysit her? Did she mean to steal her away one afternoon, knowing that Minnie could not go to the police without getting herself into trouble? Did she want to hurt Kate? To get rid of Kate so there would be no evidence of her crime?

The questions chased each other around faster and faster until Minnie's mind was a whirl of anxiety and fear.

'You're being ridiculous,' said Minnie to the blank ceiling. 'I'm being ridiculous, aren't I, Mum?'

There was no master plan. Tara didn't know and Alicia didn't know. Tara wasn't planning to harm Kate.

'Tara does love Kate, Mum. You can't pretend to love a baby like that. I've seen the way she looks at her. Babies know when they're not loved and Kate loves Tara. I just know Tara loves her as much as we do and that she would never hurt her. She probably doesn't know that Kate is hers, but now that I do I'll have to tell her. I can't keep lying. Kate might hate me when she grows up and finds out the truth.'

Minnie closed her burning eyes and let her thoughts swim.

'I have to tell her, Mum, but I can't tell her to her face. I'll write a note. When Kate and I are far away I'll write a note to Tara and to the police and let them know that the baby is safe. I'll tell them everything but only when I'm sure they won't ever be able to find us. I can change my name. I can do lots of things, but I can't give her up. I just can't.'

Outside the world descended into the silence of deep night and Minnie felt her body grow heavy and finally she succumbed to sleep. It was a fitful, fearful sleep but it was sleep nonetheless and so she didn't hear the back door of the house open. She didn't hear movement in the house. She didn't hear anything at all.

Minnie only woke up when she felt a hand cover her mouth.

'You need to get up,' said the owner of the hand. The voice was low and just above a whisper and Minnie felt her body obey the voice.

30

Liam walked slowly through the house. Brent was in the kitchen with Callum, who knew exactly how to fuck with an alarm. It hadn't looked like it was on when they came in but Callum was messing with the wires anyway.

'Why would it not be on?' Leo had whispered.

Liam had held his breath and waited for Brent to say something, but he just shook his head and pushed Leo outside.

They were all dressed in black.

Leo was in the back garden, blending in with the shadows and keeping watch. Liam's job was to work out exactly which room they needed to go into first.

'I want to know where the kid is. We'll take her in to her mother when we wake the fat dyke. I'll cover her mouth and that'll wake her up with the fear of fucking God in her. She'll tell us exactly where the money is hidden the minute I show her what I can do to that brat.' The plan had been discussed for months. Once Tara had entered the picture things had changed a little but the basic idea remained the same: use the child to terrorise the mother into telling them where the money was.

'What if she won't tell us where the money is?' Callum had said.

'Then they'll have to bury the kid next to the stupid fucking cat,' said Brent.

'Wh-what w-will we . . . do . . . after we have the m-m-money?' Liam asked.

'You don't need to fucking worry about that.'

'Seriously, man,' Leo said, 'the dyke will go straight to the police and they know everything about us—everything.'

'Don't be so fucking stupid, Leo. She's not going to go to the police.'

'How do you know that, Brent? Even if she says she won't tell they always do.'

'Not if they can't talk they don't,' said Brent, and that was when he showed them the petrol stashed in the garage.

'B-b-but they'll d-d-die,' said Liam.

'But they'll die,' sneered Brent. 'That's exactly fucking right, you stupid fuck. I'm not going to leave any trace when we go. I'll burn her pile of shit and everything in it. It'll be one big fucking bonfire. We'll be home and safe within seconds of me dropping the match. Then we can wander out in our pyjamas with everyone else and watch the show.'

Leo and Callum had laughed but Liam had seen how they could not look at each other. Liam had not understood when he asked Tara into the house that she was taking care of 'the baby', the baby who belonged to the woman with the money. It was only as he and Leo lifted the pram that he recognised the colours, recognised the pink patches, and realised that it was the same pram they had all been watching every day. Even then he thought, 'They must sell hundreds of the same pram,' but he knew that was wishful thinking. Brent had recognised the pram immediately. He told them afterwards that it was fate and then he congratulated Liam for bringing Tara into the house, like that had been Liam's plan all along. Liam hadn't planned anything. He had just wanted to spend some time with Tara. He was ashamed of himself now, ashamed of the small thought of maybe getting her into one of the bedrooms in the house. He had been such a fucking idiot.

Once Tara was in the house there was nothing he could do to save her. He had volunteered to get the keys cut because he could not sit there any longer with Tara's accusing stare.

'I remember when you were so, like fucking in love with her,' Leo had laughed on the way to the shopping centre. Liam had stared out of the window because if he had opened his mouth he thought he would cry. He was still in love with Tara. He would always be in love with Tara but he was not strong enough to save her. The only thing he could do was what he had done, what had occurred to him to do as he stood waiting for one set of keys to be cut; which was to give her an extra set of keys and tell her what Brent really had planned.

He had sent her one other text after he had told her that tonight would be the night.

'Why do you want to fucking know?' said Brent when Liam had pushed him for a time.

'We'll go when the fuck it suits me.'

'I don't want my p-p-parents c-c-calling the-the p-p-police. They want to know w-w-what t-t-t-time I'll b-b-be home.'

'Fuck, you're like a little fucken kid. I don't know, Liam. When it feels right. After midnight.'

'*After midnight*,' Liam had texted and then he had resolved to make sure they hung around the house until well after one.

He hadn't had to worry. Brent had needed a lot of time to get ready. He wanted to discuss the plan a hundred times and then he wanted to drink. 'Dutch courage,' thought Liam. 'Isn't that what they call it?'

'Please, God,' he prayed, as he placed one foot carefully in front of the other, trying not to disturb the silence in the house, 'please let Tara have taken them away.'

The whole thing felt strangely unreal; like it was actually a movie or a story on the internet. Liam could never have imagined himself breaking into a house and then just standing by whilst its occupants burned to death.

That morning Leo had wanted to back out.

'I just don't think I can handle it,' he told Brent. 'I can't get caught doing something like this. My parents would freak. They can't deal with any shit from me.'

'But you don't live with your parents anymore, mate,' said Brent. 'They basically kicked you out so they could dedicate themselves to your retard sister.'

'Don't you call her that,' said Leo. It was the first time Liam had ever heard a hint of rebellion.

Brent immediately changed tack. He put his hand on Leo's shoulder and stood really close to him. 'Imagine what you could do with this money, mate. It could change your life. You could even change your sister's life. You could go home and just hand thousands of dollars to your parents. Imagine how happy they'd be. They'd think you were a hero, mate. After all these years of them just thinking you were in the way, they would finally know that you're a good bloke, a good son and a good brother. You've always been a good mate and now you can show them who you really are.'

By the end of Brent's speech Leo was nodding. He was back on board and Liam saw his own chance to leave disappear. If Leo had left he could have too, but he would not be allowed to walk away on his own. He knew too much.

The alarm being off had given him some hope. It could mean that Tara had been and gone and that the dyke and the kid were somewhere safe. It could also mean that the police were watching or on their way, but Liam didn't care about getting caught.

So far all they had done was break and enter. He might get a few years for that but he was still under eighteen. He wouldn't be tried as an adult. Brent would be and Brent already had two assault charges against him. Brent would go away for a long time but Liam could start again. He could wipe the slate clean. Maybe he could get a job in another state and then live a different life.

Of course Brent would know it was him who had told Tara. But what else could he do?

Right now everything felt out of control. They had prepared for the night the way they prepared for everything: with alcohol and lots of dope. The joint had been passed back and forth and Liam had seen how Brent watched them, making sure that everyone had their turn. When it had come round to him he had inhaled a little and then just acted like he had taken a huge drag. He wanted his head to be clear even though Brent wanted them all to be shitfaced. Whatever you did when you were shitfaced could always be blamed on the drugs and the alcohol and that way you didn't have to look at yourself in the morning and wonder who the fuck you were. Just before they all went to change into their black clothes Brent had produced one more treat.

Four pink ecstasy tablets with little hearts carved into them.

'Fuck, last time I took one of these, I mixed it with a lot of bourbon and then I felt like I could fly. Then I went home and I beat the crap out of Russell,' said Callum.

'Your stepdad?' said Leo.

'Yeah.'

'Fuck, that must have pissed him right off,' said Brent.

'Yeah. He waited until I'd come down and then he broke my arm.'

'Wh-wh-why did he w-wait?' asked Liam.

'He wanted to make sure I felt the pain,' said Callum.

Brent laughed and then Callum laughed. Liam couldn't.

'Eat up, girls,' said Brent and they all did.

Liam held his under his tongue and spat it out in the bathroom.

Twenty minutes later they were ready to go. Brent was glassy-eyed and jumpy and Callum and Leo couldn't stop giggling, until Brent grabbed Leo by his shirt and kneed him in the stomach.

'Jesus, Brent,' said Callum.

'You want some?' said Brent.

'Nah, mate, let's just go, okay?' said Callum.

Leo straightened up and they all walked out onto the street.

Liam had heard his heart hammering in his ears. He wondered if Brent had taken anything else. He could feel the wound-up tension in the group. They were all silent. Liam could see Leo was having to concentrate to walk upright. Brent had really hurt him.

'How did I get here?' thought Liam as he strained to hear any noise in the house.

'Please God,' he prayed, 'Please God.' Fuck, he hoped He was listening—He had never, in Liam's experience, been listening to him before but Liam's penlight torch had already caught two crucifixes hanging on the wall as he walked down the hallway. Maybe God would listen in this house?

He walked past a room that he could tell belonged to the baby. There was a cloying scent of baby wipes in the air. He stepped inside, hoping that he would find the room empty. A small orange glow came from the nightlight plugged into the wall. Little stars danced across the ceiling. He wanted to stop and watch the stars.

•

Brent and Callum were pouring petrol everywhere. As soon as they had the money, Brent wanted the house to go up in flames.

'Whoosh!' he had said, laughing, when he described the scene. 'Barbequed dyke.'

'Why do we need to set the house on fire?' Callum had asked.

'There's nothing left after a fire. No one to say they saw us, no fingerprints, nothing.'

'The police will think we did it,' said Leo. 'Even if we stand there looking confused like everyone else they'll still think we did it.'

'Shut the fuck up, Leo,' said Brent. 'I told you: I've covered all the bases.'

•

Liam stepped forward to look into the cot and was startled by a movement in the corner of the room. In the dim light he narrowed his eyes and saw Tara.

'Stupid girl,' he thought.

'T?' he whispered.

She was also dressed all in black, with a black beanie on her head.

'I got them out,' she whispered.

'You-you . . . can talk again?'

'I got them out but I was too late. I was too late, Liam.'

'Wh-where are they?'

'Safe.'

'If-if-if he sees you . . .'

Tara nodded and he could see that she was crying. He wished now that he hadn't said anything to her. He should have just left things alone. Now she had saved the woman and her kid but she was going to suffer for it.

'Which way should I go?' said Tara. 'Where are they?'

Liam put his finger to his lips and walked back to the door of the room. He could hear footsteps everywhere through the house.

'I'll g-g-go and t-t-talk to them. T-take this,' he said, and he pulled his backpack off his back and fished around inside it for the hammer that he was supposed to use to tear up the floor. He handed it to Tara, who took it with trembling hands.

'D-don't let them hurt you,' said Liam.

'I'm scared.'

Liam nodded because he understood about being scared and because he knew that she should be scared.

'C-call . . . call the police,' he said, pulling her towards the door.

Tara didn't look like she was going to move on her own.

'You h-have to r-r-run,' said Liam urgently. He could smell the metallic scent of the petrol filling the house. He needed to get her out of the house.

Leaving her standing at the door of the baby's room, he stepped into the passage. He had to direct Brent away from the baby's room. He would tell them the house was empty and then they could look for the money and Tara could slip away. He would say he had left the hammer behind. Maybe they would all go back for it and then Tara could run. Tara could run and she could call the police now that she had her voice back. He wondered when that had happened.

He walked quickly back along the passage to the kitchen. The back door stood open. Brent must have called Leo in from outside because there was no sign of him in the garden.

'Good,' he thought. He had just turned to go and get Tara when he heard Brent's voice.

'Well, well—what the fuck do we have here?' Brent said.

'Oh God, n-no,' Liam whispered into the dark kitchen.

He followed Brent's voice to the lounge room. There he found Brent, Leo and Callum, all of them staring at the corner where Tara stood. Light from streetlights streamed in through the lace curtains, illuminating the scene.

Liam looked at her in horror. Why hadn't she run?

'Just what the fuck did you think you were gunna do, bitch?' said Brent. He had the hammer in his hand, and swung it once or twice before throwing it across the room.

Liam could see Tara pushing herself further and further back into the corner. How could she have been so stupid? She should have known to call the police. Why hadn't she known? They would be here now.

'If I could have explained,' he thought, 'if I could just have got the words out.'

He would have to speak now. He would have to force the words out now.

'Brent,' said Liam. He said it very loudly.

'Fuck off, Liam. Don't make this your problem as well,' said Brent, without turning around.

'Leave her,' said Liam. The words came out clearly, without hesitation.

'Hold her, Leo,' said Brent, and Leo stepped forward and grabbed Tara's arms.

Tara kicked out at him. 'Let go, you wanker,' she said. Her foot connected with his shin.

'Ow,' shouted Leo, and he let go of one of her arms to punch her in the stomach.

Tara doubled over.

Brent walked slowly and deliberately over to Liam, who could hear a roaring noise in his ears.

'Did you tell her about the plan? Did you tell her that we were gunna come tonight?'

'No,' said Liam. He looked down at his feet. He couldn't really see his shoes. His torch was in his pocket. He felt strangely like he was floating. He must have sucked down more of the joint than he'd thought.

'Actually,' said Brent, 'I think you did. I think you let your dick do the thinking for you and you told your little cunt girl-friend what we had planned.'

'N-n-no,' said Liam.

Brent was standing right in front of him now. He grabbed the front of Liam's shirt and Liam could feel how much strength he had in his arms. 'The fat old dyke isn't here and the kid isn't here so they must've known something. I know you told her.' He pulled Liam forward by his shirt and lifted his knee to connect with Liam's stomach. Liam fell onto the floor and Brent aimed three quick kicks at him.

'Just let him go,' said Tara. 'Please, Brent, just let him go. He hasn't done anything.'

Brent stared up at the ceiling. 'Ah, fuck—you're not worth it anyway, you stupid spaz. This was going to be so good for us and now you and your little girl have fucked it all up. I bet the fucken cops will be here soon. Fuck, fuck, fuck! It was such a perfect plan.'

Leo held on to Tara. He pushed his body right against hers and she heard the barely whispered words, 'Thank you, God.'

'Well, I'm not sticking around here to smile at the pigs,' said Brent. 'The only person who's gunna be found here is her. I might just have to fuck her up a little, though—just for fun. What goes around comes around, hey, T? Throw him out, Leo.' To Liam he said, 'If I see you again, you stupid fuck, I'll kill you.'

Liam could barely move. Leo stepped away from Tara and Callum took his place holding her arms. Leo hauled Liam up by the shoulder and dragged him through the kitchen.

'Shouldn't have fucked with him, mate,' he said gently as he pushed Liam through the kitchen door into the backyard.

'D-don't l-l-let him hurt . . . hurt her.'

Leo shook his head and walked away.

Liam lay on the lawn. He sucked air in and out. He needed to help Tara but he knew that if he went back inside Brent would kill him.

•

Inside the house, Brent stood in front of Tara. 'You coulda had some as well, T. I'm sure Liam woulda shared some of the money; you two coulda set up a little fucking house. But now you've pissed me right off. Fuck, I'm thirsty.' Brent was talking fast and Tara noticed he was sweating. 'He's flying,' she thought.

He grabbed Tara's face and squeezed.

'Fuck off,' said Tara.

'I don't think so,' said Brent. He turned to the others. 'Put her on the floor.'

Leo and Callum looked at him. 'Mate, maybe we should just, you know . . . leave,' said Leo.

'Throw her on the fucking floor unless you don't want any, you fucking fag,' said Brent.

Callum said nothing. He just stared at Brent like he was having trouble understanding what he had been told to do.

'Hold her down, you arseholes,' said Brent a little louder, and Callum seemed to snap out of his daze.

Leo and Callum forced a struggling Tara down onto the ground. Underneath her Tara could smell something on the carpet. It took her a moment to connect the smell with petrol. She was lying on a petrol-soaked carpet.

Tara cursed her stupidity. She had planned to alert the police and have Brent and his wanker friends caught in the act, but it had taken her such a long time to convince Minnie that she and Kate needed to leave the house.

At first when she had woken Minnie the older woman had been dazed.

Tara could see she was ready to scream so she quickly said, 'Minnie, it's me—it's Tara.'

'Tara? You're talking?'

'Yeah,' said Tara.

'What time is it? What are you doing here?'

And then Tara had tried to explain. After her months of silence the long explanation tripped and jumped off her tongue. The spoken words tasted strange.

'You can say you went driving around the neighbourhood to put Kate to sleep and then you felt tired so you pulled over to the side of the road and fell asleep yourself,' Tara said after she'd explained what Brent had planned.

'But how do you know him? When did you meet him?' said Minnie.

'My boyfriend—my ex-boyfriend—knows him. They saw me walking Kate.'

'But you said you'd walked the other way. You lied.'

'Yes,' said Tara. 'I was scared and—look, it will take too long to explain. Please just go for a drive. You can say you had to take Kate out because she was all wired up or something.'

'Will anyone believe that?' said Minnie. Tara had seen the scepticism on Minnie's face and something else—fear. Minnie had opened her eyes and seen her and been afraid of her, Tara.

'She knows,' thought Tara, but she couldn't say anything then. She had to get Minnie and Kate out of the house. She wanted to scream in frustration at the minutes that were ticking by, but she could feel Minnie's reluctance to trust her.

'Alicia used to send my dad out at midnight sometimes with Ethan in the car. He was a terrible sleeper. Dad used to drive him around until he fell asleep and then come home and try to get him into his cot before he woke up. Lots of parents do it.'

'*I've* never done it. It would be a lie.'

'You've never done anything wrong in your life, Minnie, why would they question you?'

'Oh, Tara, that's not true. I've . . . I've done some terrible things.'

In the bedroom next door Kate had murmured in her sleep.

'Listen, Tara, I need to—'

'Not now, Minnie. They'll be here soon. Go to a friend's house or something—go anywhere, but get out of here. When all this is over you can come back.'

'I can't wake June up. She'll be frightened. I know—I can go to the police. I can go to the police and get them to come back here and catch him.'

'Yes, call the police. You can say you came back from the drive and saw lights in the house.'

'What if they don't believe me? What if they ask questions?'

Tara could feel the time disappearing.

'Minnie, don't talk anymore—please just get up and go. I'll sort it out.'

And finally Minnie had hauled herself out of bed.

'I'll be there in a minute. I'll just lock the door again.'

'Come with us now,' said Minnie. 'You don't need to do anything, just come.'

'I'm coming,' said Tara.

She helped Minnie secure Kate in the car. The baby was deeply asleep and only sighed a little as she was moved.

'Right, let's go,' whispered Minnie.

Tara slid into the passenger seat, searching for her phone as she did.

'Shit,' she whispered to Minnie. 'I've left my phone inside. I need to get it. You go. I'll get it and meet you on Wilson Street.'

'I have a phone, Tara.'

'I know, but . . .' Tara got out of the car. 'I have to get it. I can't leave it here.'

'No, just leave it, Tara. We'll get it later.'

'I can't, Minnie. Just go now.'

'I'll wait for you to get it,' said Minnie.

'No, please don't.' Somewhere in the street a door slammed. 'Just go, Minnie. Wait for me. I'll be there, just go.'

'I'll be waiting, Tara.'

Tara watched Minnie reverse out of the driveway and glide down the silent street with her lights off. She turned back to the house. She had to get her phone. Her phone was filled with pictures of Kate, with text messages from Liam, with all the words she had typed over the last months. She had to get it.

The silence in the house settled over her, calming her down. She found her phone on Minnie's bedside table and shoved it hard into her pocket, relieved. She had to get out of the house and call the police—and then she had to talk to her father. 'I will never be silent again,' she thought.

She walked through the house towards the back door, but when she went past Kate's room she couldn't resist going in. She picked up the blanket left in the cot and rubbed the pink softness against her face. The blanket had that sweet Kate smell she knew so well and she thought, 'My daughter.' And then she heard the kitchen door open and she couldn't think or move. She had left it too late.

•

On the floor she felt Brent's hands move to the button of her jeans. The feel of his fingers on her skin was sickening. He tugged at the waist of her pants and Tara heard herself whimper a little. His nails were long and they scratched. She couldn't fathom what it was going to feel like when he pushed himself inside her. She felt a tear spill down the side of her face. She was so helpless. She kept struggling, kept moving, hoping that somehow he would be jolted out of his dazed state but Brent was far away, physically mauling her but mentally somewhere else. 'No,' she whispered, 'no, no, no' and then 'Please,' but no one was listening.

'Here, pull them down,' Brent said to Callum, who took over from him. Callum's hands were clumsy and rough. Tara struggled desperately but Leo held her firm. Callum was giggling quietly, like someone had told him a joke.

Once her jeans were down near her knees, Callum grabbed her breast and pushed his knee into her stomach so that Tara could hardly breathe.

'This isn't happening,' thought Tara. Brent elbowed Leo aside and leaned over her again, sticking his fingers inside her underpants and then up inside her, pushing and tearing at her. He used one hand to unzip his pants.

'God? Mum? Anyone? Help me!' Tara screamed silently.

Behind Brent, Leo danced from one foot to the other, seemingly enjoying the moment.

Tara would have liked to black out, to close her eyes and disappear, but she was wide awake and right in the moment. She turned her head as she felt herself tear inside. The pain was enormous. Her body still felt bruised from the birth; even after all these months she still felt tender. She bit down on her lip, willing herself away from this place, knowing that what was coming was going to be much worse than Brent's fingers.

'Hey,' said Leo, and he fell sideways.

Liam stood behind him with the hammer in his hand.

'Leave . . . her . . . alone,' he said.

Brent paused and looked around. Seeing Liam, he laughed and Callum laughed with him. 'You better put that down, you stupid fuck. When Leo wakes up he's gunna kill you.'

The hammer came down on Callum's head.

'Hey, you cunt,' said Callum, holding the side of his head. In the glow of the streetlight Tara could see the wet sheen of blood on his fingers. He stood up, clutching the side of his head, and swung at Liam, who dodged him. Callum went round and round a few times in a strange comical circle.

Then he lunged towards Liam, who swung the hammer again, connecting with the front of his face. Callum fell to the floor. Tara caught sight of Liam's eyes; they were wide with fear and adrenalin.

'Whoa,' said Brent, standing up, moving away. 'Are you fucking mental, Liam? You're gunna get it for this. You're gunna get so fucked up. You've really hurt them, you arsehole.'

Liam wielded the hammer in front of Brent's face.

'Just . . . go,' he said.

'Okay,' said Brent, lifting his hand in supplication. 'I just need to do up my belt, man—just give me a minute.'

Tara immediately pulled her jeans up and her top down. She wanted to curl into a ball and hold herself close but she knew she needed to move.

She stood up and stepped sideways, out of Brent's reach.

Liam nodded at Brent and dropped his arm a little, and that was when Brent crashed into him, sending them both sprawling onto the floor.

Sitting on top of Liam, he grabbed the hammer out of his hands, flung it to the side, and started punching Liam in his face. Tara stood behind him trying to block out the noise in the room. Someone was screaming. She was screaming.

'Stop! Brent, stop, stop—please, stop. Brent, stop!'

She didn't understand why no one was coming to help, why no one could hear her. The words were coming out now. Her voice was loud and shrill.

Liam's body was moving with the punches, like a rag doll, like a toy. Brent just kept hitting and hitting.

Tara scooted over to where she had seen the hammer fall and felt around for it. In the dark her hand found it and she lifted it and swung without thinking. It connected with Brent's head and he fell to the side, hitting his head on the coffee table.

The room was instantly engulfed in silence.

Brent lay still.

Very still.

Completely still.

He looked . . . dead.

'Liam, get up,' said Tara. Her voice was shaking and the tears were running down her face. 'Please, please, Liam—get up, get up, please. Oh God—Liam, please get up. Get up. Please God, make him get up.'

'Shh, T,' said Liam.

'Oh, thank God, you're alive! I thought . . .'

'Help me up, T,' said Liam.

Tara hauled him to his feet. His face was a mess but he was steady on his feet.

'Wha . . . are . . . we . . . gunna . . . do?' he slurred through swollen lips.

'You go,' she said. 'Run, Liam. Just run. Do you understand?'

'No, T . . . I'm gunna stay . . . help you.'

'No, Liam, just go—please, just go. You can't stay here. You need to go now!'

'K-Kay,' said Liam, holding up his hands.

He turned and walked towards the kitchen and then he stopped and turned back. 'Love you,' he said clearly.

Tara nodded. She hoped he could see the movement of her head in the darkness.

•

Outside, Liam started to run.

His whole body was aching but he didn't look back and he didn't stop. Tara would call the police now and it would all be over. She was talking again so she would tell everyone the truth and he knew she would leave him out of it. This was his chance.

In Brent's house he checked around for anything that belonged to him. He felt a rush of relief that he had never lived here, never left any trace of himself in this hellhole. He went into the bathroom and washed as much of the blood off his face as he could, then he wiped down the sink with a towel and stuffed the bloodied towel into his backpack.

Then he made his way back out to the street.

He should have gone back to help her, he knew, to be with her when the police arrived, but it was taking everything he had to stay upright and the police would probably not listen to him anyway.

He would wait to see Tara leave and the police arrive, and then he would run, he would really run. He might just keep running or he could go home and tell his parents he got into a fight at the party he'd said he was going to. He could tell them he wanted to redo his HSC. He could do his final exams again. He could do anything. If anyone tried to say he'd been in the house he would deny it and Tara would deny it too. He could lie with the best of them. He could do anything.

31

In the house Tara bit her lip to stop herself from screaming again. She needed to call the police but she couldn't find her phone. It had been in her pocket but now it was gone.

She crawled over to Brent, who was still motionless, and felt in his pockets for his phone.

'What the fuck?' she heard from behind her as Callum pushed himself up onto his elbows.

She turned around and looked at him. 'You had better run, Callum, and you'd better take Leo with you.'

'You little cunt,' said Callum. He started to struggle to his feet, but immediately fell back down again.

'You stupid bitch,' he said. 'Don't tell me what to do. You . . . you're really going to be fucking sorry when Brent wakes up.

I'm gunna tell the police it was all you and your fucking retard boyfriend. Jesus, fuck, he hit me. The stupid spaz hit me with a hammer, a fucking hammer. Stupid, stupid spaz. I'm gunna tell. I'm gunna tell.' Callum sang the last words and Tara looked over at him. He sounded crazy. Even in the small amount of light from the street she could see his eyes looked strange: huge and black.

'Just go, Callum,' said Tara, standing up.

'Brent said we were gunna torch this place. Whoosh! Barbequed dyke,' he giggled.

'Please, Callum. The police are coming. Don't make this worse than it has to be. If you go now they'll only find Brent here. You can run away and you won't get caught.'

'I want to see the dyke. Where's the dyke?' he said, standing up. He touched the side of his head and then rubbed his fingers together, feeling his own blood. 'Fucking retard,' he said.

Tara backed away from him. Callum was stronger than she was. She had to get out of there. She'd call the police from somewhere else.

'Where did everyone go?' said Callum. 'I want to see the fire. Whoosh!' And he laughed again.

'I'm calling the police,' she said. She stepped into the passage.

'See this?' said Callum. He held up a box of matches.

'Don't be stupid, Callum. Just get out of here. The police are on the way.'

'Stupid cunt,' said Callum, and he lit one of the matches. 'I'm not going to jail with the rest of you arseholes.'

And he dropped the match.

Flames leapt from the carpet like they had been waiting there all along. Almost immediately they were as high as Tara's waist and grabbed her side. She smacked at them and jumped over a line of fire to move further down the passage. In an instant the flames were everywhere and Tara could see Callum turning around and around. He was trapped in a circle of flames.

For one moment Tara considered trying to get to him and then she felt her lungs fill up with heat and smoke and she ran.

She pushed through the passage door and fled towards the kitchen.

She crashed through the back door and out into the night, taking deep frantic breaths.

Leo and Callum and Brent were still in the house.

They were all in there.

She turned around to look at the house. 'I can go back in,' she thought, but as she watched the metal shutters buckled and bent and the windows behind burst, sending shards of glass into the garden. The house was an inferno. It was too late.

Tara darted into the street and crouched behind a bush, trying to get her breath back. Her side was burning and she clutched at it to stop the pain.

'Daddy,' she whimpered quietly.

Then she heard someone shout, 'Fire!' and she knew that she could just let go now.

Someone else had seen, someone else was coming and she didn't have to deal with this anymore.

Behind the bush she curled up into a ball. Her chest heaved and her side burned but she didn't make any noise.

When at last she felt able to breathe properly she turned to look at the house. It was disappearing quickly.

She waited until some of the neighbours had gathered on the street and then she stood up and went to join them.

32

Liam found a large tree to stand behind. He would bolt as soon as he saw the police, but first he needed to see that Tara got out okay. He hated himself for watching, for not doing more, but he could barely stand. He let the rough bark hold him up and he waited.

He felt the air warm and looked up to see the house burning in the dying strands of night. A low moan built up inside his throat. He had not seen them leave. How could the house be on fire? Where was Tara? Where were Leo and Callum? How could they still be in there?

The noise of metal under strain and breaking glass filled his ears. Lights began to go on in the other houses on the street.

Had she managed to get out or was she burning? Was Brent burning? Had he even been alive? Who had started the fire? 'I didn't know,' he moaned. 'I didn't know,' he said again. There wasn't supposed to be a fire. He needed to go back and get them out. He had to go back. He dropped his bag and stepped forward but his knees buckled under him and he slumped against the tree. 'I can't even save myself,' he thought.

'My mates,' he said aloud. 'My friends.'

He had left them all to die. He had hurt them and left them to die and he knew that he would never be forgiven. The police would find him and he was going to spend the rest of his life in jail.

He had to run but his feet wouldn't let him leave. He needed to see her first. 'Please, let her be okay. Please, just her—please.'

The street filled with black smoke and he could hear sirens blaring in the distance.

The house was almost gone already.

He saw her then. She was holding on to her side like she had hurt herself. He wanted to go to her and hold her for a minute. He wanted to say goodbye, but there were too many people around.

As if she had heard him call her she turned and caught sight of him. He lifted his hand to wave goodbye and she did the same.

'Goodbye, T,' he said quietly, and then he turned and walked away. He walked away from the noise and chaos. He stumbled and tripped once or twice but he kept going until the sirens were background noise and the air was not perfumed with smoke. In the beginning light of dawn he smelled the jasmine and felt the heat of the day begin. It was going to be a beautiful day.

'I'm only seventeen,' he thought. 'This can't be the end for me, can it?'

He would go home and wake his parents and tell them everything. He would make them listen until he got to the end. Parents were supposed to love you no matter what. Would they love him through this?

He walked slowly into the perfect day and into whatever was coming.

33

Four streets away Tara knocked lightly on the car window, start-
ling Minnie from her prayer.

'Wait for me on Wilson Street,' Tara had said. Minnie hadn't
wanted to leave her there. She didn't know why the phone was so
important to Tara but the girl moved too quickly for her.

She had driven to Wilson Street and waited. The minutes had
ticked by. 'Where is she, Mum?' said Minnie. 'She said she would
be here. I shouldn't have left her in the house. I wasn't thinking
straight. Where is she?'

Minnie waited a little longer and then she drove around
the block and parked again. She didn't go back to her street.
Everything was quiet. 'I should go to the police right now,' she

thought. 'Something must have happened.' She would just go to the police and tell them everything. She couldn't go back to her house, couldn't put Kate at risk.

'Whose child is this,' the police would ask.

'Oh dear, Mum,' said Minnie. 'Oh God, oh God, what do I do?' She should not have listened to Tara. But Kate had to be kept safe. It was all that mattered.

She wished that she had already loaded her and Kate's suitcases into the car. That way she could have started driving and not stopped until she reached another state. But how could she leave Tara to those wolves? She needed to get help.

She had driven around again, willing herself just to go straight, to leave. Her handbag was already filled with her mother's jewellery and the money from under the floor. She could keep going. Whatever they found in the house they could have; she had enough money to buy new things for her and Kate. But something kept her going around in circles. 'Where is she, Mum? Where is she?'

It had occurred to her that Tara might be in on the whole thing, that she was going to let those vile boys into her house to steal her things, but then she had decided that she didn't care. Tara could have come into the house and taken her child but she hadn't, and she hadn't called the police to report Minnie either, even though Minnie was now sure she must know about Kate. Minnie knew she should have stayed to help Tara—the girl was too young to deal with someone like Brent by herself—but she had to make sure Kate was safe; nothing was more important than that.

'I should go back,' she thought. 'Or I should go to the police station. Someone there will help me.'

She kept circling the streets and then returning to Wilson Street to park, going around and around in hypnotic circles.

'I'll go to the police.'

'I'll go back to the house.'

'I'll drive to freedom.'

'I'll go to the police.'

'I'll go and help Tara.'

'I'll drive to the next state.'

Round and round she went.

'I wish you were here, Mum.'

'Five more minutes,' she said as she parked again on Wilson Street. 'Please God,' she prayed. 'Please, please God.' She closed her eyes and spoke to God, counting the minutes.

Now Minnie unlocked the door and Tara slid into the passenger seat.

Minnie felt her body flood with relief. Tara was safe.

'It will be on the news soon,' said Tara. 'I saw the media vans arriving when I left.'

'Media vans?'

'There was a fire. I mean there is a fire. It's still burning. I'm sorry, Minnie, but I couldn't stop it. I left it too late and Brent caught me and . . . I'm sorry.'

Minnie smelled the acrid smoke that was drifting over the suburb. She watched Tara push her hand against her side and recognised the smell of burning flesh.

'You're hurt.'

'I'll be fine.'

'Did you call the police?'

Tara shook her head.

'You could have been killed.'

'But I wasn't. I know it was stupid but it's over now . . .'

'It's over,' repeated Minnie.

'I was the one who gave them the keys, Minnie. I was the one who let them in.'

'They terrify me,' said Minnie.

'Me too,' said Tara, knowing that Minnie didn't need to hear about what had happened to Brent and Leo and Callum now.

'We need to get you to a doctor. You're hurt.'

'It will go away.'

Tara didn't mind the pain. The pain kept her focused on where she was right now. She knew she was right there sitting in a car with Minnie and Kate. For the last few months she had been missing. Only with Kate was she present. Only with Kate could she see herself.

'What happened in there?' asked Minnie.

'I can't,' said Tara, shaking her head.

Minnie closed her eyes, and next to her Tara pushed away the images of the night. The pain in her side was spreading to the rest of her body.

'Minnie, I . . .' she said.

'I know you've been talking to Kate for the last few weeks,' said Minnie before Tara could finish speaking.

'Kate's easy to talk to.'

'Ta, ta, ta, ta,' said Kate from the back seat.

Tara and Minnie smiled.

'I'm sorry about your house,' said Tara.

'It's just a house, Tara. Kate and I are safe. Did anyone see you?'

'Nah—and if they did, they didn't really see me. There were so many people in the street. I was probably just another face in the crowd.'

'Is it all gone?'

'It is, Minnie, everything is gone. It was so quick . . . so fast I couldn't believe it.'

Minnie ran her hand across her face, wiping away an escaping tear.

'I'm so sorry, Minnie . . .'

'No, Tara, love. Don't say that.'

'It was your home, Minnie. Your home and Kate's home, and it's where your mum died.'

'I know, love. Don't worry. It was only a house. Mum's not there anymore and there will be money from the insurance and we can start again. I need to start again.'

'We all need that,' said Tara.

34

'Mum, mum, mum,' said Kate from the back seat.

'It's just babbling,' said Minnie. 'She's too young for a first word.'

'My dad says I said my first word around her age,' said Tara.

The car filled up with silence.

'I don't know if that sort of thing runs in families,' said Minnie.

'Probably not,' said Tara, and she and Minnie shared a long look of understanding.

Minnie opened her door to go to Kate and then she stopped. She hung her head and said softly, so softly that Tara could not be sure she had heard the words, 'Do you want to go to her?'

Tara took a deep breath and looked at Kate. There were her chin and eyes. There was her hair colour and, when the baby smiled, Tara could see Liam's smile. There she was.

Her daughter.

Her baby.

'How long have you known?'

'Only hours really. Before I went to bed last night. I saw it in the pictures on the computer. It's so obvious I don't know how I missed it. I didn't know if I should say anything. I didn't know what to do. I know I've sinned against you and your family and against God. I don't know why you haven't just taken her and called the police. Why haven't you done that?'

'I didn't know either. Not until last night.'

'But . . .'

'It was the picture of the two of us together. I'm sure it was the same picture you saw. And then I knew and then I remembered.'

'You remembered? You remembered what?'

'Everything. I remembered the shopping centre. And I remembered your shoes. You still wear those shoes. That's where you found her, isn't it? In the shopping centre, in the . . . toilet?'

Minnie nodded. 'I thought she was a gift from God. I knew she wasn't but I needed her to be.'

'I'm glad it was you. I'm glad you found her.'

Minnie gazed at Tara. 'So what are you going to do now?'

'Mum, mum, mum,' said Kate again, holding out her arms to be picked up.

Minnie dropped her head and wiped at her eyes again. Tara touched her shoulder, gently.

'She's your baby,' said Tara to Minnie. 'You're her mum. She knows that.'

Minnie breathed a sigh that held her heartbreak and relief. She got out of the car and opened Kate's door to get her out of her car seat. The smoke made Kate cough a little and then she buried her head in her mother's shoulder.

Tara got out of the car and came and stood next to Minnie. There were more sirens screaming through the air.

'We'll need to tell,' said Minnie. 'We'll need to tell the police and you need to tell your parents.'

'You should call your friend June to let her know you're okay. She was in tears.'

'I've been an awful friend,' said Minnie.

'She'll forgive you. She'll forgive you when you tell her the truth. I think we might have to tell the truth now. The whole truth.'

'Yes,' said Minnie. 'Yes, the truth.' She knew it would feel strange after all the lies.

'You need to drop me home first. I have to talk to my dad and we have to call Alicia.'

'And then?'

'My dad will know what to do. Alicia will know what to do. Now that I've found my voice they'll know what to do.'

Minnie nodded. She was crying now. 'They'll take Kate away from me,' she said.

'I don't know about that, Minnie. My dad will help. He has a lawyer. We could tell the story to the media. We could . . .'

Minnie rubbed her face and sniffed. 'Sins and secrets never stay hidden. I always knew I would be punished.'

'This wasn't a sin, Minnie. You saved her and you kept her until I was ready and now that I know I want you to keep her.'

'Your parents won't like that.'

'I can't be a mother, Minnie, not yet. Kate needs a proper mother. She needs a mother like you.'

'Like me.' Minnie nodded.

'I want to see her, if you'll let me—I want to see her. I can still babysit.'

'You can, Tara. You can always see her.'

'It's going to be a long road,' said Tara.

'You and I have walked a fair way anyway. No sense in stopping now.'

The sirens went on and on and the sun rose, bringing a hot day to remember the heat of the flames.

They got back into the car and Minnie handed a fussy Kate a rusk to chew on.

'Well, then,' she said, and started the car.

'Well, then,' said Tara.

Minnie laughed and from the back seat Kate laughed too.

'Come on, Mum,' said Tara to the sky.

'Let's get this show on the road.'

Acknowledgements

Thanks and gratitude to Ali Lavau for her editing expertise and Laura Mitchell for her attention to detail. To Jane Palfreyman and the team at Allen & Unwin for their continued support.

Gaby Naher for always pushing me to do better.

My mother, Hilary, for reading the book over and over again and still crying at the end.

And, as always, David, Mikhayla, Isabella and Jacob.